DON'T CALL ME ISHMAEL

BOOK TWO OF THE FALLEN WORLD

Chris Kennedy

Blood Moon Press
Virginia Beach, VA

Chris Kennedy/Blood Moon Press
2052 Bierce Dr.
Virginia Beach, VA 23454
http://chriskennedypublishing.com/

Ordering Information:
Quantity sales. Special discounts are available on quantity purchases by corporations, associations, and others. For details, contact the "Special Sales Department" at the address above.

Don't Call Me Ishmael/Chris Kennedy -- 1st ed.
ISBN: 978-1950420094

Above all others, this book is for my wife and children. I would also like to thank my mother, without whose steadfast belief in me, I would not be where I am today. Thank you.

Chapter One

I awoke to blackness. Not the dark of the night, but the complete absence of light. I stretched and hit the wall about six inches above me, then to the one about three inches to my left, and then the one four inches to the right. In fact, as I shuffled around, I realized I was completely trapped on all sides by a metallic box of some sort—there were also walls at my feet and beyond my head.

A coffin. I was trapped in a coffin.

I clamped down on the panic that threatened to overcome me and took a deep breath. The air was a little stale, but not as bad as if there weren't any airflow at all. I had no idea how long I'd been in the box, but it seemed like I'd been there a while. If I could still breathe after that time, there must be a way for air to get in.

That also meant I wasn't buried—my second worry—as there wouldn't have been any air underground to flow. And I hadn't been cremated. Nor had I gone to hell, yet…unless this was some evil god's version of hell. It wasn't a good one, though, as I could fall back asleep—I can sleep anywhere—and pass the time napping. I wasn't in hell.

So I was in a box. Somewhere. I had no idea where I was, and I also realized I had no idea how I got here. In fact, I couldn't remember much of anything.

Having contained the initial panic that I was going to suffocate, I checked my surroundings more closely. The box wasn't square; the lid above me was rounded, like a...it took me a moment to find the word for it...like a tanning bed.

I didn't remember being in a tanning bed. In fact, as I thought about it, the absence of my past history was nearly complete. I didn't even remember who I was or what I was doing here. Perhaps I'd hit my head? I wiggled to get a hand up to my head—it was just possible—and checked myself out, but didn't find any bumps, bruises, or other indications of a brain injury.

Which didn't help my situation at all.

"Help!" I called out several times, in the hope that someone was nearby. If they were, they didn't come to my aid.

Leaving me trapped. And amnesic. Of course, if I couldn't get out of the tanning bed, or whatever it was, it really didn't matter if I knew who I was, did it?

With that cheery thought, I set myself to examining my surroundings as best I could. I found a small area of mesh on the wall past my head, which must be how I was getting air. It was no bigger than my fist, though, so I wasn't getting out that way.

I had nearly given up when my hand hit something that dangled from the lid of the box, up near the end past my head. My adrenaline surged, and I had to take several deep breaths to calm myself. Although I was getting air—I thought—I didn't want to burn it up too quickly if I really wasn't.

I wiggled up until my head reached the end of the box, then searched above my face and found it—a little piece of plastic tied to a piece of string that led through a tiny hole in the lid. I closed my fist around the plastic—it seemed designed to fit my grasp—and tentatively pulled.

It didn't budge.

I pulled a little harder. Still, nothing.

"Fuck!" I yelled, yanking as hard as I was able. The string pulled, and I heard a *click!* from my left. I reached to my side and found the lid had been released. I pushed on the lid above my face, and it rotated up and away. I was free!

I struggled to sit up and found my muscles were much weaker than seemed appropriate. Once I was able to dangle my feet off the side, I was able to rotate to a sitting position. It left me breathing hard, but with a view of a dim line of light, like from under a door, across whatever room I was in. It wasn't much brighter than its surroundings, but my eyes were adjusted to a complete lack of light, and I saw it immediately as a beacon of hope.

I called out again, my voice weak in the larger space, even to my ears. No one came. Again.

None of it made any sense. If I'd had an accident that caused my memory loss, I'd be in a hospital, which would have staff and a number of instruments hooked up to me to monitor my vital signs, not locked in some sort of tanning bed.

I slid off the side of the bed and collapsed to the floor when my legs didn't hold me. Turning around, I pulled myself partially up onto the bed and began exercising my legs to get some blood flowing through them. They were stiff and weak at first, but life eventually began to course through them, with a pins and needles feeling that both hurt and burned. A lot.

With a little more mobility in my legs, I forced myself to a standing position and stood there wobbling. The effort had cost me a lot of energy, and I waited a second to catch my breath while the dizziness passed.

With my heart rate somewhat under control again, I pushed off the bed and shambled unsteadily across the floor to the line of light.

I probably look like a zombie, a voice in my head said, but then realized I had no idea where the voice came from.

Great! I thought. Now I'm amnesic *and* schizophrenic.

I listened at the door for a few moments while I caught my breath, then, deciding the day couldn't get any worse, I pulled it open.

An emergency light on its last legs illuminated an office space that had seen better days. The drawers had been pulled from the desk and dumped unceremoniously where they fell, and all the books had been pulled from the bookcases. The chairs were upended and scattered about, and paperwork from the desk nearly covered the entirety of the floor.

If a mini-tornado had hit the space, it couldn't have done a more thorough job.

Among the detritus on the floor, I saw a candy bar—still in the wrapper—and realized I was hungry. In fact, I was pretty sure I'd never been so hungry before, and I collapsed around it, taking a book in the side for my efforts. I greedily tore the package open with my teeth as my fingers didn't seem to have enough strength and wolfed it down.

It then took all of my willpower to keep it down. Apparently, my stomach had been without food for so long it wasn't sure what to do with the sudden massive sugar input, and had decided to reject it entirely. An open bottle of water laying on its side provided a few mouthfuls of the precious fluid. I tried to drink them slowly and was able to keep everything down.

I rolled onto my back to let everything settle…

* * *

I may have fallen asleep for a while, because the emergency light seemed dimmer when I next opened my eyes. I realized I needed to get up and out of...wherever I was...because if the rest of the building was as screwed up as the room I was in, I was liable to break a leg trying to get out of it in the dark.

I pulled myself up on the desk and looked at the doorway through which I'd come. The door didn't have a handle on this side, and it was almost shut, allowing me to see that the pattern on the door blended well with the wall surrounding it. *Was that why the room had been tossed? Looking for the entrance to a secret room?*

I had no idea, but the thought of a secret room drew me back inside to see what might be in there. I staggered to the doorway and pushed it open. The ten-foot-square room wasn't much to behold; there was only the tanning bed—my mind refused to believe it was a tanning bed, though, now that I could see it from the outside—as well as a number of instruments and a computer attached to it by a number of wires.

There was also a second door on the left wall, and, not seeing anything of use in the dim light, I staggered over to it.

The door was unlocked, and I opened it to find some sort of combination storeroom and armory. My eyes were drawn to the food and drink section, and I shambled over to help myself, slowly eating and drinking as much as my wizened stomach would hold, and then, satisfied, I passed out again.

* * * * *

Chapter Two

The next several days passed in a haze, with me working to recover my strength and inventory the storeroom. I also began to explore the building in which I currently resided. I found some flashlights in the storeroom, along with a shelf of batteries, so I was able to see where I was going. There were two offices adjoining the room with the desk; both were in the same state of disrepair as the one I had originally found.

When I opened the door that led out of the office, though, I found a hallway with a number of bullet holes and what looked suspiciously like blood stains. I retreated back to the storeroom, closing the secret door behind me, and I decided to stay there until I was better able to deal with whatever had happened beyond my safe space.

Several days passed, and I got most of my strength back; however I was no closer to figuring out who I was. If that information existed, it wasn't in the office. I went through most of the paperwork on the floor one day. It appeared the office was engaged in some sort of import/export business, although the back two rooms showed this was some sort of cover for whatever business they were *really* engaged in. Somehow, I didn't think there was a lot of money to be made running an illicit tanning bed operation, unless we were located somewhere really far north or south.

And it still didn't look like a tanning bed, not with all the wires attached to it. Something in the back of my mind recognized it, but it was like an itch I couldn't scratch—I just couldn't *quite* come up with the answer, even though I was sure the tanning bed was the answer to all my problems.

* * *

I awoke to strange noises coming from outside the secret door—there were people in the outer office. Their voices were muffled, and I couldn't hear what they were saying, but based on the state of the office on the other side of the door, something bad had happened, and I doubted their intentions were pure.

Quickly, I grabbed one of the loaded pistols—a Sig Sauer P220, if the writing on the barrel could be believed—and went to stand by the secret door. I couldn't remember if I had ever fired a pistol before, but it felt good in my hand.

"—see that?" a man's voice asked from the other room. "There was a flash of light under that wall there."

Shit. They must have been standing in the dark, and they'd seen my flashlight. I switched it off and put it in a cargo pocket.

"Got it," a second voice, also male, answered. "It just went off." A light went on in the office, and I could see a little bit with the illumination from under the door.

"Yeah, but it was moving," the first voice said. "There's someone behind that wall. There must be a secret door there, somewhere." Even through the wall, the men had a strange accent; both men deleted the final consonant of most words and made the vowels nasally. I tried to place it. It was almost French...then I had it—Cajun. But there was really only one area that spoke with a Cajun accent—

was I in Louisiana? For the life of me, I couldn't remember ever having been to Louisiana. *Maybe I'd gone to Mardi Gras and been trampled?* While I remembered seeing Mardi Gras on TV—and it had looked fun—I couldn't remember actually going to it. It seemed like I would remember it if I'd been there. Or here, if the men's accents were really Cajun.

My thoughts were interrupted as someone began beating on the wall. "Hey, you in there!" the second man said. "Let us in."

That wasn't going to happen. While they *thought* I might be in the room, there was no sense confirming it for them, so I remained silent. They neither sounded like a rescue party nor the police…and that made them Bad Men in my book.

"Yeah," the second man said as the pounding ceased. "This section of the wall's funny. I think this is some sort of hidden door. There's no handle, so there must be a hidden catch somewhere."

"What do you think?" the first man asked. "Can I knock it down?"

"Probably," the second man said after a pause. His voice got louder as he continued. "Hey, you in there! If you let us in, we'll let you go. You can even keep some of whatever you're hoarding, except for any weapons; those are ours. If you make us knock in the door, though, I'm going to be pissed off and have to kill you. Last chance!"

I nodded to myself; they weren't with the local authorities, which made them looters…or worse. All I could see was a dim outline of the pistol in my hand, and I tried to remember if I had any experience with the weapon. Did it have a safety? I couldn't tell. If I'd ever been familiar with its operation, I'd lost that knowledge.

With a crash, the secret door burst open, and a burly man fell forward into the tanning bed room. Without conscious thought, the pistol came up in a two-handed grip, and my finger squeezed the trigger as the sights came into alignment, holding it tightly for the first double-action shot. The gun fired, and the bullet hit the man lower than intended, going through his side, just above the hip. Already cocked, the second shot required less pressure on the trigger, and the next round hit him in the chest as he spun around after getting hit the first time.

"Hey—" The second man's shout was cut off as my third round caught him in the chest. He went down, hard, and his flashlight flew through the air, randomly illuminating the room with its twirling light.

I stalked toward where the second man lay twitching, barely conscious of what I was doing, and looked into the office when I heard a noise—a third person running out the door. The flashlight he carried was going everywhere in his haste, and the strobing of it made him a difficult target. My pistol snapped up, and I fired, but he was out the door. I fired four more times through the wall, trying to judge where he would be, then the pistol ran dry.

I ejected the magazine, slapped in a new one, and allowed the slide to slam forward as I ran out the door after him. The man was just going around the far corner at the end of the hallway. Although he staggered around the corner as if he'd been hit, he was still on his feet and running. I had no idea where he was going, or if he might have other people waiting there, so I pulled out my flashlight and looked at the hallway wall. There was fresh blood, but not a lot of it. Judging by the way he was running, it wasn't a fatal hit.

I went back into the secret room. As I approached, the second man I'd shot tried to bring up his pistol. My right hand snapped up, and I fired a round through his head without any conscious thought, then stared down at my hand in horror. I'd just killed two men, with no more thought than stepping on ants. Was I some sort of psychopathic killer? Was the secret room a treatment facility—somewhere where they could do electroshock therapy on me to cure me? Was that why the tanning bed had all the wires?

I had no idea, but the one thing that went through my mind was *Flee!* I had to get out of there. If there was only one thing I was certain of, it was that the third man was going for reinforcements. I didn't know how long it would take for them to get here, but I knew the clock was ticking. Psychopathic killer or not, I still didn't want to have my own life ended, so I hurried into the storeroom.

I had already staged some of the things I thought I'd need most if I had to bug out, so it didn't take me long to throw together a large duffel bag of food, water, and a couple changes of clothes, as well as a handheld bag containing several pistols and a couple of grenades— there weren't any long arms—and all the ammunition I could comfortably carry.

I strapped on a large knife that I'd found on one of the shelves and buckled on two holsters for the pistols I wanted to have available—two of the P220s—then walked back into the room with the tanning bed to see if I could learn anything more about my would-be killers. A quick search of their bodies didn't yield anything worthwhile, although I noticed both men had blue pieces of material around one of their upper arms. I took the one that wasn't covered in blood, and stuffed it into a pocket.

As I raced back to get my gear, I realized the sight of blood and death hadn't bothered me. Perhaps I was some sort of psycho killer, after all.

Shrugging off the thought—it didn't really matter since I didn't want to die, no matter who I was—I shouldered the duffel bag, grabbed my other bag, and left the office. I turned right on leaving, figuring the man who'd gotten away had been headed toward an exit, and, two turns later, made it to where I could see daylight. Unfortunately, that daylight was broken by the shapes of a number of men coming into the building.

"There he is!" one of them yelled, and I turned and ran.

* * * * *

Chapter Three

Several shots rang out as I raced deeper into the building, but they all went wide as I rounded the first corner. I needed space and time to think, and I couldn't do that on the run, so I stopped and pulled out one of my pistols. Reaching it around the corner, I fired off an entire magazine. I don't know if I hit anyone—odds are, I didn't—but I figured that would at least give me a couple of seconds.

I reached into the bag for another magazine, but my hand hit something else instead, and I pulled out the grenade. I had found two types of grenades and had brought one of each. This one was shaped more like a soda can than an egg, but I figured it would help even the odds, so I pulled the pin and threw it around the corner.

"Grenade!" someone yelled, and there was a mass scuffling as the men following me ran. I waited for the earth-shattering kaboom, but there was only a fizzing noise, instead.

"Ha!" a different voice yelled. "It's a dud!"

Without warning, the light level in the building grew tremendously, and one of the men screamed. I couldn't help myself; I looked around the corner. The grenade had turned into a massive fireball, and one of the men was rolling on the floor on fire. Apparently, he had been too close to it when it had ignited. At least six other men were watching either the man or the flames, and I drew my second pistol and fired several times, hitting a couple of them, before return fire forced me back around the corner.

Grabbing the bag, I took off running again, passing the office suite I had come from. After a couple more turns I saw light again, and I raced toward the back door. I was half way down the corridor when a figure stepped out of a room and a gun went off.

I threw myself to the right, using the duffle bag to break my crash into the wall, and felt the bullet graze the flesh of my upper arm. The man fired again, but the bullet missed, and then I was on the floor with my pistol up. I fired three times into the center of the shadow, and he fell backward, dropping his pistol.

I scooped it up as I ran past him—a quick glance showed at least two of my rounds had hit him in the chest, and he was done—and then I was out the door and into the bright light. I drew to a stop as the sunlight hit my eyes and the enormity of my surroundings over- whelmed me. The back door to the building opened onto a major secondary road that ran from left to right in front of me. On the other side of that lay what looked like an interstate highway. Behind me, the office complex and strip mall ran for several hundred yards on both sides of me, with only a gap for a small access road in the middle. A sign proclaimed the collection of giant buildings to be the "Fremaux Town Center."

I'd never heard of it, so that wasn't any help. My choices were north and south. If I really was in Louisiana, then going south wasn't my best option—it would only take me to the swamps and eventually the Gulf, and would make me easy to track. There was also a lot of lingering smoke to the south. North it was.

But first, I needed cover, and the only cover was on the other side of the interstate. I ran as hard as I could for it, but the effort of carrying the large bag was already starting to wear on me—my stam- ina was still sorely lacking. I made it to the short chain link fence that separated the secondary road from the interstate and tossed the two bags and my assailant's pistol over it. I was just starting to climb over it when a pistol fired behind me, and the round went past my ear like an angry hornet.

No longer worrying about technique, I jammed a foot into the fence and threw myself up and over, taking scratches from the top wires across my left arm and tearing the pants on my left leg. The pistol behind me fired again, and was joined by a second one that sounded like a small cannon going off. A large divot appeared in the grass in front of me, as I grabbed the pistol and my bags, and I was off again.

I crossed both lanes of the highway while they continued to fire behind me. They hit the duffel I was carrying once, but I was a long way away and running for all I was worth, making me a difficult target. The interstate was crowned, and I threw myself into the depression on the far side to catch my breath.

There were four men in pursuit of me, and they had reached the chain link fence. I still had the one man's pistol, so I checked it—no mud in the barrel—and fired the rest of the magazine at them. It was hard to tell if I had hit any of them, but they all dove for cover, which was really all I wanted.

I shrugged the duffel bag onto my shoulders again, trying to be careful of the wounds on my left arm. I would have to bind them up soon, but I needed to get away from the men first. I turned and, staying low, ran to the east toward the trees on the side of the highway. Unfortunately, the trees were nothing more than a thin screen for a giant pond—they weren't more than brush, really—so I couldn't go any further; I was forced to head back north.

Although I was out of range, that didn't keep the men following me from firing off several rounds in my direction. I was almost to the end of the pond when a bullet smacked into the tree next to me. Moments later, I heard a new noise in the clamor following me. I recognized the sound of the rifle firing instantly—don't ask me how—and was tempted to throw myself to the side, but realized the bullet, traveling faster than the speed of sound, had already hit.

While the pistols didn't stand a chance of hitting me from where the men were, the rifleman could, and I dodged farther into the trees. I made it to the end of the pond without being hit, and staggered through about 200 feet of trees to find myself in a residential neighborhood. I tried cutting straight across it, but it seemed like every resident had some sort of fence across their yard, and most of them were too big for me to easily go over.

I had just turned around in someone's backyard, deciding it would be easier to keep to the street, when I heard a click that sounded a lot like a rifle's safety being flipped off.

"Don't move," a male voice ordered.

* * * * *

Chapter Four

I froze. After a moment, I turned my head—slowly—to look in the direction of the voice. An older man looked over the sights of a rifle he was resting on top of a large gas grill. He was probably in his early sixties, with hair and beard unkempt and gone to gray. And then I saw his eyes. Even though the man looked physically old and tired, the eyes said he wasn't a man to be trifled with—he knew what he was doing and *would* pull the trigger if given a reason. I didn't move any further.

"What the hell do you think you're doing?" the man asked.

"Running, mostly," I replied. I was too tired to try to come up with any sort of cover story, and I was pretty sure he'd already figured that much out on his own.

"I saw that," the man replied, confirming my guess. "What…no, I guess the right question is, *who* are you running from?"

"I don't know." I shrugged. "I woke up in a building that looked like a war had been fought in it. A couple of guys attacked me, and I killed them with a pistol I found in the room I woke up in. I don't know who they are—who they were—all I know is they were both big guys and had a strip of blue cloth around their arms."

"Well then, son, you are well and truly in a world of shit."

I cocked my head and looked pointedly at the rifle the man was holding. "I'm pretty sure I already knew that."

The man chuckled. "I'm the least of your problems. If you killed a couple of the Blues, they *will* be coming for you."

"I kinda figured that," I replied. "They chased me across the highway, and I'm pretty sure they'll be here soon. I'd be happy to be on my way, if you'd just point the gun some other direction."

"I haven't rightly figured what I want to do with you yet. If you've pissed off the Blues, I'd probably get a decent reward for turning you in to them." He looked at me oddly for a second, then said, "You look familiar. What's your name?"

"I don't really know," I said. Something came to me. "Call me Ishmael."

"Is that your name?"

"I don't know. I can't remember my name; in fact, I really can't remember anything beyond when I woke up four days ago. I've got amnesia."

"Amnesia, huh? Well, that's a stupid name to call yourself. Why don't you call yourself 'Fred' or something? Can you at least remember your last name?"

"No, although I'd be happy to tell it to you if I could. Especially with your gun pointed at me. I don't suppose…"

"You suppose right. I'm going to keep this rifle pointed at you until I get some answers and decide you're okay, or I decide you're not okay, and I kill you."

"Well, ask me your questions quickly then. Even though I don't want to die, I'm in kind of a hurry."

The man's brows knit. "What did you do before the war?"

"What war?"

"What war? *The big war we just had!* The Corporations throwing nukes around like they were treats for your kids. You don't remember that?"

"No, I don't. If it happened more than four days ago, I don't remember it."

"Most of the country's been wiped out. My guess is that Obsidian 'won,' if there is such a thing in nuclear war. Teledyne seemed to get its ass pretty well handed to it, although there isn't much left of Obsidian, either. Nor much of the country, for that matter. I wouldn't go any further south. New Orleans took some hits during the bomb throwing, and most of it's radioactive."

"So what are you doing?"

"Same as everyone," the man said. "We're hunkering down, waiting for the reestablishment of law by the police. The first few days were pretty bad as everyone tried to hoard all the food, water, and ammo they could get their hands on—lost my wife at the grocery store to a firefight—but now everyone's just trying to defend what's theirs and hold on as best they can." He nodded toward the house, and I looked over to see two more rifles pointed at me. That was probably a good thing, as I'd been trying to decide if I wanted to try to take the man. My reflexes were improving, but probably not good enough to beat all three. If I didn't have any other option, I'd still try it, but continued negotiation seemed the better bet. I'd also seen two young kids behind the people with rifles, and I didn't particularly want to kill their grandpa in from of them, no matter whether I was a psycho killer or not.

"So what's it going to be?" I asked. "You going to kill me, hand me over to the Blues, or let me go?"

The man turned his head and spat. "I ain't got no problem killing people who're trying to take away what's mine, though I ain't big on killing someone in cold blood." He waved the barrel of his gun toward the front of his property. "Get the hell out of here. Maybe you can still get away from the Blues."

I didn't have to be told that twice. "Thank you," I said, nodding to him as I went past. I went down to the street, turned left, and turned left again at the corner to continue north. I'd made it about a block when the gunfire started up behind me.

Sometimes, there's no escape in this Fallen World.

* * * * *

Chapter Five

"**S**hit," I said with a sigh. The gunfire was coming from the exact direction of the old man's house. He'd allowed me to go free, and now the bad guys—the Blues, I expected—had tracked me to his property.

And there were two kids in his house.

I couldn't leave him to face the trouble I'd brought, literally, to his doorstep. I dropped both my bags and put new magazines into my P220s, then threw several more mags into one of the cargo pockets on my pants. Looking up, I could see a man in the nearest house, staring at me down the barrel of his rifle through what looked to be his living room window. It was like the old man had said; everyone was forted up here.

I grabbed the other grenade out of my bag and held it up to show the man I had it, then stowed it in a different cargo pocket and tossed the bags into the man's yard. "Watch them while I'm gone," I said, pantomiming what I meant. I expected he'd be into them as soon as I was gone, and I didn't mind sharing some of the food and water. I'd be testy if any of the guns or ammo were missing, though.

Relieved not to be carrying the bags anymore, there was a spring in my step as I raced back down the street. Sure enough, when I got to the street that the old man lived on, there were a number of people surrounding his house, using the neighbors' houses for cover.

I raced across the street and back into the woods by the pond, going as quickly as I could toward the end of the pond where the old

25

man's house was. The shooting stopped suddenly, and I instantly feared for the kids' safety—a weird thing for a psychopathic killer, I know—but then I heard a man's voice.

"In the house," the voice yelled. "We don't care about you, we just want the man we tracked here!"

"He ain't here no more," the old man yelled back. "Get off my fucking lawn!"

"If you just send him out, we'll leave you in peace!"

I could see one of the Blues. He was in the trees with a scoped rifle. "No shot yet," he said into a throat microphone.

"I told you," the old man yelled. "He ain't here."

"Fine!" the man on the street shouted back. "Just let us in so we can look, then!"

"No chance of that happening! I've heard what you do once you get into someone's house!"

"Wait a minute," the man with the rifle said. "He just moved. I can see part of his head."

I was almost to the man, but I had no idea what I ought to do. I could easily shoot him in cold blood—it would be hard to miss—like any good killer; however, doing so would alert all the men scattered around, of which I could see about seven or eight. I was tired and didn't want to start the chase game all over.

The knife seemed to leap into my hand of its own accord, and I took another step toward the man.

"I've got the shot," he said into the microphone as he switched off the rifle's safety.

Without a conscious thought, I took the last step forward and palmed his forehead with my left hand, dragging his head back so my right hand could draw the razor-sharp blade across his throat.

The man's neck erupted in a spray of blood. I wasn't sure how hard to cut, so I did it too hard, grinding the knife into the bone as I finished. I jumped back—more to get out of the bloody fountain than anything else—and both the man and rifle dropped to the ground.

I quickly stepped up and grabbed the man's ear piece. It took a second to get it out because his head was all wobbly. I left the microphone around the ruins of his neck. I didn't know if it would work with that much blood on it, and I didn't want to find out.

"Take the shot, dammit!" a voice said over the ear piece.

I grabbed the rifle, happy it hadn't discharged when it fell, aimed, and shot out the man's window, missing him by at least a foot. That appeared to be the signal, as all the men on the street began firing again.

"You dumbass, you missed!" the voice said on the radio.

"Newp," I muttered to myself. I'd hit exactly what I aimed for. I found my next target—the guy talking to me on the radio. He happened to be looking in my direction as he continued to berate me—*where did I learn a word like 'berate?'*—which made it easy to see the bullet hit him in the forehead.

One of the other Blues fired, and I shifted aim to him. One hit, center mass, and he went down.

Which, however, didn't go unnoticed.

"Hey!" one of the other guys on the net yelled as I shifted target again. "Someone just shot Johnny! And it looks like the shot came from Fred!"

I couldn't find the person speaking, but I saw another flash of blue and put that man down.

The people in the house must have sensed the flow of battle shifting, because fire from the house increased, pinning several of the Blues down. I picked them off as quickly as possible. As I hit the third one, a branch snapped behind me, and I dove to the left while throwing the rifle to the right.

The man behind me fired, and the bullet hit me in the right leg. Fire lanced through my leg as I hit the ground and rolled. The man fired again, throwing dirt on me as I continued to roll. There was a third shot—from a different direction—and the sound of a body hitting the ground nearby. I stopped rolling and looked—the man who'd been shooting at me was down with a bullet wound to the chest. His hands clawed feebly for a moment, trying to stop the blood, but then he stilled.

I caught movement out of the corner of my left eye and looked to find the old guy. He nodded once to me. "Thanks for the help," he said. "Looks like I made the right choice to not kill you. You're kinda handy in a fight. My name's Sam. Sam Boudreaux."

"Umm, thanks…I think," I replied. "You're not so bad yourself."

"I fought in the war with Dellik Unified," he said as he checked the two bodies near me. One glance at the first one was all he needed before he moved on. "It was nasty. The damn Corporations are going to be the death of me yet."

I nodded. *No wonder he didn't seem bothered by the dead bodies.*

He waved toward the one I'd killed. "What war were you in?"

"I couldn't tell you," I replied. "I honestly don't remember anything beyond four days ago."

"No shit? I thought you were just trying to get the drop on me." He nodded toward the body. "You may not remember it, but it looks like you've still got some skills. People that can do that are few and far between."

"What? Cut someone's throat?"

He nodded. "Takes a particular type of man to do that."

I sighed. "Yeah, a psychopathic one. I think I was being treated for it."

"No, I was thinking more along the lines of some sort of special forces trooper. We followed them into a Dellik facility one time...they left a trail of bodies like that. And worse. Half the time, they took the heads clean off. Those guys had had some modifications and were tough sons of bitches. And the Agents? They were even worse."

I shrugged. I couldn't remember being a soldier, much less a special forces trooper. They had lengthy training, I would have thought I'd remember if I'd done it. Special forces was a nice thought, but I was still leaning toward psychopath.

"Where ya headed?" the old man asked.

"I don't really know," I replied. "All I was really doing was trying to avoid getting killed; I didn't have a particular destination in mind. Why?"

"Well, at least one of the Blues got away, so I suspect they will be back, and this time, they'll bring the whole gang."

"I thought I killed the leader."

"No, the guy in charge of that pack was the leader's brother—his second in command. Saw them together on TV once, back when we had power...and TV, too, for that matter. The fact that you killed his brother...the real leader is going to be pissed. Me and my family are going to have to leave. You're welcome to come with us. Like I said, you're kinda handy to have in a fight."

"Where you headed?"

"East. I've got family in Pensacola."

"So where are we now?"

"You don't even know where you are?"

"Nope. Told you, I—"

"Don't remember anything before four days ago," the man finished. "Got it. You're in the mighty metropolis of Slidell, Louisiana."

"Doesn't ring a bell," I replied. "Where the hell is Slidell?"

"About 20 miles northeast of the French Quarter in New Orleans."

"Huh."

"You don't remember being here?"

"No. As far as I can remember, I've never been to Louisiana in my life."

"Not even for Mardi Gras?"

"I'm pretty sure I would remember that."

"Maybe no one showed you their tits."

I shrugged. "It's possible. I would hate to think someone had, and I didn't remember it."

"Maybe they just weren't that memorable."

I shrugged again. "Maybe not. So, Pensacola?"

"Yeah, my brother was in corporate management with Obsidian. He has a winter home on Perdido Key. If anyone survived, he did. We need to get out of here before the Blues get back, and that's the best place I can think of to go. I don't know if there's anyplace 'safe' anymore, but wherever he is will be the closest thing to it."

"Wouldn't it be better to stay and fight rather than run?" I asked. "I killed at least 10 of them. How many more are there?"

"Lots. A number of the gangs merged in the aftermath of the war." He sighed. "I lied earlier, because I didn't want the grandkids to hear it. I said that we were waiting for the police to reestablish the law. Most of the local police got wiped out by the Blues—that blue band they're wearing? It's from policemen they've killed. I was hoping the National Guard would get here before our food ran out. Unless any of the Corporate troops still exist, those are the only people who have a chance against them."

"Well, shit," I said, sighing. "I guess I'm along for the ride then, as I'm sure they'll be gunning for me. How long's the drive?"

"Drive? No one drives anymore."

"Since when?"

"Since the war. How are we supposed to get gas? When you got here, you came from the direction of I-10. Did you notice any traffic on it?"

My face reddened. "Uh, no. I was kind of busy trying to stay alive at the time, but now that you mention it, not a single car drove by during the time I was by the highway." My shoulders sagged. I really wasn't up for this. "So, how long's the walk?"

"About 175 miles, give or take."

"That's a long-ass walk. Especially through country that may not currently be very friendly."

"That's a fact. Especially with children along. There's something to be said for safety in numbers, which is why I invited you along."

"Well, I can't stay here, and going south or west is out, so east sounds pretty good at the moment, especially if I'm going along with you. How long will it take you to be ready to go?"

"How's five minutes sound?"

"Four would be better."

"You remember I have kids, right?"

"Five will be fine."

You have to be flexible in this Fallen World.

* * * * *

Chapter Six

While Sam went to wrangle the kids and other folks in the house, I went back to get the rest of my gear. Of course, when I got back to the yard where I'd left my bags, they were gone.

Frowning, I looked at the window where I'd seen the man before. He tried to not let me see him—he only used one eye to look out the window to minimize his silhouette, but I caught the movement as he dodged out of sight, and when he looked again, 15 seconds later, he was looking down the barrel of the rifle I was holding. This time, I had a very clear view of him through the scope when he looked—it was a good scope and hadn't been damaged when I threw the rifle—and I held the rifle tightly with one hand as I waved to him to come out of the house with the other.

He dove back to the side, out of sight, and I sighed. I really didn't have time for this shit.

"The Blues will be back soon," I called. "If you don't want me to lead them here to you, I recommend you give me back my stuff. I've already killed a dozen people today. One more won't make that much of a difference to me." Sad as that sounded, the last two sentences were probably the truest things I'd said all day. It seemed like I should have felt something—anything—about the men I'd killed, but so far...nothing.

Even Sam had looked a little sad when he'd looked at the man he'd shot, but me? Nothing.

The door opened a crack. "Someone came and stole your bags," the man yelled through the crack.

"I told you to watch them," I replied, "so one of two things is going to happen. Either you're going to throw them out here where I can get them, or you're going to come out here and lead me to whoever has them."

"I didn't see who took them!"

"As long as I've been out here, you've been watching out one window or another. You know who has them." I made a production of looking down to turn off the safety on the rifle. "Last chance," I said. "If those bags aren't out here in five seconds, I start shooting. We'll make it easy on the Blues; they can just follow the sounds of my gunfire."

"One!"

"Two!"

"Three!"

"Wait!" the man called. "Let me see if my wife found them and brought them in."

The door shut and reopened several seconds later. "She had them," the man called. The door opened a little further, and the bags were thrown out into the yard. The door slammed shut before the second bag hit the ground. As the man appeared to have no intention of coming out to bring them to me, I made myself at home and walked in through the gate.

I could tell before I got to them that they had both been ransacked, and that things were missing from both. They had been full...now they weren't.

I slung the rifle over my shoulder and drew a pistol so I could have a free hand. Keeping one eye on the door, I searched through the bags. The clothes were still in the duffel, but some of the food and water were gone. Two of the pistols and several magazines were similarly missing from the other bag.

I sighed as I looked at the house, having armed the person I now needed to deal with. While nothing I'd seen so far had shown the man to be a killer, any person can kill if backed far enough into a corner. I also didn't know how many other people were in the house; the man might have backup. I scanned the house, looking for another set of eyes—or a gun—and didn't see one. I did, however, see a potential solution.

"Several of my weapons and my food seems to be missing," I called.

The door opened a crack again. "That was for watching them for you," the man said.

"Are you planning on going anywhere soon?" I asked.

"What? What do you mean?"

"It looks like you have two vehicles," I said, pointing to where a small economy car and a truck sat under a carport. "I'm in need of transportation. If you throw out the keys to the truck, you can keep everything you stole from me, and we'll call it even."

"I want another magazine of ammo," the man replied.

"Fine," I said. I pulled one from the bag and flipped it onto the grass.

Two seconds later the door opened a little more, and he threw the keys out.

"Go!" he ordered. "And don't try anything foolish—I have a gun on you!"

I holstered the pistol, set the rifle down, and threw the duffel bag over a shoulder. Grabbing the rifle with one hand and the pack with my other, I kept the rifle pointed in his direction as I sidled to the carport. "Stay in the house until I'm gone, then you can come get the other magazine," I said. "If I see you outside the house, I'll kill you."

I threw the bags into the back of the truck, climbed up into the cab, and started the truck. It took a couple of tries, as if it hadn't been run in a while, but it eventually fired up. I drove it down the driveway, and found Sam and his entourage waiting for me on the street. In addition to Sam, there were three kids and another, younger man, who was probably the kids' father. The kids and the young man threw their gear in the bed of the truck and got in after it, while Sam joined me in the cab.

"Would you really have killed him?" Sam asked.

I stopped the truck and pulled back the charging handle to show him the rifle was empty. He chuckled.

"I didn't want to kill him and leave his wife without protection."

The man laughed harder. "Old Man Stevens' wife died three years ago."

I started laughing, too, as we drove off.

Sometimes you have to bluff in this Fallen World.

* * * * *

Chapter Seven

We made it about 35 miles outside of town before we hit the first roadblock. I had hoped to avoid the majority of towns and cities by staying on I-10; the local roads would have been far more likely to have petty dictators set up traffic stops to exact "taxes" or whatever they wanted to call their extortion attempts.

We'd passed several off ramps to little podunk towns and gas stations (which, I thought, would be great places to get ambushed), but there was no avoiding the intersection of Highway 49, which was a major north-south connector in Mississippi. With an outlet mall and an international airport, it was too much to hope for that someone hadn't taken control of it.

"Hey, uh, Fred?" Sam asked pointing out in front of us. He hadn't liked calling me Ishmael—something about a big whale that had ruined his grade point average in school and made him go into the Corporate Army. When I told him about getting called 'Fred' by one of the Blues, he'd laughed and said it was perfect for me. I didn't particularly want to be called by the name of a dead guy—much less one that I had personally killed—but the name had stuck. Even the kids were using it now. Whatever.

I frowned at him for using that name—to which he smiled, of course—and asked, "What?"

"What's that out there?" Sam asked. He had stayed in the cab with me while his son, George, and George's three kids—John, Alice, and Eric—rode in the bed of the truck. It probably broke a number of rules and ordinances, but they were made by governments that didn't exist anymore, so it really didn't matter. They tried to stay low, and I tried not to hit any big bumps that would throw them out. It had worked so far.

"Looks like there's a road block," I replied, slowing the truck. The people up ahead had put several cars across both lanes of traffic, prior to where the exit ramps left the travel lanes. Only the ones in my lane affected me—there was a concrete divider between the two directions of travel. It was hard to tell if there were lanes through the cars blocking the highway—there probably were, but I couldn't see from where we stopped. I could, however, see at least four people behind the roadblock. I stopped the truck about half a mile from the roadblock to consider my options.

"What do we do?" Sam asked.

"Well, I doubt any of those people are out here to ensure we're well-provisioned as we go past, nor are they there to wish us a cheery goodbye as they speed us on our way."

Sam chuckled. "That seems logical enough."

"So," I continued, "I suspect they have malice in their hearts and are going to try to take what we have away from us."

"Also a reasonable deduction, seems like."

"The problem is that I don't think I want to give it to them, nor do I know whether they will let us go on, even if we gave them everything we have."

"Including the truck."

"Including the truck I so recently acquired," I agreed.

"So what do we do?" Sam asked.

"I'm thinking about that."

"Had any ideas?"

"So far, most of them are just things I don't want to do. I don't want to stop. I don't want to talk with them. I don't want to give them everything I have, including my life."

"All things considered," Sam said, "I'd rather you not give them our lives either."

"I figured you'd feel that way."

"So we're back to the same question. What do we do?"

"I'm still thinking. It seems like there's a plan in the back of my brain—like I've been in this situation before—but I can't pull it out."

"Well, you're going to have to decide soon, because it looks like one of them is coming this way."

I looked up and saw Sam was right; one of the men had left the shelter of the barricade and was coming toward us. Worse, he held a rifle at port arms.

"Not the friendliest of greetings to send someone out armed," I noted.

"Would you walk up to a bunch of strangers unarmed?" Sam asked.

"Probably not," I replied. I shifted the truck into reverse and backed slowly away from the man.

"What are you doing, Fred?" Sam asked.

"Seeing how much he wants to talk to us. And my name's not Fred."

Sam smiled, and the man started running toward us. I sped up, keeping the same distance between us. With no one else on the road, it wasn't difficult.

"You might also be trying to piss him off," Sam noted.

I looked over and winked. "I might be doing some of that, too," I agreed as I looked over my shoulder to drive down the road.

"Seems like you might have succeeded!" Sam exclaimed, his voice rising. "Kids, get down!"

I looked forward to see the man aiming his rifle at us. "Fuck!" I yelled as I spun the vehicle around.

The man fired, but my sudden movement threw off his aim.

"Guess we know a little bit more about his intentions," Sam noted, grabbing hold of the handle above the door as I skewed the truck around.

"Guess so." I put the accelerator to the floor and roared off, jerking the truck back and forth as the man fired a second and third time. Finally, I was around a corner, and I slowed the truck to a stop.

"Everyone okay back there?" I asked through the rear window.

"Little shaken and bruised," George said, "but other than that, we're okay."

"So what's the plan now?" Sam asked as I tried to catch my breath and think.

"Well, I don't see that we have too many options," I replied. "We can't go back to Slidell, and I still don't want to stop and talk to the people at the roadblock."

"Nope," Sam said. "They didn't much look like the talking types."

"Our only other option is to run the barricade."

"While they're shooting at us."

I shrugged. "I didn't say it was a good plan…"

"It's just the only one we have," Sam finished with a sigh.

"Pretty much."

"Let them know in the back to stay down," I said, driving off in the opposite direction from the barricade.

"Okay," Sam replied, "but aren't you going the wrong way?"

"Nope. Just trying not to make it too easy on them."

I had almost made it back to the prior exit when I saw them. "Persistent bunch," I noted, pointing at the collection of cars and trucks coming toward us at a high rate of speed.

"Who's that?" Sam asked.

"The Blues, I suspect."

"You're not planning to ram them, are you?" he asked, grabbing onto the 'oh, shit!' handle again as we quickly approached the on-coming traffic in a high-speed game of chicken.

"Nope," I replied as the distance rapidly decreased. Sam braced for the imminent collision, but we reached the end of the concrete divider, and I spun the wheel to the right. I had a momentary view—nothing more than a flash—of the car that went through the space our truck had just occupied. The driver's hands were on the steering wheel, his arms locked for the crash. His eyes were huge…but so was the pistol the passenger was holding to the driver's head.

Our truck slid through the grass, threatening to roll, and I straightened it out to control the slide, but then jerked it back to the left to avoid one of the Blues' vehicles that had lost control and was rolling through the median. I spun the wheel back to the right as the car came back under control and drove up onto the westbound travel lane.

"Go! Go! Go!" Sam yelled as the front window spiderwebbed.

My senses broadened—they had been completely focused on keeping the car from rolling—and I heard the guns—several of them—firing. I floored it again. The wheels spun but finally caught, and we were off again, headed back toward the barricade, but now we were in the opposite lanes of travel.

"Is this a good idea?" Sam asked, motioning to the lane we were in.

"Want to go back and ask the Blues if they'd mind if we changed lanes?"

"No!" Sam yelled as a bullet hit the cab. "Drive! Faster!"

My foot was already on the floor, so there wasn't much else I could do. I checked the mirrors—there were Blue vehicles chasing us in both the eastbound and westbound lanes. The ones on the other side of the concrete divider were a little closer as they hadn't had to slide through the median, and a couple of the sportier cars were catching up to us in our lanes. Sam and I both flinched as another round hit the cab.

"Here!" I yelled, handing Sam one of my pistols.

"What am I supposed to do with this?"

"Shoot them!" I exclaimed, motioning toward the cars coming up behind us.

"I can't hit them with this!"

"No, but maybe you can make them keep their damn heads down!"

He stuck his head and shoulders out of the window—no small feat at the speed we were going—and fired off several rounds.

The people at the barricade began firing at us as we approached, although they split their fire between us and the Blue vehicles on the other side of the concrete divider.

"Get in!" I yelled.

Sam fired two more shots.

"Get in, dammit!" I yelled, but Sam just fired again.

Realizing he couldn't hear me, I reached over with my right hand, grabbed his belt, and pulled him back toward me.

After a moment, he pulled himself back in. "*What?*" he exclaimed. "I had it!"

I pointed in front of us.

"Oh, *shit!*" he yelled. The people at the barricade had called in reinforcements—and I could see more coming—and at least five people were now firing from behind the barricade on both sides of the divider.

Sam grabbed the handle again as I showed no signs of stopping.

"You can't run into them!" he yelled. "The kids in the back!"

At least he was thinking again. He'd been too scared to realize it the first time it had looked like we were going to crash.

"I know," I said with a growl.

The barricade approached with a ludicrous rate of closure, and I could see several of the people behind the barricade break for the sides as they realized we—along with several of the Blues—had no intention of stopping.

That proved to be the undoing of one of them as I swerved to the left off the surface of the road to avoid the barricade. I hit him with the right front fender at about 85 miles an hour, catapulting him through the air. I caught a flash of him flying through the air, then he was gone, and all my focus was on regaining control of the truck again as we raced down the embankment.

One of the cars following us lost control and rolled, taking out a second Blue vehicle. I swerved to miss a light pole in the center of the embankment and fishtailed back and forth as I overcompensated. The car behind me didn't see it and slammed into it at about 70 miles an hour. The pole snapped down on impact, crushing the roof onto the driver. That car was out of the chase.

I had just gotten the vehicle under control when we hit the railroad tracks. Slightly raised, the truck hit them and leaped into the air. I don't know if we actually got airborne, but the truck got awfully light on its suspension before crashing back down on the other side.

By now the truck had slowed to 35 mph, and I easily avoided the large shrubbery in our path and jumped onto the concrete of the cloverleaf, pouring on the speed again as we approached Highway 49.

"Shit!" I yelled as I stood on the brakes; the highway had a raised concrete curb. "Hold on!"

I squared up the steering and tried to hit it as straight-on as I could. We were only going about 20 when we hit, and the truck scaled the obstacle easily as a bullet whined off the road just to the side of me.

I jumped the truck back down on the other side, crossed a small strip of grass, and then was accelerating up the cloverleaf on the other side. I crossed over to the off ramp—just in time to make it onto the bridge over the river it crossed—and continued toward I-10. As I expected, there was another barricade on this side of Highway 49, just past where the off ramp joined back in, and I swerved off the concrete to go around it. There was only one person left at it, either a young man or an older boy, who did nothing but stare open-mouthed at us as we roared past. I gave him a small salute when I saw him look at me.

We hit I-10 again, and I floored it once we were stabilized.

"Is everyone all right in the back?" I asked.

"We're good!" George yelled. "Scared as shit and our bruise collection is growing, but we're all still here."

"That turned out okay," I said. I turned to look at Sam and was just in time to see his head snap forward as the bullet hit him.

"*Fuck!*" I screamed at the world in general. As Sam slumped forward, I saw the lead Blue car, paralleling us on the other side of the concrete divider. The driver was sitting as far back as he could so his passenger could shoot at us.

I slammed on the brakes, and the car shot in front of us. Not seeing anyone in our lane behind us, I came to a complete stop and jumped out of the car. I drew my other pistol as the other car did a three-point turn and came back toward us, and fired three aimed shots at the driver.

The car went out of control after the third and crashed into the concrete divider, where it scraped its way to a stop. The passenger crawled halfway out the window and pointed his pistol at me, but I fired again and his head snapped back as the bullet hit him in the temple. I strode toward the car, hoping he'd move again, but he didn't flinch. I got to the car and shot him again in the back of the head anyway. Just because. I hadn't known Sam that long, but I'd kind of grown to like him. He was the only friend I had—that I knew of, at least—and now he was gone.

Dammit.

Good friends are hard to keep in this Fallen World.

* * * * *

Chapter Eight

"You might want to hurry with that," George said as I went through the Blues' car, claiming the weapons, ammo, and anything else that looked valuable as a spoil of war.

I was still pissed off at the man who had shot Sam, and, while I heard him, I didn't really *hear* him.

"I said, you might want to hurry!" George said again. His voice rose a bit this time, and it was enough to break into my consciousness. "*Fred!*"

"*What?*" I yelled back, exasperated, as I looked up from the back seat of the car.

George pointed back in the direction of the roadblock, and I sighed. Two more cars were racing toward us, with a third one a little further behind them. *Didn't these guys ever give up?*

A feeling of rage came over me, and I had an out-of-body experience as I watched myself jump onto the trunk of the car. The driver of the first car immediately changed direction to aim for me, with the second car a little further back and in the outside lane.

I stood on the back deck of the car and waited as they sped closer. The passenger leaned out the window with a pistol and fired at me several times. I heard one go past and changed my aim from the driver to the passenger. One shot through the head, and he dropped, limp, to hang from the window. The driver looked over at the passenger—he was close enough to see now—and I shot him once through the front windshield.

The driver had already committed to ramming the car I was standing on—apparently, he'd never been in a car wreck and didn't know how violent they were—and I jumped to the concrete divider as the two cars slammed together, balancing gracefully on the six inch ledge.

A man leaned out the back window of the second car as it approached at high speed. He had an automatic rifle, and he began spraying it in my general direction. "Get down!" I yelled to the kids, who were trying to see what was going on, then I aimed and fired. It took me two shots, but I blew out the tire closest to me, and the driver swerved slightly to sideswipe the tangled mass of cars. The man in the back was ripped violently from the window, as was the corpse hanging from the earlier wrecked car, in a spray of blood and body parts.

I dropped the magazine and slammed in a new one as the car slid to a stop. The third car arrived at the same time, going into a skid as the driver locked up the brakes. It screeched to a stop and four men burst from it, with two more coming from the second car on the left.

I did a somersault as I flipped from the concrete divider, and I landed in a crouch on the asphalt of I-10. I looked back and forth between the groups as I pulled out one of the pistols I had recovered from the earlier car and began firing both weapons.

The men on the left were closer and each of my eyes looked down a set of sights as a pistol locked onto both of them. The first man got a shot off before a round from the gun in my left hand hit him in the chest; the man on the right took two hits before he could get off a round. Both men collapsed.

A round went past my head from behind me, and I dove to the side, taking the asphalt impact on my left shoulder. Pain blossomed like the fires of a sunburst as I opened up my earlier wound. I put it aside and rolled to find the four men from the third car firing at me. A piece of asphalt from a near miss tore open my cheek, then my pistols were in-line. Both fired, and two of the men shooting at me dropped. A bullet grazed my ass as I switched targets, but then I fired again, and the two remaining men dropped.

Two of the men were still moving feebly so I climbed to my feet, limped over, and shot each of the men in the head. As I looked at the last man, I came to my senses again. The first thing I noticed was that I hurt. A lot. From everywhere.

The pistols fell from my senseless hands, and I stared at my last victim. Psychopath? Yeah, it sure seemed like it. An athletic one, I realized—I had no idea I could do a flip in the air, nor that I'd ever *want* to—but psychopath? Yeah, pretty much. Some of the men had been obviously dead, but I'd shot them again in the head, anyway.

After some time—I didn't know how much—George came over to stand next to me. He looked down at the man I was staring at.

"You're not waiting for him to get back up, are you?" he asked. "I think he's pretty well and truly dead."

"Looks like it," I agreed, not knowing what I was supposed to do next.

"You're bleeding," George noted.

I looked down. I had a lot of blood on me. I couldn't be sure, but most of it seemed to be mine, except for the spray pattern from when Sam got hit.

"Yep."

"I've got a first aid kit. Want me to patch some of that up?"

"Probably be helpful," I acknowledged.

"I'll be right back."

He came back and made me take off my shirt, then cleaned and patched me up the best he could. He was also going to put some antibiotic on my ass, but I figured I could do that myself. It wasn't much more than a scratch, thankfully, and I didn't particularly want to drop my pants in the middle of I-10.

He handed me a new shirt. "So, what do we do now? I took dad's body down the slope so the kids didn't have to see it, but I don't have a shovel or anything to bury it with."

"We don't have time to bury it," I replied. His mouth dropped open, so I added, "The folks at the road block had to hear all the shooting, and sooner or later they're going to get organized and come find out what happened. If nothing else, they'll come looking to see what they can salvage."

"I can help hold them off," he offered. "I know how to shoot…not as well as you, maybe, but I can shoot."

"When they come, they're going to come in a big group. We'll need to be gone. I killed these idiots, but if there are enough of them, they're going to win in the end."

"So, what do we do?"

"Do you know where Sam's brother lives in Pensacola?"

"Yeah, he's on Perdido Key. I live there too—he's down the island a ways from me, but I know where to go."

"Then that's where we will head. We can't go back, and I don't know of anywhere else we can go to figure out what we need to do next. See what you can scavenge from the guys I killed while I finish patching myself up, and we'll get going."

I walked over to stand behind one of the Blues' cars so the kids wouldn't see me with my pants down and put some antibiotic cream on my last bullet wound. With the pain from my other wounds, I barely noticed this one, but I didn't want it to get infected. I had no idea where the nearest functional hospital was, but I doubted I particularly wanted to go there.

I was just finishing up when I heard one of the kids. "Dad? Mr. Fred?" the voice asked from the direction of our truck.

"Yeah?" George asked, more used to answering questions from his boy. It took me a second to realize the boy also meant me. I didn't know what my name was, but I was pretty sure it *wasn't* Fred. But then again, nothing that anyone had called me felt right.

"There's a group of cars coming, Daddy," the boy said. I could see him now; it was the older one. He was standing on the bed of the truck. George must have put him on lookout duty. That made a lot of good sense; I wished I'd thought of it.

I shook my head, trying to clear it. I knew I needed to focus more, but it somehow seemed like part of me was missing. I knew some things, but others were missing. And then I'd do something like kill a bunch of people without even trying. That was the part that freaked me out the most. How could I kill like that and not remember?

I filed it away for later and looked down the road. The boy was right; there was a big convoy of cars coming. Unlike the Blues, though, they were being cautious. They probably didn't know what we were doing when we broke through their barricade—they may not have even known there were two groups that ripped through their forces, but they knew a big fight had occurred, and they wanted to make sure they could get out of whatever they got into.

In other words, they were smart. I didn't want to take this group on.

"We gotta go, George," I yelled. "Grab what you can."

I pulled my pants up, did a quick search of the car, and hobbled over to the concrete barrier. I gingerly made my way across it and back to the truck. The convoy was still about half a mile away and appeared to be in no hurry to come roaring in on us. They were probably trying to figure out how many of us were left; when they realized there were only a couple of adults, they'd probably charge us. I wanted to be gone before that happened.

"Want me to drive so you don't have to sit?" George asked.

"No, you stay with the kids in the back," I replied. One of the things I realized I was missing was a good sense of compassion. While I could recognize—clinically—the kids would probably be scared and need comforting, I also knew I wasn't the person to give it to them. George could sit with them and handle it.

When everyone was settled in the back, I started the motor and drove off. I could see the convoy of cars accelerate once we left. They stopped at the battle site and got out of their cars, while I drove off at 50 miles an hour. I don't think we left them much of value, but they were welcome to whatever was there as long as they didn't follow after us. They didn't seem to be in any sort of hurry to catch us, so I imagined they'd go back to their barricade once they searched the remaining cars. I was happy to leave both them and the Blues behind.

You take what you can get in this Fallen World.

* * * * *

Chapter Nine

We made it past Biloxi and Pascagoula without any problems. George thought that there used to be a naval shipyard at Pascagoula, which would probably have made it a target during the war. If so, the city probably ate a nuke or two. I-10 was five miles north of the city and its shipyards; I didn't figure I needed to go any closer, just in case, and hurried past it.

It was starting to get dark as we approached the Alabama state line, and I figured we needed to find some shelter for the night. Highway 90 ran parallel to the interstate, just beyond a small cleared strip, and I decided to get off the main road. I went across the cleared area, knocked down a small fence, and continued east on Highway 90. About 0.3 miles later, we came to an abandoned restaurant. It looked like crap, and the ceiling had collapsed in the kitchen, but the dining room still had a roof so we took our sleeping bags—I got Sam's—and made camp as best we could. George and I pushed some of the booths together. There would probably be an army of roaches that would come visit us once it got dark; I didn't want to sleep on the ground with the entire insect population of Alabama.

I went back outside and backed the truck in so we could leave quickly if we needed to, then took the first watch. I woke up George about halfway through the night and lay down for a bit. I didn't sleep very well, due to my wounds and the fact I knew George wasn't really prepared for a night of "watch." Ultimately, though, blood loss and exhaustion finally caught up with me, and I slept for a little while.

* * *

"That was some damn fine shooting yesterday," George said to me the next morning as we ate some cold food from our stock. He looked a lot worse for the wear. It was probably the least amount of sleep he'd had in a while, even forted up at Sam's house.

"Thanks."

"Where'd you learn how to do that?"

"I don't know."

"Can you teach me to shoot like that?" John, the older boy, asked. "Dad and—" he sniffed, "—grandpa taught me how to shoot a rifle, but we don't have that much rifle ammo, and we have a bunch of pistols now. Figured I ought to learn."

I looked at his dad, who shrugged. "That's probably true," George said. "He's got to learn some time."

"I guess I can teach you," I replied.

"When?"

I looked at his dad, who shrugged again.

"No time like the present, I guess. We're as safe here as we're going to be, and I doubt anyone these days will move *toward* the sounds of people shooting."

I told George to watch out the front of the building anyway—you never know; about half the people of the world are dumber than average—and took John and the two other kids out back for a lesson in pistols.

"How old are you?" I asked.

"Sixteen," John replied. "Old enough to kill someone if I had to. Especially if they're some of the people who killed grandpa."

"Killing's hard," I said.

"It looked pretty easy when you did it yesterday," John replied.

"It may have appeared like it to you, but I got lucky. I also got wounded myself, so I'd encourage you to try a different resolution first."

John stared at me as if I thought he were stupid. Apparently, the fallen world had already jaded him. Oh well, that might not be a bad thing.

"Okay, then," I said. "There are two things you need to know. The first is, you never point a gun at something you don't want to kill. Second, if you *do* point it at someone, you better be ready to kill them, because they're probably going to do their best to do it to you before you do it to them. Got it?"

John said he did, so I showed him how to operate the pistol. We also talked about trigger discipline and how to load and unload it. We talked so long that his younger brother wandered off and the two older children were rolling their eyes as I gave them additional pointers on the effective use of a handgun.

"What?" I finally asked after about the 30th eye roll.

"You said you'd teach me to shoot the pistol," John said. "We've been doing this for an hour, and I haven't shot it even once yet."

"I'm just getting to that," I replied. "I just wanted to make sure you didn't accidentally kill me or one of your siblings while I was doing so."

"Grampa told us about weapon safety. Blah, blah, blah, keep your booger pickers off the trigger 'til you're ready to shoot. Blah,

blah, blah." He held up a hand. "I know it's important, but I've already *got* that."

"You just want to shoot the darn pistol."

"Yes, sir," he said with a smile.

"Well okay, then," I said with a grin in reply. "Let's do that."

I took a two foot by two foot board and propped it up about 30 feet away, then came back and drew a firing line. "Here's what I want you to do on your turn." I loaded an eight-round magazine into the pistol, then aimed and fired until the slide locked back.

"See?" I asked. "Nothing to it."

"Seriously?" John asked. "You only hit the board twice."

"Did I?" I looked at the board. Sure enough, there were only two holes through it. I shrugged. "So let's see you do better."

The boy loaded and fired the pistol. Although he missed twice, the board now sported six new holes.

"That's easy," John said. "Can we do it again?"

"Sure," I said, walking up to put a new board in place. "We'll have a competition to see who's best." I went back and toed the line. This time, I concentrated as I fired off another magazine, knowing that I put all eight bullets into the target.

"You're not much of a challenge," the boy said. "You still only got four on the board, and you took about three times as long. What happened to, 'You have to be able to do this quickly?'"

"Let's see you do it then, if you're so smart," I replied.

The boy smiled as he stepped up to the line and loaded his pistol. He fired off the magazine—a lot faster than I had—then walked over to inspect the target. "Ha!" he said. "I hit it nine times—more than twice as many as you!"

"That was a great job," I replied. "I guess you win that pistol. It's now yours, but you have to clean it and take care of it. You good with that?"

"Absolutely!" he exclaimed. "I'll take it in and clean it right now."

I could see he wanted to run with the pistol, but he walked—quickly—to the restaurant and went inside, careful to keep it pointed at the ground.

"That's nice of you to build him up like that," George said. At some point, he'd come around the other side of the building to watch. "I imagine for someone like you, it's harder to miss a target than it is for him to hit it."

I chuckled. "You have no idea," I said.

George nodded. "I'm going to go inside and congratulate him, if you don't mind watching out for a bit."

"No problem," I said. "I'll take care of things out here."

George went inside, leaving me looking at the target. I had no idea what had happened. I hadn't let him win—I'd tried my level best to hit it every time, and I had missed more often than I'd hit it. I hadn't even come close to the results of someone just shooting a pistol for the first time. After about ten seconds, I turned away, shaking my head.

There are some things you just can't figure out in this Fallen World.

* * * * *

Chapter Ten

"So, what's the plan today?" George asked as we tossed our things into the truck 15 minutes later.

"We're going to drive to Pensacola," I replied.

"It can't be that far, can it?"

"It wouldn't have been that far a few weeks ago—an hour and a half, tops. The problem is that in between us and Pensacola is the charming metropolis of Mobile, Alabama."

"And?"

"And it's a big city," George replied. "I've gotta believe it got hit with a nuke or three."

"Oh."

"Yeah, oh. If it's still there, I have to imagine that there would be all sorts of barricades and such. If I were a betting man, though, my guess would be that it's destroyed and radioactive. There's also a really big bridge we'd have to go over…and I'm going to go out on a limb and guess that it doesn't exist anymore, either."

"That's a whole lot of 'we can't,'" I noted. "What is it we *can* do?"

"Well, that's what I wanted to discuss with you. We're on Highway 90. I recognized it when we got off the interstate yesterday. I've gone back and forth to Perdido Key a few times on 90. We take it east from here, then turn south on Alabama 188. That will take us to 193, which will take us to Dauphin Island."

"Okay, so Dolphin Island to Perdido Key, which I'm guessing is also an island. Please tell me there's a bridge."

"Well, about that…" he said. "There's a ferry."

"No bridge?"

"No. None." When my frown grew more pronounced, he added, "But the guys at the ferry are good people! I've never heard anything bad about them."

"And you think this ferry will still be in use?"

"Honestly, I have no idea. However, it's the only other way, without going hundreds of miles out of the way."

"I don't think we have gas for that," I noted. "I think we're at about a quarter of a tank."

"Yeah, so, unless we stop for gas somewhere, that's not only going to be our best option; it's also our *only* option."

"Well, shit."

"Pretty much."

I sighed. "Okay, the ferry it is. I hope society on Dolphin Island hasn't gone to hell like everywhere else."

"That's Dauphin Island," he corrected, "and as far as society goes…me, too."

"Well, then, I guess that's what we'll do," I replied. "And the folks there will either be sociable, or we'll have to make them sociable. If that's the only way of getting to Perdido Key, I guess we'll just have to make it work."

Sometimes, plans have to change in this Fallen World.

* * * * *

Chapter Eleven

We drove a couple of miles to the east. I had cleaned out the cab of the truck as best I could, and George rode up front with me. The weather held, so, while cool, there was no problem with the kids riding in the bed of the truck. I slowed to a stop as we approached the junction of Alabama Road 188.

"What's up?" George asked, scanning the road ahead for danger.

I pointed to the gas station across from our intended turn.

"We could use some gas," I replied. "We're probably going to run out before we make it to Perdido Key."

"I don't see any sort of defenses or issues by the pump or store," George said.

I nodded. "I know. That's what bothers me. Gas is going to be a very valuable commodity, and something to be protected. While it's possible that things haven't totally gone to shit here in rural, redneck Alabama, I doubt it. Things were shitty here before the bombs ever dropped, and I expect everyone here owns a gun or three."

"So what are we going to do?"

"You and John are going to cover me with the rifles we have from inside the truck, and I'm going to walk into the station."

"We only have a few rounds for the long guns," George reminded.

I gave George a half-smile and nodded toward the service station. "I know that, and you know that, but *they* don't know that."

"They?"

"Yeah, they. I just saw someone move in one of the windows. There are people in the station, and they're watching us. Probably getting nervous, too. I better go before they get too nervous."

I pulled the truck a little further up, then angled it across the road so it was broadside to the station. George slid over and pointed one rifle out the window, while I had John cover the opposite direction with a pistol.

"Shouldn't he be facing the pumps, too?" George asked.

"What if someone tries to sneak up on you while I'm gone?"

"I, uh…"

"Yeah, that's what I thought, too," I replied. "John, watch the opposite side and shoot anything that tries to sneak up on the truck."

"Yes sir," John said, serious. I think it had just dawned on him how "real" things had gotten.

I set up Alice with the other rifle in the bed of the truck, and had her point it toward the gas station. It didn't really matter much that she couldn't shoot it; we didn't have any bullets for it, either. I had her younger brother Eric lie down in the bed of the truck.

With them as prepared as I could make them, I walked toward the gas station. I had two pistols in my belt within easy reach, but kept my hands high. I approached the building, keeping the pumps in between us. I figured having to shoot past the pumps would make them at least think twice before firing at me. I hoped.

"Hello in the station!" I called, trying not to yell so loud that all of their neighbors could hear, too. I figured the fewer participants we had, the better. "Can I come in?"

"Slowly, mister," a man's voice replied. "Whaddya want?"

"I'm trying to make it to Perdido Key and could use a tank of gas."

"How you gonna pay?"

"How about credit?" I asked.

"You gotta be fucking kidding me," the man said with a laugh. "Ain't no such thing as credit no more."

"I have some cash…"

"And what's that gonna get me?"

I shrugged. "I don't know what you can buy around here."

"With that shit?" the man asked. "Not a damn thing."

"Well, what will a tank of gas cost?"

"What kind of weapons and ammo you got for trade?"

"I have a pistol or two I could trade you. Maybe a magazine of ammo." I reached the pump, but didn't go any closer, figuring the pump was my best cover. They wouldn't want to shoot at it if it had any gas; if they didn't have gas, there weren't any issues with hiding behind it.

"Where'd you say you were goin' again?"

"Perdido Key, why?"

"Where ya comin' from?"

Something was wrong; he was stalling. I glanced behind me to see that all eyes in the truck were on me.

"John!" I yelled. "Turn around!"

He spun around, and his pistol came up immediately. George spun around, too, as John began firing, and he slid to the other side of the truck. Both of my pistols were in my hands as I crouched behind one of the pumps. John fired four times then stopped, although I could see he was still pointing the pistol at the forest on the other side of the truck.

"You okay, John?" I called.

"Yeah!" he yelled back, still focused on the other side of the truck. "Two guys were trying to sneak up on us. I think I got one."

I turned back to the service station. "That how you deal honestly with people here?" I asked.

"Don't know what you mean," the man replied.

"Come on out here," I ordered.

"Get fucked!"

"If you don't come out here, I'm going to come in there and get you."

"Why don't you fucking try?" he asked.

I figured we were pretty much done talking by this point, so I faked like I was coming around the pump one way, then ran out the other. A gun roared—a shotgun from the sound of it, but he had fallen for the fake, and I made it out of the pumps. I felt the wind from a second blast as the pellets went past, but it was another miss, and then I was up to the building.

I fired a round through the glass door, shattering it, and the shotgun roared a third time. The rack of hydrogenated snack cakes by the door disintegrated in the blast.

"Last chance!" I yelled.

"What part of 'get fucked' didn't you understand?"

A large rock sat by the side of the building, probably used to prop the door open on nice days. I threw it through the empty door frame into the closest rack. The man behind the counter fired at the motion, like he had every other time. I fired once, hitting him in the chest, and he fell backward into the condom display stand. I avoided the glass remaining in the door frame as I stepped through, approached the counter, and shot him again through the head.

Click!

I dove behind the counter, landing on the dead man. I heard a pump action shotgun cycle, then it roared, and the condom display exploded. I tried to stand up as the pump action worked again, but slipped in a puddle of blood and fell back to the floor. The shotgun boomed again, covering me in bits of paper and metal. This time I found my footing and rose to find a woman working the action. I shot her twice, and she fell backward into a rack of snacks.

A quick search showed no one else was in the store, so I went back out and waved George forward. He pulled up to the pump and jumped out.

"You pump," I directed. "John, you go to the other side of the store and watch for anyone coming. Alice, grab that bag and grab as much food as you can from the store. Eric, stay where you are and watch for anyone coming from this side."

I ran back to the door and opened it, using the rock to hold it open, and started bringing cases of water to the truck. When I didn't see Alice, I walked around the racks to find her staring at the dead woman. The bag she'd been carrying had fallen to the floor, and she stood with her mouth open, transfixed, unable to look away.

I stepped in front of her, breaking her contact with the scene, then gently—or as gently as I could—turned her around. "Alice," I said, putting the bag back in her hand, "I need you to grab all the food you can and bring it to the truck. Don't look at the woman."

I grabbed another case of water and took it to the truck. When I came back, Alice was filling the bag. Not as quickly as I would have liked, but food was going into the bag. It also wasn't what I would have selected, but it would hopefully make her and her siblings happy.

"Tank's full," George said as I came out with another case of water.

"Good. Grab all the spare tanks you can find and fill them too. Quickly!"

I grabbed several bags from behind the counter and scooped all the energy and protein bars into one, then added the containers of peanut butter, the two bags of rice, and the four boxes of pasta into a second and a third. I scooped up the two shotguns and took it all to the truck. Alice was on her second trip, this time with every candy bar she could carry. At least they'd be good for energy.

I took another case of water to the truck, and Alice jumped as I came into the store. She turned toward me holding a package of toilet paper and several boxes of tampons. She glared at me, as if daring me to stop her, and said, "I'm taking these for me."

I nodded, and she walked past, then I stepped forward to look at the shelf. All that remained was single-ply toilet paper, which sucked, but was at least—marginally—better than using a leaf. I grabbed the rest of them, as well as the rest of the tampons, and ran them out to the truck.

I ran back to the store to find John coming in the other entrance. "People are coming!" he exclaimed.

I grabbed an armful of cigarette cartons and gave them to him. "Take these to the truck and get in!"

"I don't smoke!" he exclaimed.

"Just do it!" I yelled.

He scampered off with the cigarettes.

Movement caught my eye. "Alice, get in the truck!" She rushed out, not needing to be told twice. She was probably happy to be away from the dead body.

I grabbed the box of shotgun shells behind the counter and the three first aid kits alongside it. I threw them into a bag, then filled it up with cigarette cartons and ran out the door. George already had the truck running and the kids loaded into the back, and was sitting in the passenger seat with his rifle out the window. The driver's door was open, so I slid in, slammed it shut, and drove off in a spray of gravel.

I slowed, slightly, as I drove over the railroad tracks on Alabama 188, then roared off. I saw a few people come around the side of the convenience store, but we were too far for them to bother shooting at us. After a couple of seconds, we rounded a curve and were out of sight, and I released the breath I didn't realize I'd been holding.

George pulled the rifle back in from the window and looked inside the bags I'd brought out with me from the store. "Cigarettes?" he asked. "I didn't know you smoked."

"I don't, but something the guy asked me made sense."

"What was that?"

"He asked me what I was going to trade for the gas. I'm guessing that, for a smoker, the cigarettes will be more valuable than food these days—they're going to be in short supply. I also threw in some bottles of wine—they didn't have anything harder than that. It's not for us; it's to negotiate with. I wanted to have a better answer the next time someone asks what I have to trade."

George nodded, then looked back to check the kids.

You have to know how to operate a barter economy in this Fallen World.

* * * * *

Chapter Twelve

We drove for about ten minutes. While I wanted to go fast, I also knew that doing so would be a good way to run into something I couldn't get back out of, so I ended up going about 45 miles an hour. The area was residential, with single houses and neighborhoods located on both sides of the road. Nearly all of them looked like their owners had forted them up, and most of them had someone looking out a front window with a rifle.

I couldn't remember much of the previous world, but I didn't like this new, fallen world I found myself in.

We pulled up to the stop sign at a "T" intersection. Across the street were the remains of a fast food restaurant. All the windows had been broken out, and it looked like someone had halfheartedly tried to set it on fire. With as much grease as there was in there, they must not have tried very hard.

George snorted softly. "I guess the food supplies have dwindled enough that there's even a demand for fast food now."

As we headed south, we came to a large sign that someone had hand painted. It read, "Welcome to Bayou La Batre. The laws apply here and will be enforced with lethal force."

"Huh," I said. "Bayou La Batre? Wasn't that the shrimping city in that movie?" I couldn't think of the movie's name, just that there had been one.

"Yeah," George said with a nod. "Looks like they take their security seriously here."

I slowed as we approached the first buildings in town—another convenience store and some more fast food restaurants—since there was a barricade across the road, with four people manning it.

"Is there another way around the town?" I asked.

"Yeah, but there's no telling what's on it. It's a small road."

"If laws really do apply here, then we ought to be all right..." I thought for a second, then made up my mind. "We'll stay on the road."

As I approached the barricade, a man came out from behind the barricade and waved for me to stop. I did, at a spot marked "Stop Here" on the asphalt, and the man continued to walk toward the truck. I could see he was armed, but he kept his pistol in a holster. He looked tough and no-nonsense, from the cowboy hat he wore, on down to his boots. The fact that he was wearing some sort of sheriff's uniform only added to his air of authority.

The people at the barricade shifted as he walked toward us. They didn't have their rifles pointed at us, exactly, but they were close enough that it wouldn't have taken them long to get there.

I left my weapons in the truck and got out to talk to the man.

"Good morning," I said as he approached.

"'Morning," he replied. He nodded to the truck. "What have we got here?"

"We're traveling to Pensacola," I replied. "Trying to get to family. Is the ferry still operating?"

"Last I heard, it was. Been a while, though." He cocked his head at me. "We don't get many people traveling through, these days," he said, "and most aren't law-abiding citizens. Did you see the sign back up the way?"

"I did. It said the laws still apply here."

"And indeed they do. Are you going to have any issue with that?"

"No sir; we won't be causing any problems. As you can see, we've got three kids, and all things considered, I don't want anything more than to get them safely home."

He craned his neck to look at the truck, then raised an eyebrow. "Looks like you've seen some action. Also looks like you've done some scavenging. Kind of looks like you may have been looting."

I looked over my shoulder. Several bullet holes were visible in the side of the truck, including one in the driver's door I didn't remember being there before. Bundles of toilet paper could easily be seen from where we stood, as well as one of the stacks of water.

"We haven't been part of any 'action' that wasn't started by someone else," I replied. "And if we ended up with their stuff afterward, it was only because they didn't need it anymore, and I didn't want it to go to waste." I shrugged. "I have no trouble following the law, and I can honestly tell you I'm not looking to start any trouble here."

"Good," the man said. "Make sure you don't." He started to turn away, but then turned back to me. "I'm Sheriff Winston. If you get into trouble here, you'll come before me. Trust me, you don't want that, as I tend to settle things *permanently*."

"Makes sense," I said. "Seems to be the only thing some people understand these days."

"Indeed." With that, he turned and walked back to the barricade. He waved for the other people manning the barricade to open a way for us to go through.

I jumped back in the truck and drove through, and on into the town of Bayou La Batre. "Four people seems kind of like a small group to keep out anyone who'd want to do them wrong," George said.

"It would," I replied, "if that were all they had at that barricade. I saw two others on both sides of the road, hidden in the forest. If we'd have tried anything, we'd have been in a pretty good crossfire."

George nodded. "I guess they take their security pretty seriously here."

We drove south into town, and it was as if we'd driven into another world. People of all races seemed to be coming and going about their business—there were even children on the playground at the elementary school we passed. It was surreal to drive through after our experiences over the last couple of days. All sorts of people— blacks, whites, Asians—all getting along and interacting as if the last month had never existed. Weird.

"Almost makes you want to stop and put down roots here," George said.

"Almost," I agreed. "You thinking of staying?"

George sighed wistfully. "I'd like to, and this looks like a great place, but I promised my father I'd take the kids to my uncle's." He shrugged. "Besides, there's no telling. A gang could come and overrun this town tomorrow. Who's to say? Dad said that Uncle Luc would have enough force to provide a secure zone. I know you can't count on anything anymore, but if you could, Uncle Luc would be it."

We drove another couple of minutes in silence, then he turned to me. "You aren't thinking of staying, are you?" he asked with a touch of panic in his voice.

I shrugged. "No...not now anyway. I told your father I would help get you to Perdido Key, and I'm going to do that. Besides, I'm still looking for my past. Maybe I'll see something along the way that jogs my memory. Maybe Perdido Key will do it; it kind of sounds familiar. If it doesn't, maybe I'll travel on from there and keep looking." I shrugged. "These days, you really can't plan that far ahead. Right now, I'm focused on getting you to Florida; I'll figure out what's next after I do that."

He sat back, apparently satisfied. He was a good guy, but both of us knew he stood a lot better of a chance of getting to Pensacola with me along than by himself.

There wasn't much to the town of Bayou La Batre, and we were soon out of it and headed east. The barricade on this end of town was just past a small gun and ammo store, which somehow seemed fitting. They waved us through without conversation and we continued to the east, paralleling Portersville Bay and the Gulf of Mexico.

As we passed the sign that read, "Now leaving Bayou La Batre," I noticed someone had scrawled underneath that in red, "You're on your own." I shrugged.

You're always on your own in this Fallen World.

* * * * *

Chapter Thirteen

We made it to the flashing yellow light at Alabama 193 and drove south with Mobile Bay off to our left. The land grew progressively swampier, with trailer parks dominating the few outposts of civilization we passed. In most, the trailers had been pulled together to form a box or other geometric shape, and it reminded me of Wild West explorers "circling the wagons" to protect themselves from Indians. I had no idea where that thought came from; perhaps I'd been a history teacher in my previous life, before I turned into a psychopath. Regardless, it was obvious we weren't in Bayou La Batre anymore.

Within a couple of minutes, we were on the bridge to Dauphin Island, and I knew we were in trouble.

"What's that up ahead?" George asked, peering forward.

"Dead cars." I said. There were at least a couple cars in both lanes. It appeared as though there might be a way through the wreckage, but it would involve slowing down to negotiate the passage. The cars blocked my vision of what was in front of them, adding to my unease. But that wasn't the worst of it.

"Did you have to say 'dead?'" he asked.

"Well, it beats the ones that just pulled onto the bridge behind us." As we'd passed Cedar Point—the last strip of land before the bridge—two large trucks had pulled in behind us and were blocking both lanes of traffic. While there were large shoulders on both sides of the road, I had a feeling they'd probably move to block any moves I made to get around them.

"So we don't want to go forward…"

"And we can't go back," I finished. I looked in the rear view mirror and sighed. "Forward it is."

Whereas the last barricade had an air of professionalism, the blockage in front of us gave the impression of hoodlumism. As we approached, a woman stepped out from behind the cars and pointed at a sign on the side of the road. "Stop and Pay Tax," it read.

I could see the cars blocking the road a little better now. There were two in the left lane, with two in the right lane a little farther back, and two more in the left lane. There was just enough space for our truck to pass by, but I wasn't going to be able to do it at speed, and I could see movement behind the cars. When we slowed to go through the obstacles, they'd have us…no matter whether we paid their tax or not. Every car I could see had bullet holes, and at least two of them had caught fire at some point. This wasn't going to end well for someone; all I could hope for was that it would be them and not us.

I checked the trucks behind us—they had slowed when we did and were maintaining a respectful distance. We couldn't make a run for it that way, but at least they weren't pushing us into the trap any faster than they had to.

"You going to pay the tax?" George asked.

"Depends on what it is, I guess." I stopped the car and got out. "I think this one is going to go badly," I added. "Slide over into the driver's seat and be ready." I also told John to be ready, then walked toward the woman. She appeared Hispanic, and was only about five feet tall, with dark hair. She could have been pretty, except for the cruel look she had in her eyes as she surveyed the truck and then focused on me.

"That's far enough," she said when I was about 15 feet away from her.

"Is that so that your friends behind the cars can keep me covered?"

"Perhaps." She shrugged. "Are you going to pay the bridge tax?"

"Depends. How much is it, and how do I know you'll let me continue on once I pay it?"

"How about the little girl?" she asked. "Give her to us, and we'll let you pass."

"Not happening," I replied, trying to catalog how many people were hiding behind the cars. There were at least three, plus the woman.

"How about the little boy, then?"

I paused, as if considering, while I tried to figure out how she knew we had a young boy and a young girl. I couldn't see much behind her; her people wouldn't be able to see well into the bed of the truck. Did they have a rifle with a scope? That would be bad, as they could pick off my traveling companions before they could do much.

Still...I didn't see a rifle poking out anywhere. Then I caught a flash of something in her ear; they had a radio or three, and the truck drivers behind us were probably radioing her instructions.

That changed things. If she were just the mouthpiece, and the real leader was behind us...

"I think I'll have to pass on that, too," I finally replied. "We have some trade goods; perhaps you'd rather have some smokes or some wine? Or both?" I turned partially toward the truck as I spoke to cover the movement of my hand to the small of my back.

"Pass," the woman replied. "We want the girl."

A gun fired as I sprang toward her, but they hadn't expected me to come closer, and it whizzed past my head. I fired as I ran past her, and she fell backward as the bullet hit her in the chest.

Several guns fired as men came out from behind the cars, and I ran forward and jumped onto the hood of the closest one. I fired down into the head of the first man that came around it, dropping him. That got their attention. A bullet skimmed past me, and I dropped to the road between the car and the side of the bridge. I went all the way to the ground so I could look under the car, and saw feet moving toward me from both the front and rear. I shot the feet out from under the woman coming around the back of the car and didn't pause a second when a woman's face hit the asphalt; I shot her once through the forehead.

I rolled to my back as the other one came around the front of the car. He expected me to be in a crouch, and his shot went over my head. Before he could adjust, I hit him twice in the chest, and he fell backward.

Gunshots came from the direction of George and the truck; John was engaged in a firefight with one of the truck drivers, whose passenger was slumped against the door of the cab with a spray of red on the window. The driver stayed down low in his cab, making for a hard target, but he couldn't aim very well from that position either, so the battle was currently a draw. Eventually, one or the other would get lucky, and I didn't want to pin my hopes on a 16-year-old with one day's experience. The other truck driver was quite obviously dead.

I slid in a new magazine as I went around the back of the car. I needed to end this quickly. My hopes were answered; there didn't appear to be any more of them. I had just started to wave to George when I felt the barrel of a gun against the back of my head.

"Drop it," the first woman said.

I set the pistol on the trunk of the car next to me and raised my hands. "I thought I shot you," I said.

"You did, you asshole, and it hurts like shit."

I risked a glance behind me. "You don't look dead."

"Never heard of a bullet-proof vest?"

Come to think of it, I had heard of them, and with a flash of insight, I realized that must be why I instinctively shot everyone in the head when I could. I don't remember any of them getting back up after that, whereas the woman with the gun on me? Yeah. I may be a psychopath, but at least I made sense, sometimes.

"Now, call to your friends and tell them to stop shooting," she said.

"If I do?"

"Well, we're taking the little girl *and* the little boy now, because you made this so difficult, but if you do what I tell you, I'll let the other guy and the older boy go."

"What about me?"

"Oh, you're dead. You killed my husband and my wife. If you do what I tell you though, I won't make you suffer. Not much, anyway."

"Can't argue with that," I replied. "Not much, anyway." I waved my hands over my head to get George's attention. "Stop firing!" I yelled.

John turned to look at us, and George put down the pistol he'd been pointing in our direction.

"Good boy—" the woman started, but I spun to the right, chopping down and away from me across her wrist. Her pistol fired, off target, and I followed with a left-handed punch to her throat.

She went down, and I grabbed the pistol off the trunk. Either she was tougher than I thought, or I hadn't hit her as hard as I thought, because she was raising her pistol toward me as I looked back. I dove to the side as she fired, and I could feel a tug on my shirt as the bullet whipped past me. I hit the ground on my left side with the pistol extended and fired. The bullet hit her between the eyes, and she dropped the gun.

I shot her again, just to make sure, and climbed to my feet with my left arm on fire. Again. John was trading shots with the truck driver—mostly just wasting ammunition—and I waved at George to pull forward. He slid into the driver's seat, keeping low, and shifted the truck into gear as I rounded up all of the weapons and ammo I could.

As he reached the gap between the cars in the barricade, it must have dawned on the truck driver that we were escaping; he shifted into gear and floored the gas pedal.

"Go! Go! Go!" I yelled as I dove into the back of the truck. Something broke my fall with dual explosions, and I realized I had just smashed two bags full of potato chips.

George stayed on the gas, and the truck leaped forward into the maze. He weaved through the second rank of cars as the truck hit the cars behind us. He slammed into them, driving them forward, but we made the next turn, and they missed us. One more hard turn to get around the last row of cars, and we were in the clear. We went over a small rise in the bridge for boats to go under, then Dauphin Island was in sight.

George slowed the car. "Want to drive?" he asked through the window.

"Not really," I replied. As the adrenaline left my system, all I wanted to do was lay on the crushed bags of chips and sleep for about five days. I looked to the side. All three kids looked okay— well, not really 'okay,' but I didn't see any blood leaking from any of them—so we at least had that going for us.

"Um, I could really use a hand," George said.

Something about the way he said it set me on edge—like he was almost saying it through gritted teeth—and I rolled over and slid up to the window into the cab. He was holding his left arm across his chest while he drove with his right. He turned toward me a little, and I could see a drop of blood drip from his left elbow onto his lap. His leg already had a small wet spot there.

"Pull over," I said. I snorted as I looked in front of us; not surprisingly, there was no traffic. "The hell with that," I added. "Force of habit. Don't worry about pulling over; just stop the damn truck."

He nodded once, then slowed us to a stop. Grabbing one of the first aid kits, I vaulted out of the truck, adrenaline surging again.

"What's wrong?" John asked.

"Nothing," I said as I pulled the driver's door open. "Just stay in the back." If it were bad, I didn't want them to see it.

"Oh, my God, Daddy!" Alice screamed. "*You've been shot!*"

Well, that wasn't helpful. "Yes, he has," I said, looking back, "and I'm going to fix him right up. But I need you to be calm and not scream anymore while I do it, okay?"

She nodded her head, but tears were already flowing down her cheeks. There were also tears on her younger brother's face, and he was snuffling heavily. Even John looked like he was losing the battle to hold back his tears—both eyes were glistening in the late morning sun.

Watching me work on their father wasn't going to make it any better, either. "I need your help," I said. "I need all of your help. It's going to take me a minute or two to fix up your dad, but I don't want the bad men to surprise us. I need all three of you to watch behind us for them. Don't take your eyes off the road—it's really important. Can you do that for me?"

They all nodded, so I pointed back down the road. "Okay, then—all eyes back there. Let me know if you see anyone coming."

John nodded once to me, then looked pointedly at his siblings. "Good job," he mouthed as I passed him. He turned his face back to look behind us. I figured he understood what I was doing…but he probably didn't want to see his father's blood, either.

George slid from the front seat and leaned back against it, his face pale.

"Where are you hit?" I asked quietly.

"Upper arm," he said, squinting against the pain. "I leaned out to get one of the truckers, and the other one got me. Hit me in the humerus…"

I opened my mouth to say something, and he added, "And no, I don't think that's very funny." I closed my mouth again.

"I'm pretty sure it's broken," he added.

"Awesome," I replied. "Well, let's get your jacket off and take a look."

He moved to the side a little so I could set down the first aid kit. His face scrunched up as I slid the jacket down and off. It was bloody, but not too bad; at least it hadn't hit any of the main arteries. I opened the kit and grabbed some gauze. "Here. Hold this over the wound."

I surveyed the rest of the contents of the kit, then picked up a packet. "Here's some chewable aspirin. They're small, but maybe they'll help a bit." He opened his mouth, and I dropped them in.

I pulled on a pair of gloves. "This is going to hurt," I said. He turned his head and flinched as I probed the wound. The bullet had passed though the arm, and had grazed the bone on its way through. Aside from an x-ray or a surgical procedure, there was no way to tell if there were bone splinters inside, but nothing was poking from either of the holes, nor did my probing appear to cause more pain than it should, so I hoped it was a clean break.

I figured the worst thing would probably be infection, as there was no way to tell what the bullet pulled into the wound when it passed through. I certainly wasn't going to dig around looking and make it worse. Happily, the wound didn't look like it needed stiches so I wiped down the area around the holes with antiseptic cleansing wipes, then applied antibiotic ointment liberally and covered them with large adhesive bandages.

"Well, the good news is it isn't that bad," I said.

"Aside from the whole 'getting shot' sort of thing," he said through gritted teeth as I worked.

"Well, yeah, that. At least it didn't hit an artery, and the bullet appears to have gone through, without splintering the bone. You need to watch for signs of infection like fever or chills. If you change the bandages yourself and see an increased redness, swelling, or drainage—especially nasty, pus-like drainage, we'll have to find you a doctor. Maybe go back to Bayou La Batre or something." I don't know where the info came from, but it flowed like I'd said it many times previously.

He nodded, and I rigged up an extra jacket to immobilize his arm, then helped him back into the truck on the passenger's side.

"Are you going to be okay, Daddy?" Alice asked.

He mustered a weak smile. "Yeah, Fred hooked me up as good as new. I think I'll just sleep for a bit, though."

With the shape he was in, I didn't feel the need to correct him, but damn, I was getting tired of that name.

I got him as comfortable as I could, put away the first aid kit, and got the kids settled in the back with a snack to take their minds off what had already been a traumatic day. I couldn't believe it wasn't even quite noon yet.

Grabbing one of the bags of crushed chips to snack on, I jumped in the cab and started driving. I'd only eaten a couple of handfuls of chips before we crossed Cedar Island and approached Dauphin Island. I slowed again and sighed. The way was blocked with yet another barricade.

The more things change, the more some things stay the same in this Fallen World.

* * * * *

Chapter Fourteen

With a second sigh, I slowed the car. Again. George's eyes snapped open. "Wha…what's going on?"

"Another barricade," I said.

"Wha…what are we going to do?"

I looked into his eyes and could tell that while the lights were on, there was no one home. "Nothing," I said. "Go back to sleep. Everything's fine."

"Mmm…okay," he said. His eyes closed, and he was out.

"Well shit," I muttered as I stopped the truck about 100 yards from the barricade. Shaking my head, I got out.

"Want me to cover you?" John asked from the bed of the truck. He was on his knees, looking over the roof of the cab, and he had one of the rifles in his hand.

I motioned for him to lower it. "Put that down," I whispered. "We don't want to piss these people off or make a bad impression."

"But what if—"

"No," I said, interrupting him. "We need to play nicely with these folks. We can't go back, unless you want to play chicken with a big truck."

"Not really."

"Me, either. Also, your dad is kind of out of it; all things considered, I'd like to make nice with these people. We may need a doctor to look at his arm if it gets infected, and they may have one. We're not going to do anything that might make them think poorly of us."

I flipped my pistols onto the driver's seat and walked toward the barricade with my hands up.

"That's far enough," one of the men said as I got within about 10 yards of the barricade.

I stopped. There were at least five rifles on me; it seemed prudent.

"You armed?" the man asked.

"Not at the moment," I replied.

"There was a lot of shooting from down the bridge a bit ago," the man noted. "Care to tell me what happened?"

"There was a barricade there, too," I replied. "They wanted one of our children to pass; we decided on a different arrangement."

"Are they all dead?"

I shrugged. "All but one, I think. He's got a big semi-truck cab and wanted to run us off the bridge when we killed the rest of his friends. All things considered, I'd rather not go back to face him without some heavier armament than I have."

"Damn," one of the other men said. "He's the first person to get by them in five days; and he almost killed them all? We should go finish them off."

"So what's your story?" the man asked me.

"I woke up about a week ago and couldn't remember anything about my past. When I left the building I was in, I got attacked. I killed a bunch of them, but had to run away from the rest. I met up with a family, but the killers showed up again. I killed a bunch more, then we ran from the rest. We've had people try to waylay us several times on the way here, and we've left a lot of them dead behind us."

"That's a lot of dead people," the man said. "We're really not looking for killers here."

"I didn't kill anyone who didn't attack me or my friends first," I replied. "We also left one of our own along the way, and I got one more with a bullet wound in his arm from the folks back along the bridge."

"What is it you're looking for, exactly?" the man asked.

"We're hoping to use the ferry over to the other side of the bay. The family I'm with is from Pensacola, and I told them I'd help them get there."

"How much are they paying you?"

"Paying me?" I asked, my brows knitting. "Nothing. Why?"

"Just curious," the man replied. "You seem to be pretty handy with a gun, and I'm curious why you're with them. You don't seem like someone who would care about children a lot." He nodded toward our truck.

I looked back and could see all three kids looking at us.

I shrugged. "Like I said, I don't know who I am, so one place is as good as another. I'm hoping something will jog my memory as we go."

"Anything yet?"

"Nope." Somehow, it didn't seem wise to tell him the only thing I'd really figured out was that I was probably a psychopath.

"There's still time, I guess," he said. He peered at me intently.

"What?" I asked.

"I don't know," he said. "Now that I look at you, you seem familiar. Do I look familiar to you?"

I shook my head. "Can't say you do. Is the ferry running?" I asked, as the silence grew uncomfortable. "If so, what's it take to use it?"

"Yes, the ferry is running," the man said. "It's running on barter, though; money's pretty useless these days."

"I figured." I cocked my head at him. "But I guess you folks want something first to let us through?"

"You're a pretty smart guy," the man said. "Here's the deal. There are only a few remaining islands of civilization right now, and most of them are, literally, islands. Like Dauphin Island, here. The laws still apply here. We have police and most of the services we had before the bombing started. There's only one thing we're missing, and that's gas. We can feed ourselves pretty well, as long as we have fuel to run our boats. Unfortunately, that comes from Bayou La Batre, and we haven't received a shipment since the folks you met moved onto the bridge and started intercepting our fuel shipments.

"It's getting to the point where we were about to have to do something about them ourselves, but if you've broken up the ring, you've done us a service. If, perhaps, you were to lead a team that finished them off, since you know their disposition, we'd probably let you onto the island. You'd have to work out passage on the ferry yourself, though."

"I'm not worried about that," I replied. "I think we have some pretty good things to barter. My question is the word 'probably' you used. If I go wipe out the rest of them for you, are you going to let us through?"

The man looked at me for a moment and nodded once. "Yeah," he said. "We will."

"And how do I know you'll honor that promise?"

"I reckon you don't," the man said. He set his rifle on the hood of the car he was behind and came out to join me. I could see he was wearing a police uniform. He held out his hand. "I'm Chief of Police

Dan Bradley," he said. "My word is my bond. If you can open up the bridge again, I promise to let you onto the island."

I took his hand and shook it. "Fair enough," I said. "I don't suppose you have a doctor who could look at my friend's arm, do you? It would be a damn shame to orphan his kids if his wound were to get infected and kill him."

"We have a doctor," the chief of police said with a nod. "I'll even pay him out of my funds to look at your friend."

"You must want that fuel badly," I replied.

"We're getting low on food," he said. "Happily, it wasn't the tourist season yet, so we don't have all those mouths to feed." He shrugged. "Still, there were enough snowbirds here that it's hard enough. We're putting them to work as best we can, though."

He nodded toward the barricade and one of the men bowed. "Rod Jewell, from Ontario, at your service. I may not be able to run a fishing boat, but I can man a barricade and fire a rifle."

The chief of police nodded back to him. "See?" he asked. "Everyone's doing their part." He turned to me. "So, Mister...what did you say your name was?"

"I didn't," I replied. "Like I said, I don't know what it is."

"What do the people you're traveling with call you?"

I sighed. "Fred. But that's not my name."

"I thought you said you couldn't remember anything. It could be Fred, then, couldn't it?"

"I guess it could," I replied. "But I don't think it is."

"Well, until we have something better, that'll work for now. Nice to meet you...Fred."

I sighed again.

There are some things you just have to learn to live with in this Fallen World.

* * * * *

Chapter Fifteen

The chief called for reinforcements to take George and his kids to the doctor while the rest of us went to check on the mid-bridge barricade. Honestly, I'd seen so many road blocks in the last few days they were all staring to run together. They opened up their barricade, and I drove the truck through and parked it on the side of the road. The doctor arrived, and George's family was led off to one of the nearby buildings, a former restaurant by the looks of it.

I made a mental inventory of the back of the truck, then walked back to the barricade, armed with two pistols and plenty of magazines.

"You don't have a rifle?" the chief asked.

"We're about out of ammo for it," I replied. "I've got a couple of shotguns, but I'd rather have my pistols. I seem to do well with them."

"Up to you," he said, obviously more comfortable with his rifle. He waved to his people who were milling about. "All right, everyone, listen up. We're going to take three vehicles and the backhoe that will be arriving shortly. That's a driver and a passenger-slash-shotgun rider in each. Fred here—" I nodded, reluctantly, "—will be in the lead vehicle, since he's already been through there once. The plan is to clear up any remaining criminals, remove any blockage on the main thoroughfare, and re-establish our barricade on the landward end of the bridge. Once we've reached the other end of the bridge, we'll call back and have you move forward.

"The most dangerous time will be while our main force is in motion, so we'll want to make sure we're well dug in before we call back, so it may be a little while before we call. Any questions?"

"Yeah, Chief," another man in a police uniform said. "Why don't we just take everyone and go in one large group? Wouldn't there be safety in numbers?"

"There might be, Collins," the chief said. "There also might be more criminals there than what Fred left behind. With only three vehicles, we can get turned around quickly and scamper back here, pronto. Even if we get ambushed, there will still be a big group here that can defend the island. The worst case scenario would be to take a big force and get hit by surprise by an even bigger one while we're disorganized. If they got past us, they'd be onto the island, and that's something I'm not going to let happen."

The other man nodded, satisfied with the answer.

"Anything else?" the chief asked.

When no one else said anything, the chief said, "Mount up, then," and we jumped into our cars.

My driver's name was Tom Stevens, who was driving a year-old Mustang. "This the car you want to go into battle with?" I asked.

"You saw the bullet holes in my truck, right?"

"It may not be the one I want to get a bunch of holes in," Tom replied, "but it's the one that will get us the hell out of trouble quickly if we need to."

I nodded. "I like the way you think."

The chief walked past and handed me a set of binoculars. "If you're going to be our point person, you could probably use these."

"Thanks," I replied.

"You ready?"

"To get shot at again?" I asked. "Not particularly, although I find that it bothers me a lot less than it did a few days ago."

"You've had a busy few days."

"Too busy."

"Well, once we're done, maybe you'll stay with us a few days."

"Maybe," I allowed. "We'll see."

A large yellow backhoe drove up, driven by a man with a cowboy hat and a long stalk of grass between his teeth. "Time to go," the chief said. He turned and went to his car—a police cruiser, complete with roof-mounted lights.

Tom drove us to the barricade and the police cruiser pulled in behind us, followed by a large Suburban. The people at the barricade started the cars they were using to block off the end of the bridge and made a gap for us, and Tom slowly accelerated through it.

"Heard your story," Tom remarked, his eyes on the road. "You were some sort of soldier, right?"

"Not that I remember," I replied. Not only didn't I remember being a soldier, I was pretty sure that soldiers didn't shoot fallen soldiers in the head. There was probably some rule of warfare that forbade doing that. And if there wasn't, there probably should be.

"Just good at what you do?"

"Yeah, shooting people seems to be something I can do pretty well."

"You're on our side, though, right?" This time his eyes came over to me, and he looked intently at me for a second.

"I'm on my side at the moment," I replied, "but I'm not going to kill you, if that's what you're worried about. These assholes—" I pointed out in front of us, "—have already tried to kill me once. I'm fine with killing them."

"You'll let me know if anything changes with that?"

I chuckled. "Unless or until you try to kill me, I have nothing against you and don't want to kill you. Pull a gun on me, though, and we'll have issues."

"Got it," Tom said, smiling, as we drove up the rise in the bridge. "Don't pull a gun on the person who's good at killing people. I think I can remember that."

"Then I think we'll get along just fine."

We crested the peak of the bridge and looked down to where the barricade was. "What do you see?" Tom asked, unconsciously slowing the car as we approached the danger area about a mile off.

"Wrecked cars," I muttered, looking through the binoculars. "Doesn't look like much has changed."

The police cruiser gave a bleep on its siren, and Tom stopped the car. "What've you got?" the chief asked as the car pulled alongside us.

"Hard to see from here," I said, "but it looks about like I left it." I looked through the binoculars again. "I can only see one of the big trucks, though, so it looks like the other may have left."

"But whether that's to flee or to bring reinforcements…"

"I have no idea." I finished.

"All right," he said. "I have it from here." He turned on his lights and siren, and led us on to the barricade. I continued watching the area, ready to shout a warning, but didn't see anything moving.

"Don't get too close to him," I said. "If the chief swings his car broadside, you don't want to T-bone him."

Tom backed off a bit more, giving us some maneuvering room, then slowed as the chief approached the barricade.

"Pull in behind him," I said when he started to go into the other lane.

"But—"

I pointed behind us. "Unless you'd like the backhoe to have to squeeze past you?"

"Oh, shit," he said, whipping it back over behind the chief's car.

The third vehicle pulled up alongside the chief's car. "Guess he didn't get the memo," Tom said.

"Newp. I'd go ahead and turn around so we can leave quickly...just in case."

"Good idea," he replied. He spun the car around in a three-point turn and backed up behind the chief's car.

When I got out of the car, the chief was already out of his and talking over his loudspeaker, using his door to shield him from any potential incoming fire. "—come out with your hands up. I repeat, this is Dauphin Island Chief of Police Dan Bradley. If there is anyone in the barricade, come out with your hands up."

Seven pairs of eyes stared at the mass of tangled cars. When the truck had run into them chasing me, he had closed off the path between them and jumbled them up pretty well.

"Last chance," the chief called. "If I, or any of my deputies, see anyone alive when we come in, we will shoot first and ask questions later."

The chief waved us over. "Tom, you and Fred go around to the right. Hector, you and Juan go to the left. Rod, you and I are up the middle...assuming we can find a way through it."

"Are you deputizing me?" I asked.

"Will you do what I tell you, when I tell you?" the chief asked.

"Go to the right and shoot any of them I see?"

"Correct," he said. I nodded. "Congratulations, you're a Dauphin Island deputy. Now go shoot any of those bastards who are still here."

I chuckled and went out to the right shoulder of the road, waving for Tom to come behind me. I didn't want him in my field of fire. The search, however, was anticlimactic. None of the bandits remaining were alive, including two that now had cars on top of them. They were well and truly dead.

We met back at the police cruiser, and the chief waved the backhoe forward. There was a *screech!* as it swapped a small amount of paint going around the Suburban, and then it plowed into the mass of cars with its plow blade.

"Told ya you didn't want to park there," I said as the Suburban's owner went to take a look at the damage done to his vehicle.

"Thanks," Tom said, wiping away a speck of dust from his hood.

The police chief walked up. "Nice bit of shooting," he said. "Did they all need one to the head?"

I shrugged. "The ones that got one in the head didn't get back up again."

"True, but that really isn't what I'm looking for from my deputies in most cases."

"Maybe I shouldn't be a deputy."

"I'll take that under advisement," the chief said as the backhoe raised its blade, dumping a couple of the cars off the bridge.

"Going to un-deputize me?" I asked.

"Nope. Just said I would take it under advisement. Until we get everything set up, I kind of like your thinking."

"Hey!" the backhoe operator yelled. "*There's a body on the road!* I almost ran over it! What am I supposed to do about that?"

The police chief looked at me as if I might have an answer.

"Scoop it up and dump it over with the cars!" I yelled.

The operator looked at the chief. "You heard what the man said," the chief yelled. "Just do it!"

The man shrugged and did it, although he winced and flinched as the body squished into a car before he could get the blade under it.

It doesn't pay to be squeamish in this Fallen World.

* * * * *

Chapter Sixteen

Once the bodies were gone, the backhoe operator made quick work of the rest of the cars, but stopped when he got to the semi cab. "I don't think I can do that one," he said. "And even if I could, it's probably going to destroy the concrete shoulder wall if I do."

The policeman looked at me again. Apparently, I was the Shell Answer Man. "I don't think there's anything wrong with it," I said. "We ought to be able to drive it off the bridge."

"Well, how about getting on that, Deputy?" he said, looking at me.

I sighed, and my shoulders slumped. I wondered if I'd been able to keep my mouth shut before the bombs fell. Probably not.

The chief and I walked over to the semi cab, and I climbed up to the door. I stepped to the side as I opened it up, and the driver fell to the asphalt. The chief looked at it a couple of seconds and then back up at me. "No bullet to the head on this one?"

"It wasn't one of mine," I said with a shrug.

"Hey, Deputy?" the chief asked as I started to climb into the cab.

"Yeah?"

"Aren't you going to do something with this body? You can't just leave it here in the middle of the bridge like road kill."

"That's what it is, though, isn't it?"

He stared up at me with a frown.

I favored him with an eye roll and climbed back down. "This deputy thing is bullshit," I muttered as I grabbed the body under the armpits and dragged it to the side of the bridge. "Can you at least give me a little help?" I asked.

The chief gave me a grin, then he came over and grabbed the guy's ankles. Between us, we pitched him over the side.

I climbed back up into the cab. The driver had a half-full bottle of water in a cup holder I used to wash the worst of the blood off the window so I could see out, then I started the motor.

The chief was still standing below, looking at me. "Can you drive that?" he shouted up.

Without conscious thought, I threw it into gear and turned toward the end of the bridge. The fact that I made him scurry to avoid being run over wasn't relevant to the decision—it was just the way I needed to go. He had a smile on his face as he raced off to get into his car.

I drove slowly down the bridge to Cedar Point, speeding up slightly as the rest of the cars started catching up to me. Even the backhoe operator, seeing us all headed in the same direction, began following us after a few seconds.

Upon reaching the end of the bridge, which ended on the island of Cedar Point, I stopped and rolled down the window. The chief pulled up alongside. "What do you think?" I asked. "Do you want to end your claim here, or claim the route all the way to the mainland?"

"What do you think, Fred?"

My eyes rolled. "If it was me, I'd go all the way to the mainland. If those folks come back, they could easily put up another barricade on this island. It's not much more than a bridge—just the road and a little bit of a shoulder on both sides."

"Good point," the chief said. "Let's go to the mainland."

I put it in gear and drove off again. When I thought about it, I couldn't really remember how I shifted, or what the configuration of the truck's gears was. When I didn't, though, and just let muscle memory have its way, I could drive the truck. *Maybe I was a psychopathic truck driver before the war?* It didn't *seem* familiar, but then again, even psychos have a day job. At least, I thought they did. How else do they afford knives, guns, and such?

I drove back to the mainland, but found we had the same problem—there was nothing on either side of the road but a little bit of swamp. I drove for another half mile and finally came to what I was looking for—trees alongside the road.

I stopped the truck, pulling it across both lanes of traffic.

"Okay, I'll bite," the chief said, pulling up alongside me. "Why here?"

I pointed to the trees. The pine trees weren't big, but they had lots of branches that would help make them bulky looking.

"Knock a few of them over," I said, "and what have you got? Natural made barricade. Put enough of them down, and they will even stop bullets for you, which is a pretty nice thing to have in a barricade."

"Yeah...but this is outside my territory," the chief said.

I raised an eyebrow. "Who is going to come and push you off this land? The only people who drive down this strip are people going to Dauphin Island; you might as well check them out here, where you can turn them around easily, rather than wait until they're on the bridge, don't you think?"

"How are we going to knock them down?"

"Got any chains? Got a chainsaw?"

"I've got chains," the chief said.

"Hell, I've got chains," the backhoe operator said. He'd pulled up and caught the last bit of the conversation. "I won't need them to knock down the trees, though—just to drag them into place."

He drove the backhoe off the road on the right to where the trees were and began pushing over the ones alongside the road. I got out to watch—everyone likes watching destruction, right?—but after the first few fell, I realized they didn't quite block the road, so I climbed back into the cab and pulled it forward until the wheels were just shy of the large draining ditch on the left shoulder of the road. It was muddy as shit, so I couldn't tell how deep it was. I had just about decided to break off a stick and test the depth, when I saw a log about 100 feet away that was swimming along the ditch. Crocodile. Or alligator; I didn't know. All I knew was it was a big-ass reptile.

I decided I didn't need to know how deep the water was.

"Incoming!" Tom yelled suddenly.

He pointed up the road, and I turned to find several cars and a semi cab about a quarter of a mile away.

"Is that the one that got away?" the chief asked as he came to stand next to me.

I shrugged. "Could be," I replied. "Hard to tell from here."

All of them started forward at the same time, and I could hear the cars' engines revving from where we stood.

"On second thought," I added, "I'm going to guess that's the one that got away, and he's brought friends back with him."

"Grab your weapons!" the chief yelled.

I scrambled up into the cab and rolled down the passenger window. That gave me some elevation to shoot down on them and a little bit of cover. And no one would be stupid enough to ram something as big as a semi, right?

From my new perspective, I could see there were three cars in addition to the semi. Two of the cars led the charge; the third car hung back behind the semi, probably using it for cover. The cars continued to accelerate as they raced toward us, and for the life of me, I couldn't figure out what their end game was—we had the road blocked with trees, and then a row of cars. The cars roared closer, with one headed right at me. I shook my head. I only knew one thing—this was going to be messy.

The two cars were side by side as they came into range, and I fired. At the sound of my pistol, everyone else opened up. My first shot starred the window of the one on the left—the one headed at me—and the driver jerked the wheel to his right. He went off the road and into the drainage ditch, throwing a huge sheet of water into the air as the car slammed to a stop. I turned to the other car and saw at least one hole in its window. I added a second, and it went off the other side of the road, crashing over small shrubs and underbrush. The soft ground slowed it a little; the tree that it ran into brought it to a complete stop.

The semi continued straight for the downed trees, and I thought he was going to try jumping them, but then smoke poured from his brakes as he locked them up. The car behind him wasn't ready for the maneuver—there's no way the driver could see what was coming—and he jerked the car out from behind the semi.

I had time for one shot before the car plowed into the side of my cab, directly underneath me. I saw it coming and dropped below the window so I wasn't thrown through it by the impact; instead, I was slammed into the side of the door, face first. Things went dark for a moment or five—I don't know how long—but when I came to my senses, it sounded like a war was going on.

I shook my head, trying to remember where I was and why everything looked strange. I realized where I was after a second, and that I was only looking through one eye, which made things appear differently than normal. I wiped my face, and my hand came away red. There was a *lot* of blood on my face and in my eye, which I tried to blink out as I crawled up and looked through the window.

The truck driver was trading fire from the window of his cab with the police chief. A guy was pulling himself out of the drainage ditch. The men in the car below me were probably dead—neither of them had their seat belts on and there were two impact marks on the front windshield. Most worrisome was the car off the road to the right. Four men were coming out of it, and we were going to get flanked.

I looked around for my pistol for a few seconds, then realized my second one was in its holster. The man in the semi cab must have seen the motion as I extended the pistol out the window toward him; he jerked back. He took the round in the shoulder instead of my original aiming point; however, when he jerked back, he exposed himself to the chief, who put two rounds through his chest.

I turned and fired twice at the man coming out of the ditch. One hit him in the chest and the second in the stomach as he fell back. I could see that there wasn't a vest under his t-shirt; he was out of it.

The men in the trees were trying to get behind us. Rather than meet them face to face—four on one isn't great odds—I decided to go around behind them, too. I opened the door and pointed toward them when the police chief looked up at me; hopefully, he and the rest of the guys could keep them busy while I got behind them.

I climbed down from the cab and shot each of the men in the car once through the head. I didn't know if they were dead; now I didn't have to check. The chief's head whipped around toward me when I fired. All I could do was point at the men and shrug before running around the other semi cab and into the brush.

The shrubs and tall grass grew to a height of almost three feet, and I was able to run through them doubled over. They still probably could have seen me, had they looked, but I wasn't high enough above the grass to catch their eyes since I wasn't running toward them. I hoped.

I couldn't see the men; they had dropped into the shrubbery to sneak up on my group. Not knowing where they were, I ran for their car while I switched magazines; I figured I could start at their vehicle and follow their trail, hoping that they wouldn't be watching behind them.

I made it to where the Chevrolet hissed from something cracked under its hood. No one remained in nor near it, so I turned back toward the barricade as people began firing. Happily, the chief had seen me point toward the car, and had reoriented our men. If he hadn't, they would have caught our guys out of cover. As it was, our guys were ready for them and returned fire. Unfortunately, any bullets that went over the bad guys came damn close to me, and one slapped into a tree next to me. I remembered an adage from somewhere, something to the effect of "Friendly fire, isn't." I threw myself to the ground as several others buzzed past.

The battle became a standoff. Our guys couldn't see the bad guys in the cover of the trees and shrubs; the bad guys couldn't hit our guys who were behind the cars, and I couldn't do anything without getting shot by our guys.

I needed to get closer to the bad guys. Without thinking about how stupid it was, I jumped up onto the hood of the Chevy and waved my arms over my head. I immediately dove off the side as Tom saw the motion and took a shot at me. I heard the chief yelling something about identifying your targets, and tentatively climbed back onto the hood of the car again.

This time, no one shot at me, and I mimed not shooting at the people in front of me. Of course, one of the bad guys saw the chief looking over their heads, turned, and saw me. Our eyes locked, and he fired. As my pistol was in my holster, I did the only thing I could—I dove back into the brush. Of course, this time I ended up in some brambles and scratched up my face and arms.

It took a couple of moments for me to gather myself—and to pull off a couple of thorn branches—and then I was in motion again. The shrubs and grass were a little higher on the left, so I crawled in that direction on my hands and knees. I had seen where the bad guys were when I was on the hood of the car; assuming they hadn't moved much, I had a good idea of where they would be.

The bad guys were still firing at my group, which helped me locate them, and made it harder for them to hear me moving. While I could still hear rounds going past from my group, they now seemed to be going over a little higher. Within 30 seconds, I had worked myself into position. I could see three of the bad guys, and I thought I knew where the fourth one was.

I took a breath and let it out slowly as I aimed at the closest target. He was on one knee, and almost perfectly in profile. I fired, taking him above the ear, then shot a second man as he turned toward the sound of my pistol. The third person got a shot off that hit the ground next to me, but then I hit him twice in the chest, and he collapsed into the grass. He may not have been dead—yet—but he was well on his way.

The fourth man was the farthest from me, and rather than advance toward him, when he probably knew I was coming, I tried to scoot back and go back toward the car to get around him.

Apparently, he had the same idea, and we met at the car. His gun was already up and aimed at me when I saw him. My reflexes were faster, though, and I got my gun up. We fired at the same time, and I saw him collapse as the bullet hit him in the chest. His round caught me in the leg, and I looked down to see blood—a lot of blood.

I staggered to the edge of the woods with my hands up, hoping that none of my group decided to shoot me. I reached the cut grass of the road's shoulder as my peripheral vision began to collapse in on me, leaving me with only a small tunnel to see through. I found the chief as I fell to my knees.

"Got 'em," I said.

Then the lights went out in this Fallen World.

* * * * *

Chapter Seventeen

Death smelled like shit. Literally.

I coughed, trying to catch my breath; the odor made me gag.

"Sorry," George said from the side.

"Dear *God!*" I replied. "What the hell was that?"

"Sorry," George said again. Something on the floor seemed to have caught his attention, and his eyes refused to meet mine. A flush crept up his neck. "That one really wasn't pleasant, even for me. In my defense, they served shrimp for lunch, and I have a bit of an allergy to shellfish."

"That was a *fart?!*"

"Well, yeah. Hey, on the good side, at least you're here to smell it."

"I'm not sure I wouldn't rather be dead," I replied, looking around. If I didn't know any better, I would have said I was in a hospital. Everything was white or shiny, and smelled vaguely antiseptic. "Where exactly *is* 'here?'"

"You're in the hospital at Bayou La Batre," George replied. "The chief brought you here from the firefight. Apparently, you got hit pretty badly, and it was closer to come here."

"We also have a hospital," a doctor said, coming into the room, "which they don't on Dauphin Island. It was a darn good thing he did, too; you would have died without a hospital operating room. The bullet that hit you nicked your femoral artery. The chief slapped a tourniquet on you and rushed you here, but it was touch and go. You died once on the operating table, but apparently you're too tough—"

"Or too mean," George interrupted.

"Or too mean to die," the doctor agreed with a nod. "You're also a lot heavier than you look. Bringing you in here was a chore."

"How long?" I asked.

"You've been here a week," George said. "We got here three days ago."

I looked at the doctor. "Thank you for saving my life, and I don't want to seem ungrateful...but I don't know how I'm going to pay you."

"Well, you're in luck then. The chief of police from Dauphin Island worked out your payment already. Seems you did him a service...where you were injured, I believe?"

"Yeah. I broke up a barricade for him."

"Killed a few of the local criminals, too, I hear."

"Well, they attacked us, and it was either them or us, and I really wanted it to be them. The police chief was on my side; I'm pretty sure I was on the side of right."

The doctor chuckled. "I'm not chastising you—we're happy to have re-established ties with Dauphin Island, so you won't hear me complaining; they catch more fish than we do. Also, the world could do with a few less people looking to take advantage of the misfortunes of others."

"How much longer do I need to stay here, Doc?"

"A couple more days, then you can be on your way," he said. "That said, you're going to need to take it easy for a while—no barricade busting or shoot-em-ups for the near future, okay?"

"Got it," I said with a wink. "Next time, I'll just tell them no fighting. Doctor's orders."

He nodded once. "Make sure you do. We don't have enough supplies left to use them all on you. If the chief hadn't vouched for you, we probably wouldn't have made the effort." He nodded again then walked out the door.

"That was fairly ominous," George said.

"Yeah, I guess next time I'll have to find a new hospital to die in."

"Could you wait until you get the kids and me to Pensacola, first?"

I cocked my head and pursed my lips as if contemplating.

"Hey, uh…" George said. "You are still going to take us the rest of the way, aren't you?"

I smiled. "Yeah, I will. I didn't stay here last time, and I'm not going to do it this time, either." I shrugged. "I've never broken a promise…that I know about, anyway. Besides, this place doesn't seem to have any info on who I am, so there's no reason to stay."

* * *

We ended up staying in Bayou La Batre another week as our truck was on Dauphin Island, and none of us really wanted to walk all the way out there. The chief had said he'd be back in a few weeks to check on us, but another opportunity came up—the job of security guard on a convoy headed to Dauphin Island.

As it turned out, the only functioning refinery in the area happened to be just outside the city of Bayou La Batre, but within the area claimed by us citizens, and they traded fuel with Dauphin Island

and several other small communities for fresh fish to help feed their inhabitants. The doctor had a brother who worked at the refinery, and he'd put in a good word for me, which got me hired. I signed on for a round trip and was allowed to drive my own vehicle back on the return leg to help bring back the fish.

George walked with me to the refinery—it was about three miles from the hospital—but he wasn't much for companionship.

"I'm going to come back," I finally said as the facility came into view, and I realized why he was tagging along.

"You are?"

"Yes, I am. It's only about ten miles. We'll be there and back in a couple of hours."

After that, he was more open and jovial, and we walked the rest of the way talking about where we grew up. Well, he talked, since I couldn't remember where I grew up, but once I confirmed that I was coming back, he had plenty to say and filled the remaining time all on his own.

"Woah," I said as we got our first view inside the gates of the refinery. Two fuel trucks waited just inside, along with two police cars and a couple of trucks that had been modified for combat. Both of them had heavy machine guns mounted in the back and looked like they could put a hurting on anyone who thought to bother us.

I started feeling pretty good about the mission, as I hadn't seen anything that could match that level of firepower. If we came upon someone who could, I didn't want to be anywhere close to the fuel trucks.

Which was, of course, exactly where they put me. Somebody had the bright idea to weld platforms on top of the fuel trucks that we could man like turrets. He said he'd seen it in a movie a long time

ago. I didn't have any idea what he was talking about, and wasn't particularly thrilled with the plan.

My job was to man the rear turret on the second fuel truck, and they gave me a rifle and a couple boxes of ammo to do it with. I'd rather have had one of the machine guns, but I figured I'd make do. I also got a piece of rope to tie myself in with. Nothing but the finest for the Defenders of Fuel.

In the end, it didn't matter; we made it there without anyone molesting us. I didn't even see any cars, aside from the ones Bayou La Batre and Dauphin Island were using in their barricades. The Dauphin Island checkpoint—apparently, when the "good guys" build a barricade, it becomes a "checkpoint," instead of a barricade—had been heavily fortified while I'd been in the hospital. In addition to a number of wrecked autos they'd towed to make a drive-through maze, they'd also emplaced nail strips to puncture the tires of anyone trying to run the checkpoint, as well as several defensible positions with two machineguns and a number of other weapons. I saw a box that looked suspiciously like what a rocket launcher might come in, but I didn't have time to ask.

When the convoy came onto the island, they let me off, and I grabbed my truck. Someone—or many someones—had unloaded all of the goods we had in the back of the truck. My temper started to rise, but I decided to wait until I saw the police chief. If he didn't have it…we were going to have words. Or worse.

I hoped he had put our stuff aside, as I doubted that I wanted to fight the chief and then have to try to get off the island…especially via the ferry.

It wasn't hard to find the fuel trucks—one was down the road filling up the marina's tanks, and the other was just a little farther at the first gas station as you came onto the main part of the island. A large line of cars waited at the station; apparently, this was the first tanker they'd had in a while.

The island was out of gas...I looked at my fuel gauge and sure enough, it was nearly empty. Someone had siphoned my tank while I was in Bayou La Batre. I drove down to where the fuel truck was filling up the service station's tanks and pulled into the front of the line. Immediately, everyone behind me decided to honk their horns, and some of the braver ones got out of their vehicles to approach me.

"What the hell do you think you're doing?" The first one to reach me asked.

I held up my index finger, stopping him, and made a signal for him—and the other five drivers now approaching—to follow me, and I walked over to where the truck driver was filling the store's tank. Happily, it was the truck I had ridden in on the way to Dauphin Island, and I had been introduced to the driver before we left.

"Hi, Fred," I said. Unlike mine, his name really *was* Fred.

"Hi, Fred," he replied. Unfortunately, George had still been there when we'd been introduced. "What's up?"

"These gentlemen are unhappy that I cut them in line," I said. "I guess they've been here a while and object to me getting gas ahead of them."

"Damn right," one of the men said.

"The thing is," I replied, "someone siphoned all the gas from my tank while I was in Bayou La Batre, getting fixed up after I nearly gave my life for them, and without gas I won't be able to help haul the fish you folks need back to Bayou La Batre."

"Is that so?" Fred asked.

"He can wait his turn," the man who'd spoken earlier said in a near-yell, even though we were all within ten feet of him.

Fred nodded to the man. "Which car is yours?"

"The red one, fourth in line."

"Uh huh," Fred said. He walked over to the truck and unclipped another hose from it, then he stretched it toward the man's car. It only reached about halfway. Unlike the hoses Fred had going into the service station's tank, this one had a handle on it like at the station's pumps. He pointed the handle at the man's car, then reached into his pocket and pulled out a cigarette lighter. With a smile, he thumbed a flame from the lighter.

"Would you like to get back in your car and shut the fuck up, or would you like me to hit your car with a flamethrower?" Fred asked in a loud voice.

"Don't be a jackass," the man said. "You wouldn't do that near all this gas."

"Jackass?" Fred asked, his eyebrows rising. "I'm a jackass?"

He snapped the lighter shut, then pulled the trigger on the handle and doused the car with about three seconds of fuel. As it was a convertible and the day was hot; most of the fuel went into its open interior.

Fred turned back to the group of men around me and flipped the lighter back on again. "How many of y'all would like to watch his car burn?" he asked, holding it close to the nozzle of the fuel line.

The men went from belligerent to *very* nervous. The man whose car was now covered in fuel looked like he was going to say something, but one of the others said, "John, shut the hell up," before he could.

"I got into the gas business because I'm a bit of a pyromaniac," Fred said. "Why don't y'all get into your cars, before I decide to indulge myself?"

The men dispersed, with most of them going back to their cars. Two of them dragged John into the store, with him swearing the entire way. I just smiled at him in my own, endearing way, and gave him the finger. By that point, I didn't figure we were ever going to be friends, and as mad as he was, I was sure to hear him coming.

"Thanks," I said as Fred stowed the hose.

"My pleasure."

"What do you have in that line?" I asked.

"Regular. We use this truck as a mobile fueling stop. This hose is rigged to refuel cars."

"Can I pull my truck up and get gas from it?"

Fred shrugged. "Sure. Might make those folks happy to have you out of the line. 'Cept for the one whose car is doused in fuel. He's probably going to be mighty pissed for a while. Might want to watch out for him."

"Probably so," I replied with a smile. "Would you have done it?" I asked after I brought the truck over and started pumping.

"Done what?" Fred asked.

"Burned that guy's car up."

Fred looked wistfully at the red car. "I sure would have. Then I would have gone into the store to see if they had any marshmallows." He turned to me, and the gleeful look in his eyes sent a shiver down my back. "I wasn't kidding about being a pyro."

Sometimes it doesn't pay to challenge people in this Fallen World.

* * * * *

Chapter Eighteen

"I was going to ask you to stay on," the chief said the next morning when I got back from taking the fish back to Bayou La Batre. He'd been waiting for me at the checkpoint onto the island and had taken me out of earshot from the rest of his people at the barricade. "You have a skill set that is going to be needed more and more often in the coming years, I'm afraid." He sighed. "Unfortunately, then you had to go and douche John Wasserman's car in gas. That's going to cause serious issues for me."

"Well, technically, I wasn't the one who gave his car the fuel bath; that was done by Fred, the tanker driver."

"Fred works for Bayou La Batre, however, and he is outside my sphere of influence. Also, we want to maintain good relations with them; we like having fuel to run our boats, and right now, that means dealing with them."

I nodded; that all seemed pretty true.

"I am, however," the chief continued, "told that you were the instigator of the whole ruckus."

I shrugged. "I would say that he instigated it if you're looking for a second opinion. I was minding my own business when he and a bunch of loud mouths approached me."

The chief frowned at me. "We both know you could have handled it better."

I shrugged again. "I don't know what you're talking about. I didn't kill him, which was the first thing that popped into my mind to do. In fact, you can ask anyone there—I never laid a finger on him."

"I know that you didn't; I've already interviewed a number of people who were there, which is the only reason we're having this conversation. Aside from John Wasserman, who says you punched him and knocked him down—"

"That's a lie," I interjected.

The chief held up a finger. "Aside from John Wasserman, the rest of the witnesses all agree on the fact that you never touched him, and that he approached you."

I smiled beatifically. "See?" I asked. "It's just—"

This time the chief held up his whole hand to stop me. "That, however, doesn't absolve you from being the proximate cause of the whole event."

"Proximate cause?"

"Yeah, the one event without which none of the rest of the shit would have happened. If you hadn't driven up and cut everyone else off—"

"Someone siphoned my gas!"

This time he just talked over me. Part of me recognized the fact that he was getting used to dealing with me. Damn it. "If you hadn't cut everyone in line, none of this would have occurred. And, more troublesome to me, that seems to be the way you work. I'm worried that you're a loose cannon—you always seem to solve things with violence."

"It's something I'm good at."

"It is…which is also something that is troubling. How does a man with no past have your skills?"

"No idea," I said.

He stared at me, and I stared right back.

"You really have no idea?" he asked, when the silence began to get uncomfortable. For him; I could have stared all day.

"Honestly, Chief, I have no idea who I am or how I got to be in New Orleans. I'm trying to figure it out, and I hope something will break lose in my head, but as of right now, nada."

He continued to look at me with his "Chief's Glare." It probably worked on criminals and got them to confess—it was a really good stare—but the fact of the matter was that I was telling the truth and couldn't tell him what he wanted to know without completely fabricating it…which I didn't particularly care to do.

"So what's the deal with this Wasserman guy, anyway?" I asked, changing the subject.

"He's the mayor's kid."

"Oh."

"Yeah, and the mayor isn't happy that his kid's car—that the mayor purchased for him, no less—is a flammable swimming pool."

I could see where this was going. The mayor, who was the chief's boss, wanted a pound of flesh. It wasn't going to come from the guy who had actually done it—he was untouchable due to his connections—which only left me to provide it. I didn't know how he intended to extract it, but I doubted I'd be in the mood to give it. His expression told me that he was in a difficult position—he really didn't want to have to try to do whatever the mayor had told him to do, because he recognized that I wouldn't take it well. He knew that, regardless of whether he was ultimately successful in imposing the penalty, a lot of people were going to get hurt. But yet, it was his job, and he was still going to try.

"Shit," I said.

"Yup, pretty much," he replied.

"Guess I should be moving on."

He nodded. "The sooner, the better. I'm going to officially tell you to meet me at the police station in an hour to turn yourself in. It might take me 30 minutes after that to arrange a posse to come find you. When I come looking, I'll be meaning to take you in, regardless of the force required to do so. 'Dead or alive' as they used to say. I'm sure it would be a lot easier on everyone concerned if we were to find out that you had already left."

I nodded. I didn't particularly want to kill the chief or his men, who'd been pretty above board with me. There were two problems.

"What happened to all the trade goods I had?" I asked. "In addition to having my tank siphoned, all the stuff I had was gone when I returned."

"Don't worry about that," the chief said. "George has it where he's staying. We didn't want it to walk away…like your gas did. Not everyone can be trusted these days." He told me where George was staying. "Anything else?" he asked.

"No," I said. "I'll just need to check the ferry schedule—"

"The next one leaves in 90 minutes," the chief said. All of a sudden, his time frame made sense. He looked at his watch. "Eighty-eight minutes, now. You better get a move on. I put in a pass for you to use it about a month ago, and forgot to rescind it this morning when the mayor pulled me in. I was probably too distraught after the ass-chewing he gave me."

"Sorry about that."

The chief shrugged. "I've had worse from better. I was a Marine, back in the day." He smiled. "Nothing like a drill instructor to really administer an ass chewing." He looked at his watch again. "Eighty-seven minutes. You better hurry; there'll probably be a line."

"Thanks," I said. "I really mean that. I wish—"

"I know," he said with a nod. "I have a lot of wishes, too. I'm sure there will come a time when we'll wish you were here. That ain't now, though."

"When it comes, call me," I said. "I'll come." I turned and started off toward my truck at a jog.

"Hey, Fred!" the chief yelled. "Don't forget to meet me at the station in an hour!"

All the men and women at the barricade turned and looked at me, and I turned back to the chief to see him smiling. Bastard. He now had five witnesses he could use when the mayor asked about me. I gave him a half salute, jumped in my truck, and drove off.

* * *

I grabbed George and the kids, and we headed for the ferry at the east end of the island that ran to the other side of Mobile Bay. While the 90-minute head start had seemed like plenty when I was talking to the chief, I didn't realize that we'd have to pull the kids from the school George had signed them up for. We didn't have a lot of things to pack, which helped; some of the trade goods had been used by George, either in trade for goods and services or—in the case of the toilet paper—they'd just been used.

We pulled up to the ferry with 15 minutes to spare, but the chief had been right. There was a line leading up to the ferry service's ramp.

"Sorry," the driver of the car in front of me said. "They just said that I'm the first to load on the next ferry."

It took a second to process what that meant, and George caught it before I did. What can I say? I'd been busy thinking about other things.

"That's not going to work," George said. "We need to be on that ferry."

"Shit." It was all I could come up with. I looked around. "Who told you that?"

The other driver pointed to a man in a hat by the ramp. "Him."

"Be right back," I said.

I jogged over to the man as he started waving the vehicles onto the ferry.

"Hey," I said. "I'm in that truck." I pointed. "I need to get on this ferry."

"So does everyone else," the man said. "I'll take you on the next run."

"I can't wait," I said. "If you leave me here, you'll probably return to find a gunfight going on."

"Well, if you want on that badly, you can get on. The truck, however, stays. We are strictly first-come, first-served." He continued to wave cars aboard. There wasn't much room left.

"But I've got a pass from the chief of police!" I exclaimed.

"I know you do," the man said. "I'm aware of who you are. That's why I'm going to let you on the ferry and not charge you to do so. If you want the truck, though, you have to wait until the next run." His shoulders slumped. "Now what the fuck?" he asked.

I turned toward where he was looking. The car two in front of ours hadn't moved, and its driver was standing alongside it talking to George.

"Let's go!" the ferry service man yelled. "Get onboard now, or lose your spot!"

"I'm going to let this gentleman have my spot," the man yelled back, pointing at George.

"Well, then he needs to get his ass onboard right now, or he's going to be left behind!"

I raced back to the truck as George climbed into the passenger seat. I threw it into gear and went around the two cars in front of ours. George handed a package of four rolls of toilet paper out the window to the man he'd been talking to as we went past. I rolled up onto *Fort Morgan* and parked the truck, then looked back at the two vehicles that had been left behind in time to see the man George had talked to hand a roll to the driver of the car we'd pulled up behind. I shook my head.

A roll of toilet paper can save a man's life in this Fallen World.

* * * * *

Chapter Nineteen

"Well done," I said to George as the ferry pulled away from the dock.

"Thanks," George said. "That was Plan B in case you weren't able to talk your way aboard."

"Well, I could have gotten us aboard, but we'd have had to leave the truck behind."

"It's a long walk from Fort Morgan to Perdido Key," George said. "Especially carrying all our gear."

"Glad we didn't have to do it, then," I replied.

"And I'm glad we didn't have to stay on the island." George nodded back to the pier, where a police cruiser had just pulled up, lights flashing. I held my breath, but the boat continued on its journey. After a couple of seconds to be sure weren't going to turn around, I began to breathe again.

"Very well done," I said.

"Thanks," George replied. He watched the pier a little longer then asked, "Did you know the guy I was talking to? He said you looked familiar."

I looked back toward the pier, but the features of the man were too indistinct to tell. "I don't think so," I replied, "but I don't know; he could be from my missing memories." All of a sudden, I wanted to go back and talk with the man. I couldn't—not without having some issues with the police—but I surely wanted to. "Did he say where he knew me from?"

"Nope. Just that you looked familiar."

I watched until the pier area went out of sight, but never received any additional insight into who the man was, or where I might have known him from. I shrugged and turned away from the railing. "We need to have a team meeting," I said as I walked back toward our vehicle.

"What's up?" George asked as we reached the back of the truck where the kids were.

"I wanted to have a word with John," I replied, turning toward the boy.

"Yes?" he asked.

"I know it's been a while, but we're headed back into the unknown again, and I wanted to talk with you about our trip to Dauphin Island. On our way there, I told you to look a certain way, and you didn't. That's a problem—a big problem. We're a team, and we have to be able to count on each other to watch their assigned sectors. If bad guys get in close, we're probably done for."

A tear went down his cheek. "I'm sorry," he said.

"Do you understand why this is important?" I asked. "Your brother and sister—hell, even your dad and I—could have been killed because you didn't do what you were told."

The boy looked up and met my eyes. "I understand," he said. "It won't happen again."

"Good," I replied, nodding once. I looked at his siblings. "Do you two have any questions?"

Eric looked at me with big eyes and shook his head, but Alice held up her hand.

"Yes?" I asked.

"I need to learn how to shoot," she said. I raised an eyebrow. "I heard you talking about trade goods. You may not see the way that some of the men look at me, but that's exactly what I am to some of the men now—a trade good. If I don't know how to defend myself, that's all I'll ever be."

I nodded once. Unfortunately, she made sense. There were plenty of bad men—and women, too—who would have liked to get their hands on a young, nubile woman *before* society broke down. Now? There were probably an exponentially larger number. She had every right to know how to use a gun, or knife, or whatever she wanted to learn about in order to defend herself. I looked inquisitively at George who—unlike his son—wouldn't meet my eyes.

Finally, his shoulders slumped, and he nodded once. "Go ahead and teach her," he said, then he turned and walked off toward the boat's stern railing.

I looked back to the girl. "Okay, Alice, I'll teach you." She smiled. "You heard everything I told your brother, though, right? If I trust you with a gun, you have to do what you're told, when you're told. Can you do that?"

She nodded.

I spared a glance for her father, who was staring at the boat's wake, and I was happy I didn't have any children. That I knew of, anyway.

Kids have to grow up fast in this Fallen World.

* * * * *

Chapter Twenty

The rest of the trip between Dauphin Island and Fort Morgan went quickly; however, all the cars were stopped after debarking from the ferry. A checkpoint had been set up, and everyone had to pass through it. As the last one onto the ferry, we were also the last one off it, and we had plenty of time to watch the proceedings from the back of the line. After about fifteen minutes—the ferry had already loaded again and left—it was finally our turn.

"Purpose of your visit today?" asked a large bearded man.

"Passing through," I replied. "We're headed to Perdido Key."

"That your final destination?"

"For them, yeah," I said, nodding toward George and then the kids in the back. "They're going to see his uncle."

"What about you?" he asked.

"I don't know yet," I replied. "I may stay; I may continue onward. Why?"

"The islands—here in Alabama and Perdido Key—are fairly safe. As long as you're contributing something useful, you'll be welcome. The law still applies, and most crimes are still punished. I hear a lot of bad things about the mainland, though. The base at Pensacola ate a nuke, as did downtown Pensacola. I doubt you want to go much further that way. The rest of the mainland—that which doesn't glow at night—is pretty lawless, from what we hear."

"The entire mainland?"

The man shrugged. "Don't know. There may be good places— better ones than the areas around us, anyway—but we haven't heard about them. The people who try to cross the bridges onto the islands are pretty messed up...and they're usually being chased. You can make up your own minds on what's going on over the bridge, but I—" he leaned close to the window and his voice dropped, "—I wouldn't take my kids across the bridges. I wouldn't even go there myself. Right now, the bridges are one-way only—you can leave over them, but no one's being allowed back across."

"No one?" I asked.

"Not at the moment. We don't want any infiltrators from the warlords up north."

I nodded once. "Makes sense." I indicated the road in front of us with my chin. "We cleared to go?"

"You are," the man replied. "Just remember what I said about the laws still applying. The penalties for breaking them are harsh and pretty unforgiving. Even though we're surrounded by some pretty lawless lands, we're still trying to maintain a sense of civilization here. If you can't contribute to that, you're no good to us."

"Got it," I said with a nod.

The Guard motioned to another man at the barrier, and the second man lifted the arm blocking our passage. "Have a nice day," the guard said.

"You, too," I replied.

Civilities still apply in some parts of this Fallen World.

* * * * *

Chapter Twenty-One

After all the issues we'd had so far, the trip to Perdido Key was almost surreal in how uneventful it was. There was traffic on the main roads. It was light, but it still existed, and I wondered where they were getting the gas for their cars. We took Highway 180 to Gulf Shores and then 182 on to Orange Beach. There weren't any more barricades, although we heard they existed further to the north on the bridges when we asked about it during our stop for lunch.

Although there was a very visible police presence, there were no checkpoints or other issues until we reached the bridge to Perdido Key, which had one at the center of the enormous structure. The checkpoint seemed to be a joint venture between the two islands, but the people stopping cars on our side kept looking askance at the people on the other side of the small median, and vice versa. While they didn't appear overly jovial toward each other, at least they weren't outright belligerent.

"Interesting," I said as we waited in line for our turn to go through the checkpoint.

"What's interesting?" George asked.

"Look at the guys doing security."

"What about them?"

"The continued existence of this checkpoint is a courtesy to the people of Alabama," I replied. "The people stopping the cars going into Perdido Key are professionals—just watch the way they move;

the way they back each other up at all times. Even the way they hold themselves shows they've had training." I shrugged. "The guys watching traffic going to Alabama are just guys; the people from Perdido Key could kill them all before they even knew they were under attack."

"How the *hell* do you know that?"

"I don't know." I shrugged again. Maybe I'd had training at some time in my past if I could recognize theirs. One of the things I'd noticed about myself was an innate ability to calculate the odds of how a situation would go, and I didn't like ours if we ended up facing off against the Perdido Key guys. The Alabama guys? No problem. The Perdido Key guys were another story. "But I'll tell you one thing—if we try to mess with these guys, we're going to end up dead."

George nodded. Maybe he was learning to trust my senses. "If that's the case," George said, "how about you try to not be a smartass to them?" I guess he'd come to know that side of me, too.

"I'm certainly going to try."

I watched the men as we drew closer. While they didn't scare me—exactly—they definitely set my senses tingling, and evoked a very strong "fight or flight" response. I worked hard to control it; despite knowing the odds, I felt the need to fight, just to test myself.

"Where you headed?" asked the man checking IDs as we pulled up to the checkpoint.

I looked over to George. In all of our journey to get here, he'd never actually said where we were going.

"Sandy Key Condominiums," George said.

The ID checker jerked back a little—obviously in surprise—and I saw the man on overwatch go on alert. His hand flashed inside his jacket to whatever weapon he had there. I kept both my hands on the wheel in plain sight, all thoughts of provoking them gone in an instant. The man's reflexes were as good as, if not better than, my own. One wrong move, and we were dead.

"And what, exactly, do you think you're going to do there?"

"I'm Luc Boudreaux's nephew. I'm coming to tell him about his brother's death."

"Oh," ID Checker said. His shoulders relaxed fractionally, and the overwatch man's hand relaxed on the pistol I was sure he was holding. "Well, that sucks."

"Happens these days," George said with a shrug.

"It does," ID checker said, nodding. "What happened to his killer?"

"Fred here took care of him," George said, pointing to me.

I became the center of attention again as both men evaluated me. I tried to look as unthreatening as possible.

"That so?" ID Checker asked, after a moment's contemplation.

"Yeah," I replied, trying to sound nervous. "I got lucky."

"Lucky?" George said. "Hell, you should have seen him. He was a one man army. I don't know how many men he's killed in the trip from Louisiana to here, but I'm guessing it's in the dozens."

The man's eyebrow went up as I became a bigger threat to him, and Overwatch's hand snuggled back up to his pistol.

"So you're a tough guy huh?" ID Checker asked. He looked over to his partner. "Hey, Smitty, this guy look familiar to you?"

"A little. I can't place him, though. He kind of looks like that movie star—you know the one?"

ID Checker nodded as his eyes came back to me. "You look familiar to me, too. You ever been on TV or the movies?"

"Not that I'm aware of," I replied. All of a sudden, I didn't want to share my history—or lack, thereof—with them. I just wanted to get out of their sight. "I get that a lot, though. I just have a familiar-looking face, I guess."

"Hmm," ID Checker said, obviously not satisfied. "Are you going to cause any problems on my island?"

"Not me," I said. "All I did was finish things; I didn't start any of those fights." I kept my question of, "So you own the island, now?" to myself, which I was pretty proud of. I'm not sure when the last time I'd exercised that much restraint had been, but I'm pretty sure it was before I woke up in Louisiana.

"Uh, huh," ID Checker replied. "That true?" he asked, looking to George for confirmation.

"I can't vouch for all of them," George replied, "as I wasn't around him the entire time, but the ones I was there for were all started by other people. And he did end them all...permanently."

I saw a new look cross ID Checker's face—it was the same look a shark, or a killer—gives another one. Professional courtesy. I could also see that he was now interested in testing *my* skills, although he was too much of a professional to do it while he was supposed to be performing his duties. If I ever met him off duty, though, the nod he gave me left me with an unspoken challenge to find out which of us was better.

The nod I gave him back let him know I understood, and he smiled and waved us through. "These guys are okay, Brown," he said. "In fact, I hope to meet Fred again."

A small shiver went down my back as I drove away. I hoped that meeting never happened.

* * *

"Did I miss something?" George asked as we drove east along the key and into what used to be Florida.

"What do you mean?" I asked.

"That whole conversation on the bridge." He shrugged. "It was like I was there and talking with all of you, yet somehow you were having your own conversation with them that I wasn't a part of."

"You have no idea," I replied. I spared a glance at him. "I told you while we were waiting that I thought those guys were killers. Well they are, and I suspect they are *very* good at it. Maybe even better than me." I could see him shiver as *that* implication went through his mind. "When you told them that I'd killed dozens of people since you've known me, you made me a pro in their eyes. Then they had to measure themselves against *me*."

George shivered again.

"Yeah," I replied to his unspoken response. "Happily, they were too professional to challenge me while on duty, but if we ever meet up when they're not…"

"Oh. Shit."

"Yeah," I said. After a couple of moments I added, "Maybe, next time, you don't want to mention anything about that, okay?"

"You got it," he said in a small voice. "Sorry."

"You didn't know," I replied. "All things considered, though, I'd still like to find out who I am before someone kills me."

We drove the rest of the way in silence. Enormous high-rise hotels and condominiums lined the gulf shore on the right as we drove. I suspected most of them were empty, as trying to feed that many people would have been problematic. As the road continued on toward the north, we turned off onto the access road to the Sandy Key

Condominiums—more large buildings, next to some truly enormous ones—and were immediately stopped at another checkpoint. We stated our business with Luc Boudreaux—and nothing else this time—and were waved through.

"I have a question," I said as we drove down to the last building. "What exactly did your uncle do for Obsidian? Based on the body language of everyone here when you mention his name, he's someone pretty damned important."

George shrugged. "I don't know. He was always just, 'Uncle Luc,' you know? I knew he was in upper management, but I never really cared growing up. Then he and dad had a fight, and dad moved to Louisiana. Dad never wanted to talk about him anymore."

We parked the car, leaving the kids to watch it, went through another security checkpoint, and were directed up to a suite on the top floor. Admittedly, I hadn't seen many nice places—that I could remember, anyway—but this building was *nice*. It had the opulence of the mega rich—those people who didn't have to overstate their wealth because anyone they cared about impressing would recognize the Da Vinci and Cézanne paintings...and if they didn't recognize them, they were below notice.

Don't ask me how I knew they were Da Vinci and Cézanne; I just did.

A large, hairy man answered the door when I knocked. "What?" he asked.

"Hi," I replied, trying not to reel backward from his pungent breath. I didn't know what he'd eaten to achieve that level of rankness, but I was really curious so I could avoid it in the future. "We're here to see Luc Boudreaux."

The man's bloodshot eyes stared at me a moment, looking for recognition. "Get fucked," he said, finding none. "He ain't here."

"Hi Frank," George said from over my shoulder. "It's me, George Boudreaux. I'd like to see Uncle Luc."

"Well, look who's here," Frank said with a sneer. "The prodigal brother returns. Except it's not the brother, it's his asshole son. The boss wondered if we'd be seeing you."

"Good to see you, too, Frank." George's voice matched and—if anything—exceeded the level of sarcasm he received. "Is Luc here? I have something to tell him."

"Nope."

"Where is he?"

"None of your damn business. You and your dad left. Damn near broke his heart."

"As if something could break that son of a bitch's heart."

Frank cocked his head and frowned. "Whaddya want?"

"A couple beds for the night and to talk to my uncle would be nice."

"Not happening. Get lost." He slammed the door.

I turned to George. "And you say *I* have no people skills."

"Something's wrong," George replied. "Frank's an asshole, but he never would have kicked me out. Not without asking my uncle, anyway. He doesn't have that kind of license to act."

"Sounds like you didn't leave on the best of terms. Maybe your uncle left instructions to turn you away."

"Not a chance. He may not have liked some of my dad's choices, but he wouldn't have turned us away without speaking to us. If nothing else, he would have wanted to gloat about our return."

I raised an eyebrow.

"Okay, my family isn't perfect, either, Mr. Smart Guy, but I'm serious. My uncle would never have given Frank the latitude to talk to me like that." When I continued to look at him, he added, "I'm serious."

I nodded once, then turned back to the door. I'd come too far and gone through too much to be turned away at the door by this asshole. While I may not have been able to take the guys on the bridge—not that I'm saying I couldn't—I could definitely kick Frank's ass. Whether he was drunk, stoned, or—most likely—both, his ass was mine.

I knocked on the door again, harder this time.

The door opened again, but now the security chain was on. It didn't prevent Frank's halitosis from escaping. "What?" he asked.

I braced on my right foot and kicked out with the sole of my left. The door crashed inward, throwing him back as the frame around the chain's attachment splintered.

Frank stumbled to a stop, but surprisingly didn't fall, and he reached for the pistol in his belt. I was faster, though, and stepped forward to chop down on his wrist. His trigger discipline wasn't very good—he'd already wrapped his finger around the trigger as he tried to draw it, and the gun went off before it cleared his waistband.

"Fuck!" he yelled as he dropped the pistol and bent over to grab his groin. "You shot me in the dick!"

I put a hand on his head and pushed hard, knocking him to the floor, where he lay, still clutching himself. I stepped forward and picked up the pistol as footsteps could be heard from the hallway.

Two men raced into the room with rifles in their hands. "What the hell?" the first one through the door asked.

"Frank shot himself in the groin," I said. "I took his pistol for safekeeping so he didn't shoot anything important."

Both men focused on me and frowned. I reached to my side and gave George a small push away from me so I had enough room to move.

"Is he going to die?" the first one asked.

"Is it a problem if he does?"

"Nope," the second man said. "In fact, now that he's seen us here, it's probably more of an issue if he lives."

"Hey! Luc will have your asses when he gets back!" Frank exclaimed. "Kill them! Kill them now! Then get me a fucking medic!"

"We used to work for Mr. Boudreaux," the first man said. "He was a good man. This guy—" he indicated Frank with his pistol, "—is a piece of shit. Don't know why Mr. Boudreaux left him in charge." He shrugged. "It'd be better if you didn't shoot him again. I'll give the all clear, but if you shoot him again, you're liable to have a full security response. Some of those assholes are his friends and might not take what you're doing so...dispassionately." The men turned to leave.

"Hey!" George called. "What did you mean when you said you used to work for Mr. Boudreaux?"

The first man turned around. "Mr. Boudreaux, along with a number of his men, went north about a month ago to try and make contact with some of the other member of the company's management. He hasn't been seen or heard from since." He pointed to Frank again. "It's been long enough that some people have started trying to usurp his power." He shrugged. "I hope he comes back soon or this place is going to go to shit."

"What're your names?" I asked.

"I'm Johnson; he's Jones," the first man said.

"I understand your concern," I replied, "as does Mr. Boudreaux." I nodded to George. "That's why Mr. Boudreaux sent his nephew, George, to manage things until his return."

"Is that right?"

I gave him my best smile. "That George is Mr. Boudreaux's nephew? Absolutely."

"No," Johnson said. "I know that's Mr. Boudreaux's nephew. I've seen him before, although it's been some time, and I recognize him. I'm asking whether Mr. Boudreaux sent him."

"Let me put it to you this way," I said, allowing the smile to fade, "I say that he did, and I'm willing to fight anyone who calls me a liar. I personally know the new Mr. Boudreaux, and I'll vouch for him. You wanted a new, good, interim boss? Here you go."

Johnson gave George an appraising look. "I've worked for worse, and I wouldn't have any issues working for the new Mr. Boudreaux. Nor would Jones. Some people will, though, and you'll have to deal with them."

"I'm looking forward to it. Where might I find these people?"

"They like to use Room 702 as their party room."

My smile returned. "Party? I love a good party. I think I'll stop by."

Johnson looked at Jones. "I think I'm going to like working for him."

"Me, too," Jones replied. "Assuming he survives."

"True." He looked at me, then stared hard at me for a few moments. "You know, you look familiar."

"Yeah, I know. I've been getting that a lot. I look like that movie star from TV, back when we had them."

"No, although now that you say it, I see a certain resemblance. What I was talking about, though, was you look like a guy that I saw in one of the corporate wars I fought in. We reached a point where both forces couldn't go any further. After about a week of stalemate, this guy came around. I don't know what his name was—I may not have ever even heard it. Anyway, he said, 'I want you to attack in two hours.'"

Jones shrugged. "I thought it was stupid—both sides had tried several times by this point, and neither could move the other—but my colonel said, 'That guy's a company man—an Agent. If he says to attack in two hours, we attack in two hours...and we'll be successful.' We watched that guy meet up with two other guys, then the three drifted off toward the enemy lines."

His eyes lost focus, as if he were watching something from long ago.

"So, what happened?" I asked when he didn't continue.

Jones twitched; he'd been so lost in his thoughts, he seemed surprised to see me there. "What?" he asked.

"What happened with the attack?"

"We attacked in two hours and barely lost a man. When we got to the other side, we found whole sections of the enemy line where no one was still alive. Except for the fact that there wasn't a crater, it looked like a bomb had exploded in their midst—they were scattered about in pieces."

"And those men had done it?"

"I don't rightly know—we never saw them again. If they didn't do it, though, I don't know who did. And if they *did* do it..." he shook his head.

"And I look like that Agent guy?"

"No, but you look like one of the two men he met with. As they split up, one of them—a man that was the spitting image of you, minus a few years now—walked by and smiled at me, just the way you did now. He never said anything, so I can't tell if the voice is the same; he just gave me a sarcastic half-salute and walked off." Jones paused a second then added, "We have to go—we've got sniper duty on the roof now—but I just want to say one thing. If you're him, I'm awfully glad you're on our side. Me and Johnson will be *very* happy to work for you."

The men turned and left, and I turned back to Frank.

"I can be of use," he said. All his earlier combativeness had disappeared as his will to live kicked in. "You don't have to kill me."

I walked over to where he lay. He'd wet himself, and the blood and urine made a nasty puddle on the floor. Someone was going to have to clean it up, but that someone wasn't me.

"You are going to be of use," I replied as I bent over and twisted his head suddenly. The crack as his neck broke echoed throughout the room. "You're going to serve as my example."

Examples are important in this Fallen World.

* * * * *

Chapter Twenty-Two

"Um, are you sure you know what you're doing?" George asked.

"As to putting you in charge?" I asked. He nodded. "Yeah, I do. I kill the troublemakers and set you up as the legitimate heir to fill the power vacuum."

"That's not what I meant."

"You asked if I knew what I was doing. I have a plan and am implementing it."

"What I really meant was more along the lines of, 'Do you think this is the right thing to do?'"

"Obviously, we couldn't wait for your uncle to return with Frank still alive; he would have had you killed as soon as he could. And me too, unfortunately. I didn't intend for him to shoot himself, but once that happened, there really was no going back. Either he was going to die, or we were."

"I'm glad you chose him, then."

"Me too. Like I already told you, I don't know who I am, and I don't have any intention of dying in that state."

"So what do we do?"

"It's too late to do anything now, but the first order of business tomorrow, assuming we're still alive, is for you to start learning the ropes."

"Um, still alive?"

"You heard Jones; there will be people who object to the change in management."

"I did."

"They will probably make an attempt on your life tonight. My intention is to stop that attempt and give any people who have issues with your installation a number of reasons to believe they should accept it as the path of least resistance…and the one most conducive to them living a long and somewhat happy life. As much as we can in this shitty world, anyway."

"You know I have three kids, right? While I would like to survive the night, I would also very much like it for them to do so, too."

"What's your point?"

"My point is that it might be easier to get back in the truck and drive across the bridge to Alabama…or maybe back to Dauphin Island or Bayou La Batre. Somewhere where the laws are functional and the people aren't actively trying to kill us. You know, like here."

"They aren't trying to kill us here yet. Aside from Jones and Johnson, who seemed to be okay with it, no one else knows about him." I nodded to Frank. "By the way, I am *not* cleaning that up."

"And this would be a great time for us to leave, while they are still in that state."

"It would also be a great time to hit the assholes here and install you as the leader of this island, where laws also still apply…and will even more so, once we get rid of the people who would corrupt them while your uncle is gone."

"And then what?"

"What do you mean?"

George shrugged. "What happens when my uncle returns? He and my father didn't part under very good terms, he might not be happy to see me."

It was my turn to shrug. "Who knows? We'll burn that bridge when we come to it. He may never show back up again—you saw that Frank obviously thought he wasn't coming back, or he wouldn't have been taking the liberties he was. Besides, I want to stay around and meet your uncle. If I look like this guy who was friends with an Agent—i.e., a company guy—your uncle, as upper management in that same company, might have some information on who I am. Hell, maybe he even knows me. Like I said—"

"You're not dying without knowing who you are."

I smiled. "Exactly."

George sighed and seemed to slump a little. "Okay, so what's the plan if we stay here?"

"The first thing is to nip any of Frank's assholes in the bud, so fewer assholes come after us tonight, or tomorrow, or whenever they decide to make their play. If we get all of them at the start, we don't have to worry about them later."

"Which means we…"

"We go to Room 702, tell them how it's going to be, and kill everyone who disagrees."

"Do you always have to solve your problems with violence?"

"In the world I woke up to? Yeah, it seems like it. Talk was great in the old world—before everything worthwhile got nuked—but people just seem to respond better to violence now. I've also found that people aren't as likely to try to kill me if they're dead."

"So why don't you install yourself as the new boss?"

"That's not my job. You're the relative of the bigwig; I'm not. It therefore falls to you to be the new boss. After I kill all the assholes downstairs, no one's going to want to work for me anyway. I'll make a great enforcer and bodyguard for you—for the time being, anyway—but people will be too afraid of me to work well for me. That's my plan, anyway."

"For the time being?"

"Until you are safely installed. After that, I will follow up any leads I can find to figure out who I am." I shrugged. "I only promised to help get you here; I never promised to stay. Now, stop stalling. Are you in or out?"

George contemplated a couple of moments, then straightened his back and stood a little taller. "I'm in. What do you need from me?"

"Stay behind me, don't get hit by any stray bullets, and shoot anyone that looks like he's going to shoot me."

"I can do that."

"Good. Follow me then." I reached over Frank's puddle to grab his shirt collar and began dragging him to the door, but then looked back at the mess it was making.

"I know," George said, before I could speak. "You're not cleaning that up."

"Nope. The real first order of business for you is to find the cleaning crew and get that cleaned up, so your kids can move up here where they can be better protected."

"I can clean that up."

"RHIP. You're not cleaning it up either."

"RHIP?"

"Rank hath its privileges. The big boss doesn't clean up piss or blood. That's what you have minions for."

"I get minions?" George asked. "I'm liking this job more and more all the time."

"One thing, though?" I asked.

"Yeah?"

"I'm not your minion. I'm not cleaning that up."

"I think we've established that."

"Okay, just checking. Let's go then." I continued dragging Frank out the door, then down the stairs, the back of his heels thumping down them as we went. It wouldn't have been hard to find where the men were; even with the door closed, the sounds of their partying could be heard in the stairwell. It wasn't that the soundproofing was bad—they were just that loud.

We reached 702, and I pulled out one of my pistols and adjusted my grip on Frank's collar before motioning George to open the door.

He tried the handle. "It's locked."

"Of course it is." I shook my head. "See? Violence is needed, more often than not."

I let Frank's head drop onto the concrete walkway with a solid *thwack!* I didn't figure he cared anymore, and neither did I. Then I squared up and kicked in the door. Inside was a hallway, leading to a large room full of people. The furniture had been pushed back to the walls, leaving the space open. Several kegs of beer were in the middle of the room, and most of the people either had a beer in their hand, were smoking hand-rolled cigarettes, or both.

"Stay here," I said to George as I grabbed Frank's collar again and pulled him into 702. Between the music and people yelling to be heard over it, no one noticed me kicking the door in and dragging a dead body into the party.

It looked like a good party.

More violence was required, so I dropped Frank again, drew my pistol, and fired a round into the ceiling. As George's new room was 801, I wasn't worried about putting a hole in his floor...or anything that might drain through it.

The yelling stopped as everyone turned to look at me, and the music stopped a second or two later.

"Hi, Everyone," I said. "I just wanted to let you know that there's been a change of management." I nodded back over my shoulder. "George Boudreaux is here to take over until his uncle gets back from his trip. Frank here—" I indicated him with a kick, "— had issues with the change of management. I was hoping to avoid any further unpleasantness, but heard that some of you might be opposed to such a change."

"And who the fuck do you think *you* are?" asked a large, hairy man as he set his beer down. He looked a lot like Frank, and I could see he was going to be a problem. He jumped to the top of my target list.

"People call me Fred," I replied. "Aside from that, I'm one of George's friends, and someone who would like to see a stress-free shift of power."

"What about him?" a second tough asked, pointing to Frank.

"I can assure you," I said, "Frank isn't feeling any stress at the moment. Now, I'm hoping that everyone will play nicely and go along with this."

"Or what?" asked the first guy. I noticed his hand had gone behind his back.

I fired, and a round went through his forehead. His head snapped back, and he collapsed, dropping the pistol he'd drawn.

"Or that is what is going to happen." I sighed theatrically. "Look, I'm hoping we can all just get along."

"And if we can't?"

"My first thought would be to kill you, but Mr. Boudreaux says I need less violence in my life. Because of that, I am willing to give anyone who wants to leave a 30-minute head start. You'll have 30 minutes to grab any of your things and get off the island. Anyone who is still here in 30 minutes had better be willing to follow Mr. Boudreaux's orders, or we're going to have issues. The kind where one of us—probably you—gets a terminal case of lead poisoning." I smiled. "Now, would anyone like to take me up on my generous offer of letting you leave before things get ugly?"

A few hands went up. After a couple seconds of looking around, a couple more went up.

"Okay, you're free to go. As long as you don't draw your weapons, you can even take them with you." I nodded toward the door. "Go ahead; get out of here. George, if any of them draw their weapons, shoot them."

"I intend to," George said from behind me.

Six people nervously walked to the door and out. I could hear at least a couple of them break into a run once they were clear.

"Okay, that leaves you folks," I said, looking around the room. About 9 people remained—six men and three women. "Are any of you still here because you would like to continue in the employ of Mr. Boudreaux?"

Five hands went up.

"Welcome to the new and improved management team," I said. "Please put your weapons on the floor—carefully!—and go out to the hallway outside. I'll be with you shortly."

Four of them did so, but one tried to take me. I shot him twice, but that set the room into motion as the rest of the thugs all went for their guns. I dove to the side as the first man fired, and shot him in the chest. From my spot on the floor, I hit several more, and George tagged at least two from the doorway.

Seeing no movement, I got to my feet. At least two of the people who'd wanted to join our team were dead. Oops.

"Fuck...you..." said the second man who'd spoken. He had two rounds through the chest and had collapsed into a sitting position against a couch. "You can't kill us...all. We've got...friends. They'll get...revenge..." I shot him once through the head. The time for threats was over.

I saw movement out of the corner of my eye and dove to the side, but wasn't fast enough. My right leg burned as the round went through the meat of my thigh.

I hit the ground and rolled as he fired twice more. Both rounds went over me as my pistol came around and the sights lined up on him. It wasn't a "him," though, it was a "her," and I shot her twice in the chest. One of the rounds passed through her and shattered the glass door behind her onto the balcony, the falling glass coating her dead body as she collapsed.

"Fuck!" I yelled as the pain hit my leg.

I pulled myself to my feet and put new magazines into my pistols. "If you're with me, raise your hand." Two hands went up. I limped around the room and put a bullet into the rest of the people's heads, just to be sure, then spun as best I could to the doorway as footsteps sounded outside.

"You in the room, it's me, Johnson!" a voice said.

"Easy, George," I said. His pistol was up, pointed at the doorway, and his eyes were huge. Johnson was pretty smart—George probably *would* have shot him. "C'mon in," I added a little louder.

"One of your kids just got snatched!" Johnson exclaimed as he came around the corner.

"What?" George asked. "By who?"

"By one of these guys' friends, I suspect," Johnson said, indicating the bodies scattered throughout the room.

"Shit," I said as I hobbled to the door. "Where'd he go?" I asked, more to the point.

"He jumped in a car and is headed out."

I raced out the door and looked over the railing into the parking lot, with Johnson and George right behind me. "Which direction?" I asked.

"He's headed toward the bridge," Johnson said, pointing to the north. "There! The green Volkswagen!"

I looked and saw the convertible blow through a stop sign then race off toward the bridge. It went behind a stand of palm trees, then it broke into the clear, a long way off. There was a man driving, and I could see a girl in the back seat. *Damn it, I liked Alice.* "Give me your rifle," I said, the pain in my leg forgotten as the adrenaline kicked in again.

"Shit," Johnson said. "That's just a waste of damn ammo. You can't hit him from here."

"Give me the gun," I repeated. I could see another patch of palm trees ahead of the man, and knew if he made it to that cover, he'd be home-free to the bridge. I didn't know how I knew, but I knew I could hit him, but I needed to shoot *now*.

"Shit," Johnson said. "That's a long damn shot, and you're just as likely to hit the girl. Ain't never going to happen."

"Give me…the fucking gun…*now!*" Something in the way I said the last word seemed to move him—a tone of command, perhaps—and he handed me the rifle.

I gave it a quick glance. AR-15 clone, probably chambered in either a .223 or NATO 5.56 round. Whatever NATO was. But it was a light round, and more easily affected by the wind.

With a grunt, I put the rifle to my shoulder. It felt right, as if I'd done this before. A lot. Maybe I'd been a soldier before the war. I sighted on the fleeing man. The palm leaves weren't moving near him, so no wind. That would help.

I led him as I'd been taught…taught? *I* had *been a soldier!*…took a breath and, as I let it out, slowly squeezed the trigger. The rifle fired, surprising me so much I almost dropped it, but somehow I held onto it long enough.

"Told you it was too far," Johnson said as the car streaked toward the bridge.

"Nope," I said. "He should have dodged." The words had no sooner come out of my mouth, then the man pitched forward onto the steering wheel. The car lost speed, then swerved to the right and slammed into a palm tree.

"Well, I'll be fu—"

"Not by me you won't," I replied, starting toward the stairs. "We need to go quickly," I added. "Not sure I killed him, and we don't want him to get away."

George and Johnson ran to where the car rested against the tree, just ten feet shy of the start of the bridge. I hobbled as best I could, and got there to find George hugging Alice. The round had taken the kidnapper through the spine, just where it entered his head. He never knew what hit him and was probably dead before the car hit the tree.

"Dayum," Johnson said. "That was one hell of a shot. A head shot from that distance? I would have said it couldn't be done."

"Me, too," I muttered. I'd been aiming lower—between his shoulder blades—to get a center of mass hit. Even with all that, to hit a moving target that far away…it was still a pretty nice shot. Maybe I'd been some sort of sniper.

"Maybe Jones was right about you," Johnson asked. "Maybe you were one of those company people. If nothing else, you must have been a sniper or something in the army."

"Maybe," I said with a nod. "Either way, though, I don't remember doing it."

"Well, you sure shot the shit out of him."

"Yep."

There was a tapping on my back, and I turned to find Alice looking up at me, her eyes huge. "Thank you for saving me, Mr. Fred," she said. "Daddy says he's ready for me to have that pistol training you promised me, but never did."

There's never enough time to do everything you want to in this Fallen World.

* * * * *

Chapter Twenty-Three

The thugs, when they came that night, were very good. Not professional grade, but very good for amateurs. I had napped during the time between Alice's rescue and when everyone else went to bed, besides getting my leg wound treated, and I was—if not 100%—at least in the upper 80s.

Two people were lowered from the roof at the same time someone opened the door to the suite of rooms. While I couldn't see the front door from my vantage point in the coat closet, I could easily see the man and woman on the back porch through the sliding glass door. Neither had night vision gear on, but the moon was full and bright, and it gave the scene enough light for them to see. Not enough to see me through the missing two slats of the closet door, but more than enough to see into the room.

They checked the door—it was locked—then waited with their pistols drawn. Two men came into view from the hallway by the front door. I suspected there would be at least one more there, maybe two, as lookouts. It's what I would have done, anyway.

The two from the front door both had night vision goggles on, and one stood at the entranceway to the main room, while the other crossed to the sliding glass door onto the balcony. That was my cue, and I aimed, closed my eyes, and fired at the man on overwatch.

I opened them to find him slumping, while the man at the glass door spun around. The two people on the porch were pointing in my general direction, but the other thug with NVGs on had his back to them and couldn't see what they were doing. They couldn't shoot at me, as he was between us.

As the man's eyes searched the condo, I took care of that problem by shooting him while he was looking at the other side of the room.

He slumped, giving the two on the porch a line of fire into my position, but I was already in motion as they began firing, and I heard the sounds of glass shattering and rounds hit the walls behind me as I dove through the hole I'd made in the closet wall leading to the second bedroom. I crawled to the door and raised my pistol as one of the men walked into the main room. He quickly scanned it once, then moved toward the closet door as his partner walked in from the porch.

She stopped to look around and had a split second to see me and draw in a breath to warn her partner before I shot her in the chest. She fell, and I was up and back to the hole in the wall into the closet as the man spun, trying to find out what had killed her. I shot him from about two feet away, close enough to see his blood and brains spray out, even in the dark.

"What's going on?" a voice said from the hallway. "Did you get 'em?"

I didn't say anything.

"Steve?" the voice asked. "Richard? Jackson? Are they dead?" He paused. "Joan?"

"They're all right here," I replied in a stage whisper. "Why don't you come in and get them?"

"But...*argh!*"

I could hear what sounded like a body hitting the floor.

"Is it safe to come in?" a man's voice asked from the door.

"Depends on who you are," I replied, moving quickly to the bedroom door in case the person was trying to figure out where I was.

"I mean you no harm," the voice said. "I met you earlier at the bridge. My name is Williams. I'd like to talk with you. The person who was standing lookout is no longer a threat."

"Come on in," I replied, "although keeping your hands up and empty of weapons is the best way to ensure you keep breathing."

"I will do as you ask," Williams said. "I am unarmed."

He came into the room with his hands up, and I came out of the room, covering him with my pistol.

"I assure you, I am unarmed," he said. "May I turn on a light?"

"Go ahead," I said.

He flipped on the overhead light and smiled as he saw me. "Thank you," he said.

"For what?"

"You just won me a gallon of fuel," he replied. "My partner—" he nodded toward the door, "—bet me that they'd take you out. I bet on you."

"*What?*" I asked, the pistol never moving from his chest. "You knew all these assholes would attack us, *and you just let them?*"

Williams shrugged. "One of two things was going to happen. Either you would kill them off—as you have—showing that your Mr. Boudreaux is fit to rule, or they would have killed you off, proving he wasn't." He shrugged again. "The fact is, if you couldn't take care of these assholes, you—and he—probably weren't fit to deal with the other problems this island—and this world—have right now." He smiled, and it looked a lot like mine—the look of a predator. "Besides," he continued, "I bet on you—I thought you could do it. If you want to be mad at someone, be mad at Brown. He's the one who bet against you."

"You did, huh? Bet on me?"

"I did. When I saw you at the bridge, I had a good idea you were an Agent."

"Well, that's great and all, except for one thing—I'm not an Agent."

Williams waved a hand at the devastation throughout the room. "The evidence would suggest otherwise." He paused, then added, "Maybe not an Agent, then, but at least you have corporate training."

"The fact of the matter is, I don't know who I am. I woke up in a back room in New Orleans right after the war, with no memory of who I am. None."

"Interesting..." the man said. "Hey, Brown," he called, "Get in here. Slowly."

The other man from the bridge came in. If he was armed, he at least had the courtesy to put his weapons away. I holstered my pistol and took off the goggles, which were hurting my head.

"Hi," Brown said. "I'd say it was good to see you again, but you cost me a gallon of gas."

"I heard," I replied, "although I have to say I'm happy to disappoint you."

"What's up?" Brown asked his partner.

"Fred here woke up in a New Orleans back room right after the war, with no memory of who he was."

Brown turned and studied me. "Really?" he asked. "That's interesting. No memory at all? Not even a childhood memory of a time or a place?"

"None," I said, shaking my head. "It's a clean slate."

"Interesting," Brown said.

"That's what your partner said," I noted, starting to get a little annoyed with their secrecy.

"What's interesting?" George asked, coming out of the other room, where he'd been barricaded in. He shut the door, probably hoping the kids couldn't listen in.

"Your friend's history," Williams replied. "How long have you known him?"

"A couple of months. Since right after the war."

"So, nothing before his memory loss?"

George shook his head. "Why?"

"What have you noticed about him?" Brown asked.

"You mean, like being handy with a gun or knife?"

"That's a start. What about leadership? Does he like to be in charge, or would he want to be someone...a little more outside the normal chain of command?"

George chuckled. "I told him that he should be the one in charge here, and he didn't want any part of it. Said he wanted to go find out who he was."

Brown and Williams looked at each other and a wry grin passed between them.

"What's so funny?" I asked, my annoyance level building quickly. If I didn't start getting some answers soon, I was going to shoot someone. Probably Brown; he seemed the slower of the two.

"He could no more be the leader of this endeavor than we could. His training—and even if his brain doesn't remember it, his body does—is in killing people and solving problems. He's an Agent—just like us—and organizational leadership just isn't his thing."

It's funny, the people you meet in this Fallen World.

* * * * *

Chapter Twenty-Four

We moved into the kitchen so we could sit down. After all I'd been through today—complete with a good amount of blood loss—followed by the revelation I was an Agent, it was either sit down or fall down.

"So if I'm an Agent," I said, "not that I'm agreeing with you, but if I were one, how is it that I don't remember any of it?"

"For the same reason we don't remember our other lives," Williams said. "Part of the process of creating an Agent is that your former personality—everything about who you were and all your memories—are stripped away, and then the Agent psyche is imprinted over the top of it. While you're an Agent, you're an Agent. Then, when your mission is over, the Agent psyche is removed and all of your old memories are given back to you via the imprinter so you can go back to being who you were again."

"That's not me, though!" I exclaimed. "I don't have either my old memories or the memories of an Agent."

Brown shrugged. "Obviously, the process got interrupted for some reason. Maybe it was the war; maybe there was some other big power hit, although most facilities that do imprinting have a backup power source."

"Even in the back room of some weird import/export operation?"

"That's where you were when you woke up?" Williams asked.

"Yeah."

"Oh, well that makes sense, anyway," Williams said. "Sometimes, Obsidian would sneak an imprinter into the territory of one of the other companies, and then the Agent would travel to that place as his normal self—not someone who would have any of the characteristics of an Agent—and then they'd do the imprinting there. That way, they can sneak the agent into the target area without being noticed."

Brown nodded.

"I can see that, I guess," I said. "But why don't I have either set of memories, then?"

Williams shrugged. "Like Brown said, something must have interrupted the process. When you woke up, was there something like a tanning bed nearby?"

I nodded.

"That was the imprinter. Your state—somewhere in between person and Agent—is a result of an incomplete imprinting. You need to go back and finish the process."

"He could be imprinted as an agent anywhere, though," Brown said.

"True," Williams agreed with a nod. "But what if he wasn't becoming an Agent? What if he was coming back from a mission and was getting his civilian psyche back?"

"Oh. He'd have to do it at that imprinter."

"Exactly."

"Wait," I said, not entirely following. "What are you saying? That in order to become 'me' again, I would need to go back to the imprinter I woke up in?"

"Yeah," Williams said. "That's exactly what I'm saying."

"Well, shit. That isn't happening, because when I left there, the building was on fire. I set off a thermal charge as a distraction while I was trying to get away…that building is gone."

"Well, then there isn't going to be anyway to get your psyche back," Williams said. "Not that I know of, anyway."

"Unless Obsidian keeps a spare copy somewhere in case of something like this," Brown noted.

Williams shrugged. "That makes sense. Of course, that being said, I don't know if Obsidian would have done it."

"Who would know?" I asked.

"Mr. Boudreaux would have known, certainly," Williams replied. He looked at George. "The other one; not this one."

"In the interim—until he gets back—what do I do?" I asked.

"You could find an imprinter and go the rest of the way to Agent," Brown said. "You have already been prepped for psyche implant. That way, you'd have your full knowledge of your skills, not just the muscle memory, like you do now."

"You mean, I'd actually understand what it is I can and can't do? Like using weapons and—"

"There are a variety of skills," Williams interrupted. "We don't talk about them in front of people who aren't cleared for that information, though, and Mr. Boudreaux's status is still…to be determined. He doesn't currently have a need to know." I must have looked frustrated, for he added, "Suffice it to say, though, the list of skills that we have—" he looked at Brown, who nodded, "are extensive. Anything from destruction…insurrection…to skills in the bedroom."

"Really? Bedroom skills?"

Brown shrugged. "You never know what you're going to need to win the hearts and minds of someone. Remember those old spy movies? How did the spy win the hearts of the beautiful enemy agents?"

I nodded. "Okay, I get it. Until I get my own memories back, how do I get my Agent memories?"

"Well, you could have used the one here, like both of us did," Williams said, "but it broke. We're both stuck in Agent mode until Mr. Boudreaux gets back." He shrugged. "I don't know where the next closest one is. Somewhere up north, I'm sure."

"Charlotte, North Carolina, would have had one," Brown said. "That's where corporate HQ was."

"Yeah, but they got nuked," Williams said. "They had to have. I have a hard time believing Obsidian's HQ is still standing."

"True," Brown agreed. "It would have to be further north of that, then."

"What about Miami?" George asked. "Didn't Obsidian have an office there?"

"They did," Williams agreed. "That's why it got nuked, hard. I heard the whole area, even deep into the swamps, is radioactive. I wouldn't go there. Your best bet is to find Mr. Boudreaux."

"I thought everyone here assumed he was dead," I said.

"We do," Williams replied. "Still, that's the best chance you're going to have. He would know where any of the imprinters were, and if there were one that had your original psyche. Most of them probably don't."

I nodded. All of that seemed to make sense in a perverted sort of way.

Sometimes you have to find a dead man to really live in this Fallen World.

* * * * *

Sometimes you have to find a dead man to really live in this Fall-en World.

* * * * *

Chapter Twenty-Five

"**O**kay, so that's what I'm going to do," I said. "I'll go find Mr. Boudreaux, the elder."

"Good luck," Williams said. "I have to be honest with you, though. The odds on him still being alive are pretty long."

"The odds that you'll find him are even longer," Brown noted. "Or that you'll live long enough to make it to wherever he is. And then that you'll make it back."

"True," Williams said with a nod. "You're not even a real Agent. You may have some of the muscle memory, and some of the training may still be in your brain, somewhere, but you don't have active memory of it."

"I know two people who do, though," I replied with a smile. "Would you guys like to come along and help protect little ol' me? It sounds like that's the only way you'll get your old personalities back, too."

"There's only one thing wrong with that," Williams said. I raised an eyebrow. "That assumes we *want* our old personalities back. I can't speak for Brown, but I don't want the old me back—not now anyway. I've never met the old me, you understand, but I can tell you for a fact that he doesn't have my skills. In today's world, I need the new me to stay alive. It also lets me help others stay alive and maintain this sanctuary. Maybe someday we'll bring back the old world—complete with all its issues, but all its strengths, too—but that won't be for a while, and this world needs me to be Williams until that time."

"While I agree with my partner," Brown said, "there's a second factor in play here, too. Mr. Boudreaux, our legitimate boss, told us to stay here and protect the colony, for that's what this really is now. We're an island of civilization among the ocean of barbarism and chaos that surrounds us. We were told to 'stay,' and to go against that would violate our orders. It would lead to…consequences if we were to do other than as we were told."

I pondered that a minute. "That's why you supported that piece of shit, Frank, then, isn't it?"

Brown nodded, then sighed. "Yes, he was a piece of shit, but he was left in charge, and our orders were to support the legitimate person in charge. While he was alive, that was Frank."

"And now that he's dead?" I asked.

He jerked a thumb toward George. "Now that's him. Williams and I talked about it and came to the conclusion that if you defeated the play on your lives by Frank's supporters, that made him the legitimate successor to Frank, especially since he was related to Mr. Boudreaux."

"So I don't have to worry about coming back and finding you've killed him and assumed the leadership of this colony?"

Williams laughed. "Nope; that ain't us, man. I can take over and lead a foreign country, but not my own—it's not in my programming. Besides, my mission orders are to support the legitimate leader; I can't take over. It would lead to the same consequences Brown mentioned earlier."

I looked over to Brown. "And you have the same programming?"

"My programming is slightly different from Williams—we have different imprint psyches, so we're different in what we can do and how. Still, though, my mission parameters are to support the legitimate authority, and I will support Mr. Boudreaux up to the point that the original Mr. Boudreaux shows back up—if he does—then my allegiance will switch back to him."

"As will mine," Williams added. "In the morning, though, we will make it known that we support the new Mr. Boudreaux, and one or the other of us will tag along with him for the next week or two until he gets established, in order to prevent a reoccurrence of that." He nodded toward the other room.

"We will also help get you up to speed on what's what, and who works for you," Brown added, looking at George. "I'll start with the cleanup crew—we'll get someone up here right away to clean up the bodies and mess. The plasterers and the sliding glass door installers will probably have to wait until tomorrow, but it's warm enough that you and your family should be okay until then.

"Speaking of family," Brown continued, "we'll also get someone as a protective detail on each of your children. We are limited in the number of Agents we have, but we have some pretty good 'normals' running around as well. They will be able to see to your family's safety."

"Can they also teach his daughter to shoot?" I asked.

Brown nodded once. "That can be done, too, if Mr. Boudreaux wishes it."

"I do," George replied.

"Then it will be so," Brown replied. "And, with that, I think we're finished here for the night. Anything else can wait until the morning. I would like to get the cleaners up here so your children don't have to see the dead bodies or blood and guts everywhere. They won't ever have a normal childhood, but they will have the best one possible in the current world."

The two Agents nodded, got up, and left, leaving us to our thoughts.

"I understand your need to find out who you are," George said, "but can you stay around for a few days, just to make sure everything goes as advertised? While Brown and Williams seem like good guys, I trust you a lot more than I do them."

"Better the devil you know?"

"You're not a devil, nor are they—you're all products of a corporate mentality gone crazy. If what they say is true, they—and you—are exactly what this world needs to help people pull it back together again."

"Um, I hate to mention it, but 'the people pulling it back together again' now includes you. You're the one in charge of this mess now."

George sighed. "Yeah, I know. Even though I have no idea what I'm doing."

"You can still run away to Bayou La Batre or somewhere else."

"And give up private bodyguards for my children?" George asked with a smile. "Not in this world. I'll struggle along somehow."

"Lean on the Agents," I suggested. "Even though they may not be programmed to lead, they obviously have training in how to run an organization. I'll go find Boudreaux and be back soon."

George gave me a wry smile. "We both know the odds of you returning are small. They're even smaller that you'll find Boudreaux and the information you're looking for."

"Still, though, I have to try."

"I understand."

Although an old world concept, "finding yourself" is just as important in this new Fallen World.

* * * * *

Chapter Twenty-Six

"It's not too late to change your mind and come along." I said to the group that had come to the base of the bridge off the island's east end to see me off. George and his kids, Williams, Brown, Johnson, and Jones looked somewhat awkwardly at me and each other.

"Up there?" Williams finally asked with a smile, jerking his head to the north. "No thanks. I'm fast, but even I can't outrun a bullet. I might dodge a couple, but eventually, if you throw enough of them my way, one of them's going to hit me. Do enough damage to me, and even I can be taken down." He feigned a shudder. "I'll stay here, thanks."

I turned toward Brown. "Don't look at me," he replied with a smile. "My job is to support this idiot." He nodded toward Williams. "And even *I* can't help you up there," he added, "if half of what I've heard is true. Be careful and trust no one."

I nodded. That was good advice most places, these days.

George looked at his feet. "Sure you want to do this, Fred?" he asked. "I looked at a map someone dug up last night—it's got to be the better part of 350 or 400 miles of walking to get to Chattanooga."

"Am I sure?" I asked. "Not really. I do, however, want to know who I am. Or at least who I was. Failing that, if I can at least get an Agent load, that will give me something to go on, rather than this limbo I'm currently in."

"Careful what you ask for," Williams said. "Being an Agent isn't everything you might assume it to be. There are also a good number of Agent imprints, so just being 'an agent' isn't necessarily what you're looking for."

He nodded to his partner. "Brown is a good load, but he is optimized for supporting another, primary Agent. While he's great for teamwork, and together we're far more than either is separately, it may not be what you want alone in the wilds.

"He's right," Brown said. "And not all of the imprinters you find will have the load you want. The bigger ones, sure, but most of them probably got wiped out in the war." He shrugged. "Williams is also right in that support is what I do." He handed me a small box. "This is for you; I hope it will help you along the way."

"What is it?" I asked. I turned it over and found it was some sort of electronic device with a number of buttons and a display screen that showed "0.072."

"It's a nuclear radiation detector, electronic Geiger counter, and personal dosimeter," Brown said. "It will tell you how much radiation you're getting and warn you if you're going into a danger zone. That number there—0.072—is the new normal background radiation reading per hour. It used to be about half that. If you see the number climbing rapidly, go a different way. If the horn goes off, run like hell."

"Got it," I said. "Any places I should avoid?"

Brown laughed. "Big cities, mostly, or military facilities. You can just about count on the fact that they got hit. Of course, both of those have other issues, like people who'll want to take everything you own, so you might want to avoid them, anyway." All of a sudden

I didn't feel much like setting out. Maybe not knowing who I was wasn't such a bad thing.

"It's easy to use," Brown said, pointing to the Geiger counter. "Turn it on and read the dial. I don't know how long the batteries will work, so I wouldn't leave it on. Of course, it's rechargeable…if you found somewhere on the planet where there's still electricity. It also can log into the worldwide server…if you find somewhere with WIFI." He chuckled. "Basically, just turn it on and read the dial, then turn it off again."

I nodded. "Okay; thanks." I turned to the bridge and squared my shoulders, mentally preparing myself for the journey and the challenges I expected to face. Radiation was probably the most benign and avoidable.

Williams and Brown started laughing uproariously, and I frowned as I turned to them. "*What?*" I finally asked, annoyed.

"You…you were…" Williams couldn't get his thought out, and he started laughing again.

My frown deepened, and I began tapping a foot. I looked at George, who appeared as clueless as I was, and Johnson didn't appear to be in on the joke, either. Whatever they were laughing at was lost on me, and my annoyance grew. "Do I need to kill someone to find out what the hell is so funny?" I asked when I couldn't take it anymore.

"I…I think he's serious," Williams was finally able to get out as the laughter ran down. "You better tell him."

Brown reached into his pocket and pulled out a keychain. "We couldn't believe you actually intended to walk 400 miles each way, especially having been shot a few days ago. I mean, sure, it's a new world and there are checkpoints and barricades all over so you might not want to be in a car…but we could at least give you a start so you didn't have to walk the *whole* way." He tossed me the keys, then turned and pointed at the dark blue, older model Ford he'd driven up in.

"It isn't much to look at," Brown added, "but it's got some nice upgrades you can't see. The windows are bulletproof up to anything smaller than a fifty cal, and there are kevlar shields protecting the driver's compartment and the motor. It's also a pretty sturdy motor and should keep running for at least a bit after it takes a hit. The tires are both self-sealing and self-supporting; they should give you a run-flat ability that ought to get you away from whoever is trying to kill you."

"Thanks," I said, my annoyance replaced with something that felt surprisingly like gratitude—something I wasn't sure I'd ever feel again.

"It will also help you carry your gear," he said nodding toward the pack I carried. "I've thrown some extra ammo for your pistols and some additional food into the back seat."

"Thanks," I said again, almost overcome. "I really mean that."

Brown shrugged off my thanks. "No worries, man; it's what us helper types do. If you really want to thank me, you'll bring it back in one piece. It's my car, after all, and that means I'm going to have to be riding with Williams now."

"Hey!" Williams exclaimed. "What's that supposed to mean?"

"I don't know what you eat," Brown replied, "but you stink. I mean, your farts in a car with windows that don't roll down? You're just awful." George's younger kids giggled.

I hefted the keys. "All right, well, I guess I better get at it," I said. "I'd like to get as far as I can during the day, where I can see what's coming."

"Thanks for getting us here," George said. "I'll never forget it."

"I hope not," I replied. "I'll be back soon, and you still owe me beers for that."

"Good luck," Williams and Brown said.

"Safe journey," Johnson added.

"See you soon," Jones said, the most positive of the group.

I made it two steps toward the car before Alice ran forward and wrapped her arms around me, bumping my bad leg in the process. The display of affection was as emotionally moving as her embrace was physically painful. "Don't go!" she exclaimed.

"It'll be okay," I said as George worked to detach her. "I'll be back soon."

"Promise?" she asked, looking up at me with tears brimming in both eyes.

"I promise."

"Good," she replied. "Don't forget."

"I won't." With that, George disengaged her, and I tried not to hobble as I walked to the car. I got in, buckled up, and drove off with a wave.

* * *

Two of the support Agents at the barricade on the bridge saw me coming and opened a lane for me to pass through. Apparently, Luc Boudreaux had imprinted a number of people in the aftermath of the war, with a number of specialties, creating his own private army of operatives, and all of them were now being put to work defending the island and the services needed to function.

There were a number of stores and businesses that had existed on the other side of the bridge, but all of them had been cleaned out by Boudreaux's forces as the bombs began dropping. If nothing else, Boudreaux had been somewhat of a visionary. When it all went to shit, he'd made an army and took control of all of the resources he could, whether that was food, fuel, or personnel. He'd even stripped the local medical center, previously located just off-island, as well as the closest hospital, and had brought all of their equipment, supplies, and personnel he could convince to come back to the "safe" side of the bridge.

A large number of the locals had stormed the bridge, demanding access to all the things he had "liberated." Those who had usable skills had been offered a place on the island, while those who didn't had been turned away. When they returned later, armed and bent on taking it back by force, Boudreaux's army of specialists had been ready for them. A short and vicious firefight had ensued between Boudreaux's forces, who were firing from behind cover, and the locals, who were in the open, which had quickly turned into a massacre. The locals had finally charged the barricade. None of them had made it.

I couldn't see the stains anymore as I drove down the backside of the bridge.

While I didn't know what I'd find further inland, Williams had given me an operational brief the day before on what to expect within a mile from the bridge—nothing of note. The remaining locals had tried a few times to set up roadblocks and barricades, but two of Boudreaux's specialists were snipers. They had quickly taken out the defenders, and then Williams and Brown had led a party down and had removed the barricades and collected their weapons. Although Boudreaux had taken one of the snipers with him on his expedition, the other remained on the island to ensure the locals didn't get restless.

Although the stores had been looted and a number of them burned, there were still people in the area. As the Ford roared by, a number of them came to stand by the road. No weapons were displayed—they obviously knew what happened to people who brought weapons within sight of the bridge—they simply stood, looking at the ground with their hands out, silently begging for whatever handout I would give them. Most had emaciated children with them, and normal people with operational psyches would probably have wanted to stop and give them food and water.

I wasn't one, though, so it was easier for me to drive by.

The people did a good job looking sad, and they probably were, but I only had enough to get me where I was going and back—maybe—and there was a good chance that if I had to abandon the car, I would also end up in the same position—looking to scavenge wherever I could. Of course, I was armed and had the muscle memory of skills I'd had in the past. I wasn't as fast, or as skilled, as any of the Agents, but at least now I knew why I was better than the run-of-the-mill human being.

I continued on 292, heading north, and then turned left onto 293 as 292 bent around to the east. Like George, I'd also found a map of the area, and I had spent a good amount of time deciding on and memorizing my projected route of travel. I still had the map—it was in my pack—but hadn't thought I'd need it for a while. Of course,

I'd been expecting to be walking, so I was going to need it far sooner than I had originally thought.

As I drove, I was reminded of a series of popular movie remakes from my childhood, about a guy who drove around in a post-apocalyptic world. While his world was barren and mostly desert, the road I travelled was mostly forested; still, to look at the burned out houses and buildings, and sections of forest that had burned down with them, gave me a phenomenal sense of unease. It wasn't a matter of "if" there were people out here who meant me harm—there absolutely *were* bad people who would like nothing more than to capture and kill me—it was more a matter of "when" they would show up to attempt it. The further I went, and the longer it didn't happen, the more the stress of knowing it *would* happen built. It was like an itch I couldn't scratch, which had me wanting to look over my shoulders and in every other direction simultaneously.

The Company people on Perdido Key even had reports of cannibals operating on the outskirts of Pensacola; I intended to avoid them at all costs.

To that end, when I reached the main east-west highway, I turned west, away from the city. To have gone east would probably have been quicker, but it also might have meant going through areas which had been irradiated, as well as the area where the cannibals were supposed to be operating. While I had toyed with the idea of doing it off-road when I thought I would be on foot, the chances of running into a trap that would have been difficult to get out of rose exponentially with me in a car. The roads were where they'd be watching…and where any of their traps would be set.

The problem with going west, though, was Perdido Bay, and the large bridge I'd have to go over to get into Alabama. If there was going to be trouble, it was going to be there. I didn't have long to think about it—the bridge was less than two miles away—and as it came into sight, I could tell my fears were justified; there was a barricade on the close end of the bridge.

Unlike the bridge into Perdido Key, though, the bridge here was relatively low-lying; it had a center drawbridge section to allow waterborne traffic to pass, so it didn't need to be high off the water. The barricade, therefore, didn't need to be in the center of the bridge so that the defenders could keep an eye on both sides; instead, it was on this end. Cars had been placed together to block traffic, and they had been augmented with several trees which had been felled and dragged into place.

I approached slowly, trying to determine the number and nature of the barricade's defenders, and I saw two men and a woman, all armed with pistols, on the side closest to me. I could see when they noticed me—they all ran to the other side of the barricade to use the cars for cover. I slowed to a stop, scanning the forested neighborhoods on both sides of the road for additional defenders. I didn't see any, so I decided to wait a few minutes to see what their intentions were; the way they had the roadblock, I certainly wasn't going to be able to smash the car through it. Perdido Bay was over half a mile wide at this point, so trying to swim across it with all of my gear and food was contraindicated. If I wasn't able to get across the bridge, I was either going to have to find a boat to steal—which would probably be defended—or go back the other way and through the outskirts of Pensacola. As neither of these were my preferred choices, I waited.

After a couple of minutes, one of the men came back around the barricade to stare at me. I waved, trying to present a good first impression. I don't know if I was successful or not, as he held out his hands in a "What are you doing?" sort of manner. I tried to put down the window to talk to him, but it was stuck in the "up" position, probably due to the bulletproof glass. Failing that, I waved at him again.

He turned and said something to the other people at the barricade, then turned and said something to me. As I couldn't hear him, and lip-reading wasn't my thing, I waved to him again. He gave me an exasperated look, as if I were some kind of moron, then waved me forward toward his position. Not wanting to be where all three could easily fire on me at once, I waved him forward to where I waited. His hands dropped to his side and his head cocked to the side with a quizzical look on his face, as if trying to determine what my malfunction was. Apparently, no one else had been comfortable sitting and waiting outside of pistol range, and he didn't know what to do with me. As having a car had put me way ahead of where I thought I'd be at this stage, I was content to wait.

Which seemed to exasperate him more. Finally, after turning and talking to his compatriots again, he asked something I didn't have to be a lip reader to understand: "What is your fucking problem?"

I smiled and waved him toward me. After staring at me openmouthed for another few seconds, he set his pistol on the car and walked toward me. He tried to stop about 20 feet in front of the car, but I waved him over to the driver's side door. By this point, he was getting used to doing what I told him to and—even though he looked like he expected me to be some sort of pervert who was going to flash him when he got close—he came to stand next to me.

"Are you some kinda idiot?" he asked with a strong southern accent. "Or is there just somethin' wrong with ya?"

"Sorry," I said, talking loudly to get my voice to penetrate the glass. In addition to stopping bullets, it also was pretty good at stopping sound; something I really hadn't noticed until he was alongside and talking to me. "The glass is bulletproof, and I can't roll down the window."

"Well, why didn't ya get outta the damn car?" he asked.

"I didn't know if you'd shoot at me. I'm safe in here."

That, at least, seemed to make sense to him, and the expression that he thought he was dealing with an imbecile left his face. "Whaddya want?" he asked.

I gave him my best smile. "To cross the bridge," I replied, as if the answer weren't patently obvious.

That response, however, was one he was mentally prepared to deal with, and a crafty look went across his face as he craned his neck to see into the back of the car. I sighed, wishing I'd put my supplies in the trunk; there was no way he'd missed them.

"It's gonna cost ya," he said.

"How about if I just don't shoot you?" I asked. "Would that work?"

He shrugged. "Prob'bly not. The woman at the barricade is my wife. She'd prob'bly be happy she was free to date again, but that ol' nag ain't gonna let ya through."

I shrugged. I hadn't really wanted to shoot him—he hadn't done anything to deserve it and ammo was precious these days—I'd just wanted him to know it was an option I was considering as we started the negotiation process.

"Well, they can't shoot me," I said. "The windows are bulletproof, and the car's armored."

"It ain't armored enough to slam through those cars and trees," he replied. "It'd take a hell of a lot more than what ya got to do that."

I nodded, willing to concede the point as it was pretty obvious. If it had a blade on the front…but it didn't. "So what's the price?"

"The ammo in your back seat," he said with a big smile, looking at the three boxes of 9mm rounds.

"Not happening," I said, wishing again that I had put it in the trunk. "But I'll give you one of them."

"Not enough," he said. "Our lowest rate for crossing the bridge is two boxes. Take it or leave it."

"Tell you what," I said. "We both know that a box of shells is a considerable fortune these days. Normally, I'd leave and come back in the middle of the night and kill all of you, but I just don't have the time today. I'd like to cross the bridge, with a minimum of fuss, and be on my way. By giving you a box of bullets, I'm not making you use any extra bullets to shoot at me, and I'm establishing a relationship where we can work together, and I can come back and forth through here, over and over, and pay every time I do. That's called developing a loyal customer base. I could go other ways…but I choose to give you my patronage."

The man looked at me like I was speaking a foreign language. "What the hell's that supposed to mean?" he finally asked.

"It means I'm going to come back this way in a few days, and I'll give you another box when I cross back over. How about that? No one needs to die, and neither of us have to waste precious ammo convincing the other person how serious we are. How about that?"

"How 'bout ya give me the box, plus five loose rounds?"

"Fair enough," I said, wanting to be on my way. "Move the barrier, and I'll set the ammo down right here."

"How do we know ya won't try to run the barricade since ya have your bulletproof car?"

"If I do, it will be awfully hard to come back across when I get back now, won't it?"

"I reckon it would," he said after considering it for a few moments. "Done."

He went back to the barricade and they moved the vehicles back far enough for me to pass through. I opened the door and set the ammo on the ground, along with an extra one and a note that said, "Thanks for your honesty," hoping they didn't try something as I went through.

They waved as I went through the barricade, and I waved back as I drove off, happy that I hadn't had to resort to violence. It was rather refreshing. Sure, they were extorting money from passersby, but at least they were honest about it.

And sometimes everything *is* as it seems in this Fallen World.

* * * * *

Chapter Twenty-Seven

My good luck lasted about four hours longer. I'd been shot at a couple of times along the way—that I knew of, anyway; there may have been more—including one marksman who took a divot out of the window next to my face when I slowed for the crossroads in Elsanor, Alabama. I suspect he was on the roof of the convenience store, where he had a view of both the major roads that crossed there, but I never saw him and didn't stick around to look. If he was that good, I needed to be somewhere else.

The other time I was shot at was when I stopped for gas at the intersection of Highway 47 and I-65. I had stopped along the way to hide the food and ammo on the back seat, and what to my wondering eyes should appear in the trunk, but a rifle that Brown had stashed there for me. The note along with it read, "In case you need to reach out and touch someone. I hear you know how to use it." It appeared to be the one I had used to kill the kidnapper, or one that looked just like it.

When someone began firing at me with a pistol from a small copse of trees across the street, I ran to the trunk, pulled out the rifle, and ended the threat. It looked like the sights had gone a little up and right—the shot that should have been a near-immediate kill only resulted in a gut shot. He was going to die, but it would take a while for it to occur. He screamed a lot as he dropped into the undergrowth, but I wasn't going to go wandering in there after him. I quickly finished pumping the gas and drove off. Somewhere during that time, he stopped screaming, although I didn't know if he were dead or just trying to draw me in.

If it were the latter, I didn't give him the satisfaction—I just drove off, got onto I-65 and headed north.

* * *

Montgomery hadn't been spared the nuclear hammer, and my Geiger counter began clicking upward as I approached the city. I was surprised at how close I got to the city without running into any roadblocks; the high level of radiation might have had something to do with that. Luckily, Montgomery was a spider web of roads, so I cut over to Selma and up onto Highway 22, avoiding the rad-filled city.

I had just passed through the little town of Maplesville, Alabama and was going around a curve in the road when I came upon a roadblock thrown up across Highway 22 along a stretch that ran through a wooded area. It was manned by at least three men, and, before I could spin around and head back the way I'd come, a second group of at least four men drove a long truck across the road behind me, blocking it. The truck was a lowboy-style equipment carrier—a long, flat platform used to move heavy equipment like dump trucks or bulldozers.

The men had modified it to hold a series of big cages on the front of the truck bed and what looked like a .50 caliber machine gun on the back. A witticism flashed through my head—Ma Deuce is your friend—but at that particular moment she was *far* from being friendly to me as the gunner chambered a round. There was no way through the blockade in front of me, the woods blocked both sides of the road, and the machine gun behind me was about to fire. Although the glass in the car had proven capable of withstanding rounds from smaller rifles, I doubted it was enough to stop the M2's rounds, so I did the only thing I could—I grabbed my rifle and my pack off the seat next to me and ran into the woods.

The machine gun fired a few rounds as I scampered into the trees, drawing some yells from the roadblock—apparently, it had never dawned on them that if they actually had to *fire* the M2, the rounds were going to go by and through their target...and into their compatriots. That had the unintended benefit of slowing the pursuit a little as they dove for cover. Then it was off to the races.

After a couple of minutes, I stopped to look back and could see flashes through the trees; armed men were in pursuit of me. Most appeared to have rifles, which was hardly surprising in this part of the country as most of the men—and a decent part of the women—would be hunters.

I fired twice at the closest men, hitting one of them, then turned and ran. A couple of them returned fire, and I heard a bullet *crack!* past me. That gave me the adrenaline to sprint faster, and I left the men behind. I suspected that if I could break contact with them, they would have to slow down as they would have to worry about me stopping to ambush them.

I ran as far as I could, then slowed and turned east, walking as fast as I could. I was wrong about them slowing; however, and soon heard several of them crashing through the forest. I threw myself behind a fallen log and watched them go past. Although they may have hunted previously, it didn't appear any of them had any tracking skills; they just blundered on past, and I let them go. Once they were out of earshot, I got up and loped as best I could to the east. After a few minutes, I came across a small dirt road that ran perpendicular to my course, and I took it back to the south.

As I approached Highway 22 again, my senses screamed that I was being watched from a cluster of storage buildings to the right, but I never saw anyone so I continued on. As I reached the pavement of 22, I realized that I hadn't gone as far as I thought I had in the woods—the roadblock was no more than a quarter of a mile to the right, and I could easily see several men walking around near it.

I tried to melt back into the forest beside the road, but then a male voice said, "That'll be far enough."

I froze, and all my senses went to high alert.

"Set the gun down, then put your hands up and turn around."

Not knowing anything about the man—or men—behind me, I complied and turned around to find a man dressed in camouflage holding a shotgun on me from about fifteen feet away. Too far for me to do anything about, and—depending on what he had loaded—too close for me to escape.

"Are you with 'em or against 'em?" he asked.

"Who?" I asked.

"The men down at the roadblock."

"Considering they just shot at me and stole my car, I would definitely have to say I am 'against' them."

"Really? You had a car? With gas? Ain't many of them around no more."

I shrugged. "I came from down south. There's still some gas there."

"How do I know that was you they was shootin' at, and that you're not one of them that just got lost?"

"Do I either look or sound like I'm from around here?"

"Nope. That's for sure." He looked at me for a few seconds, studying me. "Okay, I guess I'll take you to the boss."

"But I thought you believed me. Why are you taking me to the boss?"

"Well, I don't know you, and my orders are to shoot you if I think you're one of *them*, or take you to the boss if you're not."

I smiled. "Well, that's a good choice then! Let's go see the boss."

He motioned with the gun. "Get walking," he said.

"What about my rifle?"

"Don't worry; I'll get it." The man chuckled. "It's too valuable to be leaving it in the woods."

Nothing gets left behind in this Fallen World.

* * * * *

Chapter Twenty-Eight

We passed a barricade across the road about a half mile later, manned by the sentry's people. The sentry—whose name was Tim—and the rest of his people all called the other group, "Them," as if they had no names. The barricade faced "Them" and was manned by five men with long rifles and another M2. Although the barricade workers looked relatively relaxed, there was always someone alert and scanning the road behind us.

We walked at least an hour east along Highway 22 toward the town of Clanton. It looked like some of the cities I had passed through to the west, in that everything seemed at first glance to still be functional, with one exception—there was a complete lack of motorized vehicles, except for one tractor I saw working a field.

"No access to gas?" I asked over my shoulder as we walked. He'd allowed me to put my hands down after the people at the barricade had searched me and removed my pistols, but he still made me walk in front of him and watched me carefully as we walked.

"Not my business to tell you or give you any intel," Tim said. "You can ask the boss when you see her, and she'll tell you...if she wants to."

He had responded similarly to other questions about the town's capabilities and how many people were in Clanton, so I hadn't really expected an answer, but I was bored and had wondered. The sun was setting as we reached the outskirts of the city, and I was feeling a lot like the city—I was pretty much out of gas, too.

"So," I said as we finally reached the town proper. "A little food, nap, and shower might be better for me than going straight to a meeting with the boss."

"Not gonna' happen," the man said.

"Why's that?"

"We ain't got enough food to waste on you if you're going to be killed or exiled, nor the manpower to babysit you while you sleep."

"How about a jail cell somewhere, then?" I asked. "Then you wouldn't have to watch me."

"Funny you should say that," Tim replied as we approached a large two-story building. "We're here."

I looked at the front of the building as we came around the corner and saw that it said, "Chilton County Courthouse."

"The boss is in here," Tim said, motioning with his gun for me to enter.

We walked inside. There were lights on in the building—one of the few I had noticed with them, but the metal detector didn't appear to be working, so an armed man searched us while a second one stood nearby with a shotgun in his arms.

The guards held onto our weapons and called a third armed guard to escort us to the boss' office. The boss turned out to be Mayor Stephanie Gould, who met me in one of the courtrooms. I was brought in and seated at the Defense table, while she waited in the seat where the judge normally would have sat. If I'd had any intentions of harming her, I would have been quickly dissuaded—an armed guard stood to either side of her.

"So, who is this?" she asked.

"He says he doesn't know who he is, ma'am," Tim said. "Calls himself Ishmael, although he said other people sometimes call him Fred."

"You don't know who you are, eh?" the mayor asked.

"No ma'am, I don't," I replied. This didn't seem the time to be a smartass.

"Convenient," she replied. "I'm sure there are many people who have used this period to try to wipe away some of their previous sins and start over."

"No ma'am; it's nothing like that. Apparently, I worked for one of the companies, and they slicked my memories right before the bombs started falling. I don't exactly know what they did, but those memories haven't come back yet."

"That seems like even better proof that you were doing something objectionable. Perhaps you were someone antisocial, and they were trying to adjust your personality to something less objectionable."

"No ma'am. I was an employee of the company—a special forces operative or something like that—and they were going to give me some specialized training that I never got."

"Uh huh," the mayor said, obviously not buying the story. "So, what exactly are you doing in my town?"

"Just passing through. I am trying to track down one of the company officers who went by here some time shortly after the bombs fell. He has the answers to who I am and possibly how to make me whole once again."

"He went by here that long ago, eh? And he hasn't been seen or heard from since?"

"That's correct. He was headed to Chattanooga, probably up I-65 just east of here."

"Well, in that case, you might as well turn around and head back home. We have cannibals living to the west and north of us. If he passed through here and hasn't returned, then he isn't returning. He probably got caught and eaten."

"With all due respect, I don't think so, ma'am. He had an armed guard that would have been able to take on most people or groups that tried to stop him. He was corporate management; the people he had with him were the best."

"Well, that may be so; communications from here to the north are nonexistent." She shrugged, then she looked at me strangely, peering down her nose at me. "Did you say you were a special forces operative?" she finally asked.

"I said that they say I was an operative, but I don't remember being one." It was my turn to shrug. "I have some of the skills through physical muscle memory, but I don't remember actually being one."

"But you do have some skills…"

"Yes ma'am, I do."

She nodded. "Every week, several of our people go missing, and they are never heard from again. We suspect—hell, we know—that it's the cannibal groups that are taking them. They sneak in, grab them, and go back to their safe areas. What's worse is that one of the groups controls the area that has our hospital in it. Not having the hospital puts our medical teams at a disadvantage. The time has come to end the predations of the cannibals living near us, and we're putting together a group to attack them. I would like you to join the team."

"I see." I looked at her for a moment, then cocked my head. "I'm sorry to sound mercenary, ma'am, but what's in it for me?"

"I guess I could be crass and say that we'd kill you if you didn't, but then you might cut and run when the opportunity presented itself, leaving my people in the lurch. I don't think you would just put your life on the line for our people, though, simply out of the goodness of your heart. As such, how about if I appeal to your desire to complete your quest? My men tell me the cannibals captured your car. If you help us, we will try to recover it during the attack on the cannibals to the west of here, and you can have it."

I noticed she hadn't said they *wouldn't* kill me if I didn't go along with the plan…only that she hadn't said it. Still, getting the car back would greatly improve my chances of making it to Chattanooga—especially if all the supplies I had were still in it—and if I let the locals lead the attack, I could probably survive it and be on my way. Boudreaux had left months before me…another day or two probably wouldn't make a difference on whether I found him or not.

"Does getting my car back include all of the supplies I had in it, even if they've been pulled out and redistributed?" I asked.

"Absolutely," the mayor said with a small smile. She could obviously see she had won and was feeling magnanimous. After all, she was only giving me something she didn't have, and there was only a small chance it would even be found. She also probably figured there would probably be an equally small chance I would still be alive at the end to collect.

"I'm in," I said. She didn't know me very well.

But then again, who do you really know in this Fallen World.

* * * * *

Chapter Twenty-Nine

The next couple of days passed quickly as I was integrated into the planning process for the attacks on the two groups of cannibals. The ones currently holding my car belonged to the smaller group that was based out of Maplesville and had slowly been expanding toward Clanton. Although Maplesville was about 15 miles away, apparently they were aggressive enough—or hungry enough—to be raiding into the environs of Clanton. Fifteen miles was a long way to go in a world without cars...but hunger will make you do those kinds of things.

The other group had occupied the intersection of I-65 and Highway 145 about three miles north of town. As I would have had to go through there on my journey north, helping them wipe out that nest of cannibals would actually be a benefit to my future travels. Between getting my car back and removing a hindrance to my journey, the attacks—assuming they were done well—would set me up to proceed. As long as I wasn't dead.

The first attack was to go against the cannibals to the north, who we actually had some intel on. A couple of weeks ago, they had taken a girl, but her father had freed her. He'd snuck in and released her, but he'd been taken in the attempt as he fought a delaying action to get her away. He was probably dead now, but she had made it back to town and had told us about what she'd seen. There were a couple of auto dealerships on the east side of I-65 that were being used by the cannibals. One was their living space and headquarters; the other was their larder.

The girl had been kept with a number of other people who had fled when her father rescued her, and was able to escape when the cannibals tried to recapture all the escaping victims.

The cannibals had barricades on both I-65 and Highway 145, and there were a large number of guards on them. Our primary goal wasn't to rescue the people they'd taken; our goal was to kill the cannibals. Sure, we wanted to free whoever we could, but we wanted to permanently end their threat even more.

The main force went up I-65, with a smaller group taking Highway 145. Once the main attack started, they were supposed to hit the barricade on Highway 145. That would still leave the northern barricades on both roads, but we'd try to scoop them up as we finished the attack on the car dealerships.

As night fell, we went into the woods on the east side of I-65 to move forward into our attack positions. Although the forest wouldn't get us all the way to the dealerships, it would get us close.

"Why don't you go walk ahead of us a bit?" the leader of the attack, a man named George Jacobs, asked after a few minutes of being in the woods. Jacobs also happened to be the chief of police for Clanton in his day job. A burly man of average height, I'd already seen that he could pass for Santa Claus when he was happy...or a grizzly bear when he wasn't. These days, I was sure he needed to be much more of the latter, and he was good at it. Apparently, he'd been a submariner back before the war, but had come home in time to avoid being caught in it when the missiles started flying.

"What for? So you can talk about me?" I asked with a smile. Although I thought they were being straight with me, I'd pretty much lost my belief in the goodness of humanity by this point. Even if they had decided to kill me, I didn't figure that would happen until after the second attack, so I wasn't really worried—much—about what they were going to say.

"No," Jacobs said, "so we don't run into an ambush. Militaries have a point man in front of the rest of the squad; I'm nominating you to be our point man."

"Why me?" I asked. "Why don't you go?"

"Because on my best day, I'm not half as quiet as you. They'll hear us coming a long way off. You? You'll probably sneak right up on any sort of ambush before they hear you coming."

I hadn't really recognized it, but now that he'd called my attention to it, I realized I *was* a lot quieter than they were. It wasn't something I was intentionally doing…my feet just kind of came down naturally quiet and avoided stepping on things that would make a noise of their own accord.

"Being loud now isn't going to change my opinion," Jacobs said.

"What do you mean?"

"You were as quiet as a mouse, right up until I mentioned it to you, but then you got as loud as the kids."

"I hadn't realized I was doing that," I said. So, when I didn't think about it, I was quiet, but when I wanted to be really quiet, I thought about it and was noisier. I shook my head, not sure how best to resolve the conundrum. Weird. My subconscious was better at tradecraft than my conscious mind.

I moved to the front of the formation, consciously trying to be unconscious about what I was doing, and periodically having some success at it. As we approached where the barricade was on I-95, I became even better at my woodcraft—I was too worried about the people out on the road to think about moving through the woods. I kept my attention on them, and my other senses helped me navigate through the trees. I even felt confident enough to motion the rest of the group to stop, while I checked out the barricade.

I moved like a ghost to the edge of the forest and reconnoitered the situation, getting a good count of the men and their positioning. I was feeling pretty good about my skills as I stood up to leave…

But then one of the men at the barricade had to pee—I was close enough to hear him say it—and he walked straight toward me. I edged further back behind the tree where I was sheltering, praying nothing was sticking out that he could see. He walked to the edge of the trees, unzipped, and let fly, using the tree I was hiding behind as his target.

Which was okay…until he started spraying it around from side to side as if painting the tree. Apparently, at least part of my backside was sticking out to where it could be seen, and I felt the stream hit me several times as he worked the flow back and forth. I forced myself not to move, and I swear I heard a giggle from deeper in the forest, but the man couldn't hear it over the impact of his urine on the tree.

After what was probably only 20 seconds, but what seemed like an eternity, the man finished, zipped up, and went back to the barricade, allowing me to sneak back to the group.

"Hey, Pissboy!" one of the men whispered. "Did you get a good count of how many people had to go to the bathroom up there?"

I started toward him, intent on…I'm not sure what, but two of the men grabbed me. "Quiet," Jacobs said, pulling me to where I had to look into his eyes, dimly visible in the moonlight. "Ignore him and focus."

I tried to pull away, but he had a grip like a vice. "Let it go," he said.

I took a deep breath and let it out quietly, focusing myself. "Okay," I said. He relaxed slightly, and I pulled away. I gave the offender another glance just to let him know we weren't through yet, then returned to the point.

"How many are there at the barricade?" one of the men asked. He was the leader of the team that would hit the barricade, and I had forgotten to brief him about what I'd seen. I gave him a quick update on manning and positioning at the barricade, then started off again with the rest of the group.

The forest opened up just past the barricade, and we came upon a house. It was dark and didn't look lived in, so we continued past it. Thankfully, if it were lived in, the owners didn't have any dogs to alert them. At the end of their driveway ran a road that passed perpendicularly. After scanning it for a few moments, I led the group across it. The forest dropped down to almost nothing, just a line of trees that served to screen another house from the highway.

Unlike the earlier house, though, not only was this one lived in, there were people awake within it, and it looked like there was a party going on inside it.

I kept an eye on the house as we moved quietly down the line of trees, going slowly from one to the next. I reached the end of the trees—it bordered on a giant lot full of cars no one could drive anymore—in time to see a group of people moving from the car dealership to the house. As I watched, I realized it wasn't a group going to the house; it was six men, dragging along another man and woman. Both were fighting and trying to get away, but it looked like their arms were tied behind their backs and they had to have been gagged—as much as they were fighting, they would have been yelling, if they could.

In a flash, it dawned on me—the group in charge of the cannibals had obviously taken over the house next to the car dealership, and were using it as their headquarters. Although it was a single story ranch house, it was built on top of a hill and had a basement. I could see a garage door under the house, toward which the two prisoners were being dragged.

A red haze came over my vision, and I realized I couldn't let what was about to happen actually occur. It wasn't that I didn't *want* it to happen; I absolutely *couldn't let* it happen.

I worked my way over to Jacobs. "You guys go on with the assault," I whispered. I indicated the people going into the house. "I'm going to take care of that."

"Our mission is to kill the cannibals, not set people free," he whispered back. Even though low, his voice was intense. "We don't have the people to spare for another target."

"I know that," I said. "That's obviously their headquarters, and I'm guessing it's full of the cannibals. There may be more there than anywhere else! You want me to help kill cannibals? *That's what I'm going to do!*"

Somehow Jacobs had missed the fact that those were the cannibals; perhaps he hadn't seen where they came from. After a second, though, he nodded, realizing what I said was true. "Okay," he said. "Do you want help?"

"No," I replied. "I've got this." Realizing I had no idea what was inside the house, I added, "But please swing by after you're finished in case I need it."

He nodded once, and I ran across the yard toward the basement entrance. There was one window on the end of the house that someone could have seen me through, but it was one of the few that were currently dark.

Reaching the house, I shielded my watch as I flipped on the light to check the time. I still had 10 minutes until the attack was scheduled to begin. I squatted between a bush and the side of the house, staying in the shadows. Every bone in my body strained to go—to save the people from something awful—but I knew I had to wait. Our attack was a multi-pronged assault; if I went early, I might screw it up for some of the other teams.

After waiting what I thought was 10 minutes, I checked my watch. Thirty seconds had passed. Shit. I sighed, steeling myself to patience.

And then the woman screamed, and before I could stop myself, I was in motion.

The basement garage had a roll down door, but it was open and I entered through it. The garage was surreal. Most of the things inside it looked like what you would have found in a normal garage before the Fall, although the number of barbeques—five—was more than most people would need. Then there were the implements to hold people hostage, as well as a wide variety of cutting tools sitting near a deep sink mounted on the wall. There wasn't much light—only what was coming from under the door at the end of the garage—but there was enough for me to see they all had dark stains on them.

I set my rifle next to the door into the house, checked my pistol in its holster, and drew my knife. I was early, but maybe I could keep it quiet.

I tried the door; it was unlocked, and I opened it quietly. The room on the other side might have been a game room at some point; in the sick, twisted minds of the cannibals, it probably still was. The main features of the room were the two pool tables, upon which the prisoners had been tied after being stripped naked. The carpet had been removed from the floor and rolled up on one side of the room; it probably made cleaning up easier.

The man was already dead—that much was easy to see—but it appeared several of the men wanted to have some fun with the woman while she was still alive. One of the men was on top of her, while two more stood to the sides, cheering him on.

They didn't see me approach; the first time they noticed my presence was when I reached around to draw my knife across one of the men's throat. The resulting spray coated the woman and the man on top of her; I threw the man I had just killed to the side, and shoved the rapist off the woman and into the cannibal on the other side of the table. The rapist's pants were still around his ankles, and the two men went down in a pile.

The woman screamed again, but I was pretty sure everyone in the house was used to the sounds of screaming from the basement— she'd done it several times before I entered—so I figured I was okay. I raced around the table to where the pantless man was trying to get up and stabbed him several times in the back. He collapsed onto the man under him, blocking the pistol he was trying to bring to bear. I stomped on his wrist, making him drop the pistol, then grabbed his hand and bent it around one handed while pushing the dead man off him with the other.

As the body rolled off, I rolled the cannibal onto his stomach with his arm twisted behind him. Holding it in place with a wrist lock, I said, "Quiet, unless you want me to kill you. Do you understand?"

"Yes," the man said in a squeaky voice.

"Good. How many people are upstairs right now?"

"About ten," he said.

"Are you sure?" I applied a little more pressure on his arm.

"*Yes!*" he hissed. "There are about ten people up there."

"Thanks," I said as I drove my knife through his heart.

"Why?" he asked, his voice weak.

"You're a fricking cannibal," I said. "What did you really think was going to happen?"

I let go of him, wiped off my knife, and used it to cut the woman's hands free. She was a mess—beyond the blood sprayed on her—with cuts and bruises across her body.

"Thank you!" she cried as I released her arms.

She tried to hug me, but I pushed her back. "The time for thanks is later," I whispered. "After we get you out of here."

I freed her legs, and she ran to a pile of clothes and started trying to put them on. Unfortunately, they had cut her clothes off, leaving nothing in a condition to be worn except a pair of shoes.

"Take the shoes and get out of here," I urged. "Run straight across the back yard to the stand of trees. Wait for me there. If I don't come out, go south. There are other people out there who will help."

"I want to help you," she said.

"You'll help me more if you leave," I said, taking hold of her shoulder and guiding her toward the door. I opened it just in time to hear gunshots coming from outside. "Go!" I said, giving her a small push in the right direction. I grabbed my rifle and turned back toward the play room. I had a date with some cannibals.

It was time to bring some order to this Fallen World.

* * * * *

Chapter Thirty

I could hear people racing around upstairs, and knew they'd heard the shots, too. While they might not be worried about it yet—*who knew how often they shot someone here?*—they soon would be. If they had any sort of communications devices, they would be getting the word that an assault was underway, and they'd react to it. I didn't know whether they'd try to assist in repelling the attack, or if they'd fort up and prepare to defend the house, but I didn't want to give them time for either.

I had just started up the stairs when the door opened, and two men came racing down the open, wooden steps. They were too close to shoot, so I did what I could and leaned forward covering up my head with my free hand, and stood up as they came down on top of me.

Neither of the men really had a chance to see me, so they didn't realize I wasn't one of their people, and the shouts they gave were more grunts of surprise as they tried to avoid me. One failed completely, and stepped onto my back—he was thrown off balance headfirst down the rest of the stairs after leaving a boot print on my left shoulder blade.

The second was almost able to stop himself, and a booted foot came down on either side of my head. I head-butted him in the groin as I stood while grabbing him and pulling backward. His hand scrabbled for the railing, and he almost saved himself, but I braced with my free hand, and lifted his feet off the steps. He went over me, managing to reach down and grab a handful of my shirt as he fell, pulling me along with him. Unlike him though, I still had control of my center of gravity and leaned forward to grab one of the stairs. He flipped over me and slammed into the stairs below us.

Knowing the others upstairs would have heard the thuds, I spun around to finish them off. The first man was done—he was at the bottom of the stairs with his head at an unnatural angle. The other was sliding slowly down the stairs on his back, stunned, his eyes pinched shut in agony.

"You guys okay?" a male voice yelled through the door at the top of the stairs.

"Uh, yeah," I called, trying to mask my voice by making it deeper and mumbling slightly. I ran down several stairs, just in time for the man's eyes to open as I stabbed him. His eyes went huge, and slowly dimmed as the light went out of them. Sheathing the knife, I started back up the stairs.

"Hey! You guys—" the voice from earlier yelled as someone moved into the doorway.

I had just reached the door, and I grabbed a handful of his shirt as he looked down at the men below, then pulled him down the stairs after them.

The "Woah!" he yelled ended abruptly as he face-planted into the stair frame. A loud crack indicated something was broken—hopefully another neck—but I didn't have time to look.

A number of voices on the second floor were now asking questions. They were interested—not alarmed yet, but they knew something was odd—and my time was quickly running out.

"What the hell?" "What's going on down there?" rang out from above me as I picked my rifle back up from the stairs.

I flipped off the safety and threw the rifle to my shoulder as I reached the top of the stairs. I saw that the stairway emptied into a kitchen, and as I came around the corner, I began firing as cannibals came into view. One woman at the sink; two rounds to the center of mass. I spun toward the table, and saw I was screwed—four men were sitting there, all facing the stairs. They were already in motion as I spun toward them, with the one closest lurching toward me blocking most of my shots at the rest of the group.

I fired at him and put two to his gut and one in his face as he dove at me, then I side-stepped, trying to get a shot at the others. One fled out the open door to the back porch. Although he wasn't as much of a threat, I was already lined up on him so I fired twice; I thought at least one of them hit him.

I spun back in time to see the one on the left going around a corner into a hallway—too late to get a shot at him. The last man flipped the table on end, intending to use it for cover. While the thin wood provided him some concealment, it didn't provide cover—in fact, it did nothing to stop my bullets as I shot him several times through it. He slumped, letting the table fall onto its face. I could see one of my rounds had hit him below his eye; he was done. The woman was similarly finished; she lay looking skyward, unmoving.

A noise from behind made me spin, and I found the guy who'd gone down the corridor. Apparently, the corridor wrapped around to the formal dining room behind me, and he'd tried to circle around while I was busy with his friends. He had his pistol out, and he came around the corner with his gun blazing as I threw myself to the side, firing a couple of times on the way down. Although the bullets didn't hit him, they caused him to stop and dive back around the way he came.

As quickly as I could, I shot through the wall five times in the direction I thought he might be. I was rewarded with a "Fuck! I'm going to kill you for that!" so I figured I'd hit him, but not badly enough. I sprayed another handful of bullets through the wall, hoping to force him either out of or away from the corner. When I didn't hear anything else, I set the rifle down and drew my pistol as I got up. I ran quickly to the corner and risked a peek. I immediately noticed two things—they were going to need a new dining room table and, more importantly, the man was gone. Figuring he was trying to sneak around behind me again, I ran around after him, and caught up to him as he burst into the kitchen.

"Die, Motherfucker!" he yelled as he sprang out shooting.

"You first!" I yelled. I gave him just long enough to start to look in my direction, and put one through his head. He collapsed like a marionette with its strings cut.

Which left me staring out the glass door from the kitchen onto the back porch at the other six people I'd been told were up in the house. Several of them had drawn pistols and were starting to aim at me. I fired twice, causing them to dive down and cover themselves as the glass door exploded into shards on them, then I dove back toward the dining room to dodge their fire.

Six people were more than I wanted to face with just a pistol and knife; I needed my rifle! I got up quickly and raced through the dining room to the other side of the kitchen. The cannibals were just coming through the remains of the door. I traded fire with one of them as the rest dove out of the way; he grazed me on the arm, but I hit him in the forehead. I loosed a few rounds at them one-handed, just trying to keep their heads down as I grabbed the rifle in my left hand and ran back into the dining room, slamming another magazine into the rifle once I was out of sight.

But now I was trapped. They were in the kitchen, but they also had a good view of the foyer and the front door, which was on the other side of the dining room. Had I known there were that many more, I would have run out the front door instead of shooting the last one of the first group with my pistol. And yelling at him had been stupid, too.

Oops.

Twenty-twenty hindsight didn't help me much; I needed a plan, and I didn't have any time to think up anything, so I threw my pistol toward the front door, then charged out into the kitchen from the other side. The clatter as it hit the tile in front of the door caused all of the cannibals to look that way, then I was upon them, my executioner's mask upon my face.

I killed the first two while they were still looking at the pistol lying on the floor, then a third as he started to turn. Realizing he'd been had, the fourth threw himself onto his back so he could aim at me and got a shot off that was close enough to my ear for me to hear it go past. I shot him four or five times—I wasn't entirely sure, I was so scared at that moment—then lowered the rifle to take stock.

Which was when the remaining cannibal, who'd followed me through the dining room tackled me. He hit me hard and high from behind, wrapping his arms around me, and drove me to the floor. Happily, his momentum carried us into the living room, so when my face broke our fall, it was at least on carpet rather than the simulated wood of the kitchen.

I lay there, stunned, as my air *whooshed!* out of me, and the cannibal took the opportunity to release me and climb onto my back. He grabbed my head in both of his hands and rammed it into the floor. I saw stars, and then more stars as he did it again, but he had gone too far up my back, and I got my hands and knees under me and boosted upward, throwing him off me.

He was faster getting to his feet, but had to spin back around and we came up at the same time to face each other—me with a knife in my hand and him armed with nothing more than a frown. I smiled as I advanced on him, but he took a step back and yanked a lamp off an end table—pulling out the plug—bashed the lamp shade off, and came back at me, using the broken glass at the end of the lamp like a blade of his own.

He now had a substantial reach advantage over me, and I gave ground as he advanced, looking for something to even the odds.

Unfortunately, I tripped over one of the bodies behind me. As I started to go down backward, he saw his chance. He rushed forward and tried to stab me in the stomach with the broken lamp, but I pushed off on the faux wood floor and slid backward; the lamp dug a chunk out of the flooring between my legs. As he recovered, I levered myself up with one hand and drove my knife into the meat of his left thigh, which was as high as I could reach.

He stumbled backward, his left hand going to the knife, but he managed to trip over the same corpse I'd fallen over, and *he* went over backward. I jumped to my feet, ran two steps forward, and scooped my rifle up from where it had fallen. He was just starting to get back up as I turned toward him, and three rounds in the chest put him back down.

I stood up, stretching, and took a deep breath, only to see motion from the corner of my eye. I flinched, but couldn't avoid it, and the object hit me in the stomach like a punch. I looked down and saw it was a meat cleaver as it fell to the floor—someone on the porch had thrown it, but the handle hit me, not the blade. I looked up, and the man I had shot in the back earlier was standing on the far side of the deck, just visible in the dim light spilling out of the kitchen. A grill was set up out back, and it looked like someone had been making barbeque.

He looked at me, and I looked at him; he looked as spent as I felt, and had a look of genuine disappointment on his face—he'd been sure the cleaver would kill me. I could see a dark stain on his shirt; he probably had been losing blood while I fought the rest of his friends, and I could tell he didn't have much left as he reached over to pick up another knife. He drew back his arm to throw it at me, and I shot him in the face. He went backward and over the low railing around the deck.

I bent over, trying to catch my breath, while still looking for more of the assholes—there seemed to be an endless supply of them—when I noticed something beyond the blood dripping into my left eye. Gun fire was still coming from the car dealership next door. I sighed.

Guess I'd have to go help with that, too.

There was no rest for the wicked in this Fallen World.

* * * * *

Chapter Thirty-One

I reloaded my rifle quickly—no sense charging into battle without ammo—and wiped the blood from my eye. Apparently, I either had a cut or a bleeding carpet burn on my forehead from where the asshole had banged my head on the floor. Nice. When it wouldn't stop, I tore off a strip from one of the cannibal's shirts and made a bandage out of it, seeing as how he wouldn't be needing it anymore.

Before I left the house, I searched the rest of it, as I didn't want anyone sneaking up behind me again. I found one more of them hiding in a closet. He came out...with two 9mm holes in his chest. Seriously, there were way too many of these people—it was amazing they hadn't already depopulated all of Clanton; they must have had access to some alternate food sources, at least for a while.

When I got down to the car dealership, I found the attack group huddled together in the parking lot. "What's going on?" I asked Jacobs.

"At the moment, nothing," he replied. "One of them saw us coming and ran into the building with the hostages. Looks like there are two more in there with him. They're threatening to kill all the people if we don't leave." He took a closer look at me. "You okay?"

I rolled my neck, trying to keep a clear head. More hostages. If I didn't already hate these people, I would now. Something about taking hostages just irritated the crap out of me. "Yeah, I'm okay," I said. "Pissed off, mostly."

217

"How many were in that house?"

"I don't know," I replied. It all seemed a blur. "Ten or twelve."

"How many got away?"

"None." I shrugged. "None that I'm aware of, anyway."

"You killed ten or twelve *by yourself?*"

"Yeah. Turns out it's something I'm good at." He stared at me, mouth open. "I know, right?" I asked. "I had no idea either."

"Want to be our sheriff?"

"Not really," I replied. "I'd rather kill the rest of these people and get some rest. I feel like shit." I nodded toward the north. "What about the barricades?" I asked. "Heard anything from them?"

"Yeah, the two southern ones are clear, as is the northern one on Highway 145. They all came running up once the gunfire started. They were in the open and didn't last long."

"So, just the northern group on I-65 is left, besides whoever's in the building?" I indicated the car dealership with a finger.

"I sent some people to check out I-65, but those guys had split, and I don't particularly want to chase them through the forest at night. Do you?" I shook my head, and it made me dizzy. Note to self—don't do that again. "I have someone going back to town to get some dogs to track them. We'll find them in the morning."

"Awesome," I said. They officially became Someone Else's Problem, and I focused my attention on the building. "So, three total bad guys in the building?"

"We think so, based on the return fire we've taken. There might only be two, and they're running around like crazy in there trying to pretend like they have more people." He shrugged. "Could be more, too, I guess, and they're just hiding out to ambush us."

"Well, I'm tired of this shit, and I'm tired of these assholes," I said. "It's time to do something about it."

"Got something in mind?"

"Yeah," I replied, studying the building. "I'm going to kill them all."

Final solutions work best in this Fallen World.

* * * * *

Chapter Thirty-Two

Jacobs looked at me and cocked his head. "If you don't mind me asking, how exactly do you plan to do that?"

"I guess I could just go up and ask them nicely," I said. "Maybe I can win them over with my charming personality."

"It's possible," Jacobs said with a nod. "Then again, it's possible monkeys may come flying out of my ass, too. Neither one's very likely, but they're both possible."

I chuckled. "When we're done with this, I could see about getting you some monkeys, if that's what you'd like…"

"No, I think I'm good without 'em," Jacobs said. "Figured out how you're getting in?"

"All things considered, I'd rather not go in the front door," I replied. "As the whole thing's glass, I expect they'll see me a long way off. I'd rather go in a back door, but I suspect they'll all be locked, and they'll hear me breaking in."

"You could also just have Anderson open the door," one of the guys sheltering behind the truck next to us said. "I think he works there…or worked there, before the fall."

I looked at Jacobs and rolled my eyes. "That might have been good info to have prior to now."

He held up his hands, and his eyes went wide. "That's the first time I've heard about it!"

We both turned to glare at the man behind the truck. "Don't look at me," he said. "I just found out on the way up here. He wasn't at the original planning meeting, and I forgot he used to work here."

"Do you know where he is?"

"I think he's on the other side of the parking lot."

Wonderful. "Okay," I said. "I'll go look for him, *and then* I will go kill the remaining assholes. And *then* I'm getting some sleep."

"Sounds like a good plan."

I gave the guy behind the truck another glare—he shrugged and mouthed, "Sorry"—then I was off, running between the cars. I worked my way around to the other side of the parking lot, without anyone knowing who Anderson was. I finally made it to the last person.

"Have you seen a guy named Anderson, or do you know who he is?"

"No idea," the man said. "Mighta been him," he added, pointing to a body lying on the pavement between the car he was hiding behind and the building. There was a lot of space between us...and obviously someone in the building was a decent enough shot to shoot that far.

Shit.

I sighed. Apparently, nothing was going to be easy tonight.

"What'd you need him for?" the man asked.

"Someone said he used to work in that building and might have a key to get in."

"Well, if he does, it's probably there with him. I heard him say something about being able to get in there."

"Really?"

"Mmm hmm."

I looked at the body. Anderson—if that was really Anderson—was an average-sized guy. He'd be heavy, but I could drag him back to cover. It would probably be safer than standing out in the open searching his pockets.

The guy was only armed with a pistol, so I handed him my rifle. "What's your name, and do you know how to shoot one of these?" I asked.

"Yeah, and I'm Bob."

"Good, then cover me, Bob."

"You're going out there?"

"You know another way to get the keys out of his pocket?"

"Nope."

"Me neither."

"So you're going?"

"Yep."

"Well, shit. Good luck. You know he got shot out there, right?"

"I figured as much. You going to cover me or talk me to death?"

"Trying to keep you from doing something stupid," Bob said, "but if you're all fired-up to do it, I guess you're gonna do it." He shrugged. "Your life," he muttered as he braced my rifle on the hood of the car and looked through the sights. "All right, I'm ready."

"Here I go... *now!*" I exclaimed as I ran out across the lot. I'd taken four steps before the first shot rang out from the dealership. I was already zig-zagging, so all I could do was hope the guy would miss. I heard the round go by—so it was a miss—and I could hear Bob fire back with my rifle. That, at least, appeared to get the shooter's attention, as the next couple of rounds he fired didn't come anywhere close to me.

I made it to Anderson's body, grabbed him under the armpits, and began pulling. Anderson was a lot heavier than I thought he was going to be, and there wasn't much way for me to zig-zag with his corpse. The pavement exploded next to my feet as a round hit, and Bob started trying to light the shooter up with rapid fire, making the person shooting at me stop momentarily as he tried to evade the lead headed toward him. Before he could shoot again, I made it to the safety of the cars.

"Damn, that guy's heavy," I said, dropping him to the pavement.

"Eww," Bob said, as Anderson's head hit with a thud.

As I started rifling through the body's pockets, Bob asked, "Is that Anderson?"

"I don't know yet," I replied. I hadn't found any keys, but I did come across his wallet. I pulled it out and found a driver's license that belonged to Fredrick J. Anderson. I dove back into his pockets, looking for the keys.

"Hey, Mister?"

"What?"

"Find the keys?"

"Not yet; still looking, Bob." I'd checked all the pockets and was going back for a second round.

"Hey, Mister?" Bob asked again.

I was nearly frantic looking for the keys. I needed the stupid things to finish my mission, but they weren't anywhere to be found. I ignored him.

A second search proved as fruitless as the first. I started a third, my frustration rising to an overwhelming level.

"Hey, Mister?" I ignored him again, searching the rest of the body. Maybe the keys weren't in his pants pocket, but a pocket somewhere else.

"Hey, Mister?"

"*What the hell do you want?*" I yelled, turning on him. "*Can't you see I'm busy?*"

Bob sheepishly looked down. "Sorry," he muttered. "Just thought you'd like to know that there's something that looks like a set of keys out on the pavement."

"*There's a...*what?" I dropped the body again and looked over the trunk of the car. There, where the body had been on the pavement, sat a set of keys. They may have been in Anderson's hand and fallen out when I moved him—or somewhere else—but a set of keys was definitely sitting out on the pavement.

Well, shit. "Sorry about yelling," I said. "I've been a bit out of sorts, lately." *And where the hell did the urge to "finish my mission" come from?* I needed to get the hell out of here, find Boudreaux, and get my personality back. The one I had—or the absence of one—was starting to crack.

"We all have," Bob said. He shrugged. "Want me to cover you while you go get them?"

"Unless you'd like me to cover you while *you* go grab them?"

"No thanks," he said. "I'm pretty happy here."

"Okay, then, cover me."

"You got it," he said, taking up his position again. "Go."

I raced out as Bob fired into the building. A shot came back, then, when Bob didn't return fire, several more came from the dealership—including some fired from a second weapon—and I sprinted for all I was worth, dodging as I went. No more shots came from my new "friend" Bob, and the fire from the dealership picked up. I grabbed the keys without stopping and raced off in a different direction, causing several shots to go wide, but then they were back around me again. A round slammed into a car as I dove over its hood. It wasn't graceful, but it accomplished the job. A bullet shattered the windshield next to me, and then I was behind the car and—mostly—safe.

"What the…" I tried to catch my breath. "What the hell did you stop firing for?" I asked.

"I ran out of bullets," Bob said. "Got any more?"

Some people need a little more initiative in this Fallen World.

* * * * *

Chapter Thirty-Three

I took my rifle from Bob—grabbed it back would have been more accurate—and crouched while I ran over to the back of the building. While the front of the building was all glass and clear lines of sight, the back was the opposite—there wasn't a single window on it, making it easy to approach. I contemplated following it around to the front and dodging inside through the broken glass, but if there were people in back with the hostages, it would give them time to kill some or all of them—we had no idea how many of them there were—so I decided to stick with the first plan.

The back of the dealership had a number of roll-down doors for their maintenance department, but only one door that people would use. I crept up to the door—no sense giving away my presence if there was someone listening—and looked at the door handle. There was a bolt and an opening for a key on the knob.

There were seven keys on the key ring. Two were definitely vehicle keys; it wasn't them. Two looked like they fit something smaller—combo locks, maybe? I didn't know, but I knew they weren't door keys. That left three, and I tried the first in the bolt. It didn't move. I tried the second. Also a no-go. I held my breath as I tried the third, but it not only fit, it turned the bolt. I left it locked and tried the same key in the door knob, and found it turned as well. Success! I stopped as an idea came to me, and I hoped that I hadn't turned the bolt or knob far enough for someone to notice if they'd been looking.

I crept away from the building and circled back around to Jacobs.

"I have the key," I said.

"Hell of a lot of shooting over there," he noted.

"Yeah, nothing's ever as easy as it seems," I said. "Or as easy as it should be."

"Nope," he agreed. "It rarely is."

"Regardless, I have the keys. I need you to give me some covering fire, so their attention is focused on the front of the building, and I can sneak in the back. Can you do that?"

"Sure thing."

"Give me five minutes, then do it," I replied. He nodded, and I loped off, trying to save some energy for what was to come. I knew I didn't have much left.

I made it back to the door and inserted the key, then stood there feeling very exposed. Sure, the building was ringed with "our" people...but everyone was in cover except me. It felt wrong, somehow.

After a couple of minutes, the forces around front began firing, and I slowly twisted the key in the bolt, unlocking it. I then slid the key into the door knob and turned it. The knob turned and the door opened. I slipped inside and shut the door again quickly, hoping no one noticed a difference in the volume of the gunshots, then drew my pistol in one hand and my knife in the other.

There was a small corridor behind the door, and I crept down it slowly as gunfire from out front trickled off to nothing. In this fallen world, ammunition is far too precious to waste. Even for covering fire.

The hallway ended in a series of cubicles full of people, of which the top half was glass. There was a large open area between them and the front of the building. That was also glass, and a large portion of it had been destroyed in the night's gunfire. The women in the cubicle at the end of the passageway I was in—five of them—noticed me, and they all stopped and stared at me as I sneaked up to it. Not wanting the cannibals to come find out what they were staring at, I motioned at them to turn around. All of them did, except for one who continued to stare at me. I pointed at her, and her eyes grew large, shocking her out of whatever dream state she'd been in. I then mimed for her to turn around, which she—finally—did.

I continued to advance and heard voices.

"What do you think they want, Harry?" one voice said in a stage whisper.

"I suspect they want their people back," a second—probably Harry—replied in a sarcastic tone.

"We can't hold out much longer here," a third voice said. "What if we kill all these people? Think they'd leave then?"

"They might," Harry replied. "They might also assault the building or hit us with heavier weapons if we no longer had the hostages."

"So what are we going to do?" the first voice asked.

"We're going to sit here and wait for the boss to come rescue us," Harry replied. "He's probably rounding up folks from the barricades right now and is going to hit them from behind."

I reached the end of the hallway, but stayed back in the shadows. As the men continued to talk, I could tell that two of them were off to the right, while one was close by to the left. I edged forward a little, trying to get a better view.

The first thing I could see was the door to the cubicle in front of me. There was a wooden beam on the floor going over to the wall across from it. The door, which opened out, was blocked from doing so by the brace—a simple method of keeping everyone in. I couldn't see any of the other doorways, but I suspected they were similarly blocked.

One of the cannibals was also visible—the first one who'd spoken. He was closest to me on the right, and he looked like he couldn't have been more than 16 or so. Probably someone's son who hadn't known any better than to go along. Now, though, he was part of the problem, and he had to go.

I couldn't see either of the other two cannibals, but knew Harry—the leader of the three—was to the left and the third was to the right on the far side of the kid.

I paused at the end of the corridor, not entirely sure how I was going to do this. Some flash bangs would be nice, but I didn't have any. I flinched away from the opening as it dawned on me—I wasn't sure how I knew what flash bangs were. I seemed to recall using them...but then the memory—if that's what it was—disappeared.

Which left me back at the same place—with geographically dispersed bad guys and no way to get at them simultaneously. Taking the kid would be easy; but it would probably put me into sight of at least one of the others, and probably both...and I guessed they were both bigger and more lethal threats.

I still hadn't decided when the one on the left said, "I'm going to see if I can sneak out the back and make it to the boss' house." The voice was closer and moving toward me; I barely had time to swap my weapons before he walked around the corner.

Happily, I had the benefit of knowing he was coming, and as he drew up in surprise, I stuck my blade between his fourth and fifth ribs, angling it upward to pierce his heart. Not what I particularly wanted to do, but all I had time for.

"Oh," was all he had time to say as his eyes opened wide, and he fell backward.

I tried to catch him, but the momentum was wrong and he was a big guy; all I succeeded in doing was to allow his corpse to pull me out of the cover I'd had. My head turned toward the kid, and our eyes met. I don't know if he'd ever seen someone die that close, but his eyes were huge. The gun in his hand started up toward me, and I had no choice—I put two into his chest as I fell forward and rolled to a stop next to the cubicle.

I got to my feet as quickly as I could, staying low, but the third man was gone. I looked around frantically, but couldn't see if he'd tried to run off—not a good prospect with the building surrounded—or was trying to sneak around the cubicles to get behind me. I backed into the corridor I'd come out of, knowing that my back was protected then, but then I realized there was a third alternative I hadn't thought of as I looked back—he'd gone into one of the cubicles and now had a gun to one of the hostage's head.

The girl, a thin child of no more than 12, had long blonde hair and was crying hysterically, while a woman—probably her mother—screamed, "Please let her go!"

"Shut up!" the man yelled back. His eyes met mine, and he smiled.

"Take me instead!" the woman yelled.

"I said, 'Shut up!'" the cannibal replied. "If you say anything else, I'll fucking kill you *and* her!"

The woman opened her mouth again, but nothing came out.

"That's what I thought you said," he sneered.

With his arm around the girl's waist, he lifted her up like a shield and walked from the cubicle, then shut the door and kicked the brace back into place so no one else could get out.

"So, Mr. Tough Guy," he said, looking at me, "if you let me go, I'll let her go once I'm clear. Otherwise, she dies."

"And that would bother me, why?" I asked. "She's not my daughter."

"Yeah, but you're one of the good guys. I'll bet you don't want her to die."

"All things considered, no I don't," I replied. "With that said, though, I don't want you to get away, either." He glared at me, and I sighed theatrically, then put my pistol in its holster. "All right," I said. "The boss and all his cronies have already gone, but if you let her go, I'll send you on your way to meet up with them."

"You mean it?"

I nodded. "Yeah, it would be my pleasure."

"I'm not letting her go until I get to where they are, though."

I shrugged. "Fine. Come with me." He nodded, and I walked out toward the front of the building.

"We're coming out!" I yelled, hoping no one decided to try to shoot him—or me—as we walked through the shattered glass at the front of the store. No one did, so we started walking toward the cannibals' house.

"What the hell's going on?" Jacobs asked as we neared the car he was hiding behind.

"This is the last of them," I replied. "I told him I'd show him where the bosses went and would send him off to meet them."

"You did, huh?" Jacobs asked. His voice held a hint of sarcasm, and I hoped he wasn't going to blow it. "I can't let him take the girl."

"He said he'd let her go when we got there."

"That so?" Jacobs asked.

"Yeah," the cannibal said, grunting.

I smiled. Even though she was small and not struggling anymore, the girl had to be getting heavy. And it was still a long way to the house.

"Well, make sure you do," Jacobs said. "We'll come find you if you don't."

I continued walking toward the house, about 100 yards away.

"Where are we going?" the cannibal asked. He was really struggling to hold the girl up now.

"Up to the house," I said. "I think they left a note for anyone who wanted to follow them."

"Faster," the man urged. "I want to see this note."

"Sure," I said, picking up my pace a little. As we approached the house, I said, "Shit," and bent down and pulled my shoelace before he could see what I was doing. "Damn shoelace came untied."

As I hoped, we were close enough that he kept walking, going by me as I bent to tie it. And then—probably thinking himself safe—he set the girl down to walk on her own, clearing my shot. In a flash, my gun was out. He must have heard it rasp against the leather, for he immediately reached forward to grab the girl, and my first shot went past his head. The second shot didn't, though, hitting him in the spine between his collarbones, and he flopped to the ground.

I raced forward and flipped him over, and his eyes glared at me.

"You're probably thinking I lied when I said you'd see your boss soon," I said. "I didn't. You're about to see him...in hell." I stepped in between the little girl and the cannibal so she wouldn't have to see it, and shot him between the eyes, so he could see it coming.

Ammunition may be at a premium, but I always have one to spare for the cannibals and hostage takers of this Fallen World.

* * * * *

Chapter Thirty-Four

I woke up in a bed that wasn't the same one I had been sleeping in.

"Good to have you back with us," a voice said. It sounded like Jacobs.

I rolled toward the voice and squinted one eye open. It was Jacobs. "Where…"

"You're in St. Vincent's, our hospital. With the cannibals taken care of, we were able to reclaim it. Good thing for you, too. You lost a lot of blood and almost died."

"Don't remember…"

"It looked like you got shot a couple of times and had a knife wound too. I saw you walking up with that girl you saved, then you just collapsed."

Girl I saved…I thought hard and several pictures ran through my head. A car dealership. A young girl being carried by a man. That same man as I killed him. The rest of the night filled in around them, and I remembered walking away from the cannibals' house, but that was it.

"I think I have most of it," I replied.

"Do you remember who you are?"

"Yeah, I'm…" No, I didn't remember that. I sighed. "No, that part hasn't come back." Of course, if the agents in Pensacola were right, I wouldn't ever get it back without an imprinter machine and my stored psyche.

"Should we go back to calling you Ishmael?"

"No, I'm growing to hate that name."

"So what should we call you?"

I sighed. "They were calling me Fred; that name's as good as any, I guess." I tried to sit up, and Jacobs came over to help me. The tubes running into my arm from the bag above me didn't help. Well, they probably helped me, in the long run, but they made it harder to sit up.

"Easy," he said. "You've been out for several days. The doctor said it was the damnedest thing, though—you healed faster than anyone she's ever seen."

"I've always been a fast healer."

"Yeah, not like this. It kind of freaked her out a little."

"*Mpff*," I grunted as I swung my legs off the bed. My body was stiff, but there wasn't a lot of pain. I stood, and the world canted to one side and wobbled a little. Jacobs held onto my arm like he thought I was going to dash off somewhere, but just standing was good enough for the moment.

"When do we hit the other cannibals?" I asked when the world had steadied again.

Jacobs chuckled. "You're a real go-getter, aren't you?"

I shrugged. "Robert Baden-Powell said to leave the world better than you found it; I'm just trying to do my part."

"Robert who?"

"Baden-Powell. You know, the guy who started the Boy Scouts?"

"How the hell do you know that, and yet not know who *you* are?" Jacobs asked.

I smiled, searching my memory for more. Nothing came. "I have no idea," I said, leaning back onto the bed. Darkness seemed to crowd in from the sides, and a nap sounded good. "When did you say…the other attack…was?"

I never heard the answer.

* * *

I woke up again—later that day? The next day?—I didn't know, but I felt a lot better. The world didn't seem to want to spin as much.

"I timed that well."

I turned and found a dark-haired woman in a lab coat. Short and stocky, she looked at me with her head cocked to the side as if trying to figure out what species I was. My first thought was, "People still wear lab coats?" but then I realized who the person had to be.

"You must be the doctor," I said.

"I am," she replied. "I'm Doctor Briggs. And you are?"

"I don't know," I replied. "Call me Fred. I got tired of Ishmael."

She chuckled. "I can see why. It wouldn't take me long to want to get rid of that name." She paused. "Jacobs tells me you don't know who you are or where you're from. Is that true?"

"Yes, ma'am, it is. I woke up in New Orleans after the war, but I have no idea how I got there or what I was doing there."

"It wasn't home?"

"I don't think so. It didn't feel like it anyway."

"Where's home?"

I stopped to think. No one had asked that before. *Where was I from?* I shrugged after a few moments of introspection. I had no more idea of where I was from than what my name was.

I held my arm with the IV out to her. "Any chance of getting this out?"

"I'll send in a nurse to get it," she said. "Even though you should probably have it for another couple of days. You almost died, you know?"

I gave her my best smile. "I'm a quick healer."

The smile didn't work; she frowned at me. "Just so you know, we don't have a whole lot of medical supplies left here, and I can't be using them all up on one person. Try not to stand in the way of any more bullets or knives, okay?"

I tried again with the smile. "Yes, ma'am. I'll be good."

It failed again. "Why do I doubt that?" she asked.

She left, but a nurse came in a few minutes later and disconnected me from all of the apparatus. I had obviously been out of it—I didn't realize there was equipment monitoring my vital signs. I nodded to the machinery. "How is all that operating?"

"We have a generator out back," the nurse replied. "It will work…for as long as the fuel supply holds out. Then it's going to be back to the dark ages for medical care."

"So, happily, I almost got killed at a good time?"

She shook her head. "There's never a good time to get killed."

She obviously hadn't spent much time journeying around this Fallen World.

* * * * *

Chapter Thirty-Five

Things were happening when I reached the police station, as there were the better part of a hundred men in the parking lot. Most seemed to be cleaning weapons, checking ammo, and talking nervously—the kinds of things people did when they were about to go into combat. Most of them at least looked like they knew which end of the gun the round came out; in the deep south, that was somewhat to be expected, I guessed.

I pushed passed several and made my way into the building, and thought to bypass the person on door duty.

"Where are *you* going?" he asked.

"I'm going back to see Jacobs," I replied.

"And who are you?" he asked. "I don't recognize you."

"I'm Fred," I said, for lack of a better answer. He eyeballed me a little more, and a questioning eyebrow went up. "I was part of the raid on the cannibals up north," I added.

"Oh," the man said, his other eyebrow joining the first in surprise. "You're *that* guy. Well, I'm sure the chief will want to see you. Let me go get him."

The man came back with Jacobs in less than two minutes.

"How ya doing, Fred?" Jacobs asked. "You look kind of pale—are you sure you should be up?"

"Looks like you guys are about to go get my car back. I want to make sure I get all my stuff that was inside it, too."

"We are," he said. "But I don't think you're going to be up for it."

"When do you leave?"

"We're going to take a bus over to the first checkpoint in about an hour, and then we'll hit them at about two in the morning."

"I want in," I said. "Except…"

"Except what?"

I held out my empty hands. "No one at the hospital seems to know what happened to my weapons. I'm sure I could be more of an asset if I was armed."

Jacobs chuckled. "I'm sure you could. Happily, of all the stupid questions I've received today, that's one I can answer. Your weapons are in my office. I've been holding them for you. Come with me."

He led me back to his office, where there were several men waiting.

"These are the team leaders," Jacobs said. "This is Hubbard, Wade, and Mullins, who will be in charge of Alpha, Bravo, and Charlie teams, respectively. Gentlemen, this is Fred."

"So what's the plan?" I asked after we'd all shaken hands, and they had brought in an extra chair for me. I have to admit I was ready for it.

"We've had a couple of folks watching the town and their checkpoint," Hubbard said. "Every three days, they've been sending teams out. Most of 'em come our way, as our town's the biggest one around, aside from Montgomery, which I wouldn't want to be in or around right now. It's our goal to capture one or more of the teams and use them to hit the checkpoint they have on Highway 22, then roll everyone into Maplesville and wipe them all out."

"Everyone?" I asked. "Men, women, and children?"

Jacobs' face was grim. "Everyone old enough to be eating solid food. If we find any babies, we'll bring them back and raise them. Aside from that, though…"

"It's the way it has to be," Wade said. A big man, he looked equally grim.

I shook my head. "Seems kind of… I don't know."

"It's legal," Jacobs said. "There was a trial at the courthouse, and we gave them notice that they had to cease and desist. Anyone that turned themselves in by last week would have been spared."

"Anybody turn themselves in?" I asked.

"Not a one," Mullins, a large black man replied. "We had hoped they would…but no one came."

"And now, since they have a taste for it," Wade added, "they have to be put down. It's just the way it has to be. Besides—" he looked around at the other men, "—we hear they are led by a monster."

"Well, yeah," I said. "Anyone that would lead a group of cannibals isn't—"

"No," Mullins said, cutting me off. "Not a monster of a human being, but a real, honest-to-God monster. Some say he's part crocodile—that he crawled from the swamps to lead them in this new world."

"Part crocodile?" I asked, rolling my eyes.

"Could be," Jacobs said.

"How's that?"

"Geno Freak."

The other men flinched away from Jacobs, as if in fear of the term. My eyebrows knit. I couldn't remember ever hearing it before, yet somehow that term sounded familiar.

"Geno Freak…" I muttered, then shook my head. "I got nothing."

"It was a fad ten to fifteen years ago with the young folks. They would splice different types of animal DNA into their bodies to become one with the animals—kind of like the ultimate furry experience. You weren't just dressed up as one—you *were* one."

"I hear a 'but' coming on," I said.

"Yeah, there's always a 'but,' isn't there?" Jacobs asked with a half-smile. "Sure it gave them whatever they wanted—fur, claws, hell, even fangs—but it was illegal. Not just because it was immoral, but because it didn't work. Human body just couldn't support the splicing and most people didn't live any more than another three to four years in their new 'condition.' I don't want to say that the fad 'died out' quickly…but it did. And thankfully so."

"So, if it's one of these Geno Freak things, how would it still be alive?"

Jacobs shrugged. "Supposedly, the lizard ones were able to live longer. If this *is* a Geno Freak—not saying it is, but if it were—that might be why."

I chuckled. "Okay, so if I see a guy running around with a crocodile mouth full of teeth, I'll just go ahead and put him out of his misery."

"That shit ain't funny," Mullins muttered.

"Sure it is," I said, laughing. "A guy running around with a crocodile head? That's a damn funny mental picture."

Jacobs shook his head. "No, it isn't funny. Not only is it just *wrong*, it's also possible the Freak had other things modified, too. It—if it exists—will probably be inhumanly strong. Probably faster than normal, too. Maybe like a snake striking. If there is a Freak there leading them, it's going to be tough to put down, but put down it must be, along with any of its followers or, Heaven forbid, any offspring it might have had."

"*Those things can sire more?*" Mullins asked, aghast.

"I don't know," Jacobs said, "but it's a genetic mod. If he were to sire children, it's possible that could be passed on."

"So kill them all, and let God sort them out," I said with a smile, trying to lift some of the blackness that came over the room with that thought. I wasn't sure that killing everyone in Maplesville was the best way to go about it, but it was their town, and they would have to live with it. "Whatever you guys say," I replied. "I just want my car and my stuff."

"Fair enough," Jacobs said. "The mayor already told you that if you help us, you'll get it back. I will make sure that happens."

"Then what do you need me to do?" I asked.

Sometimes you have to make hard choices in this Fallen World.

* * * * *

Chapter Thirty-Six

An hour later, we loaded into several buses from the local high school and went through a number of back roads to a church on the west end of town, then walked the rest of the way to the buildings I had seen right before being captured by Clanton's sentry. One of the biggest buildings was a warehouse, and we mustered inside of it. From there, a number of Hubbard's Alpha Team members spread out into the local countryside to wait in ambush for the hunter/gatherer teams coming from Maplesville.

I slept.

It wasn't that I was lazy; it was more that I'd been assigned to Bravo Team. The people in Alpha knew the lay of the land there, and in many cases knew the people they were there to protect; they made far better members of ambush teams than I would have.

And I was tired. It's not every day I almost die, after all. More like every month or so, I reckoned. Still, I knew I'd need my energy later, so while the rest of Bravo and Charlie teams huddled in the dark, talking via whispers, I slept, and it was a good sleep.

Eventually, though, like all good things, it had to come to an end, and someone shook me awake far sooner than I would have liked. I could see via the moonlight coming through a couple of windows that the other members of my team were gathered near one of the doors, and I grabbed my gear and walked over to find out what was going on.

246 | CHRIS KENNEDY

"Okay," Wade said, "I have good news. Alpha managed to capture two of the groups, and a third group was killed. They grilled the people they captured, somewhat literally, and were able to get some information from them. We now know that they hunt in groups of five, and that they don't take more than five people at a time. While they rest up for the attack on Maplesville, it's now up to us to take out the checkpoint. In one hour, a group of ten will walk up to it, dressed as one of the teams and its victims, and, while their attention is on our folks, the rest of us will hit them from behind, as planned. Any questions?"

I didn't have any. Although the plan hadn't been mine, the part of it where the group distracted the people at the checkpoint had been something I had added when the team leaders discussed the plan with me, so I was very familiar with it.

"Let's go," the leader said to my group as the meeting broke up, and the others sorted out who was doing what, based on the descriptions we had of the people who had been caught coming from Maplesville. We even had the clothing from two of the groups, so they would be dressed authentically. The people from Maplesville didn't need the clothes anymore.

I had five of Clanton's best hunters and woodsmen with me, and we slipped out the door into the cool night air. One of the men lived just east of where we were and had been hunting this forest all his life; he led us to the north to where a small house sat, and then to the west. We didn't have to worry about anyone sounding an alarm from the house—the family that lived there had been some of the earliest victims of the Maplesville cannibals and, since it was on the front line of the confrontation, the house had been vacant ever since.

We went west for another hundred yards or so, and then turned toward the checkpoint to the south. The group crept like wraiths through the forest, using the cover of a breeze blowing through to move from tree to tree until we were within fifty feet of the cannibals' checkpoint. We were downwind of them, and I could smell them. Perhaps it was their equipment, but I was willing to bet it was *them*. They were rank, and we didn't have to worry about if the wind shifted direction—they wouldn't be able to smell us over their own stench.

The leader gave us the halt sign, then the "go to ground," and we got onto our bellies and into position. As one of our better marksmen, I had drawn the M2 gunner as my target, and I sighted in on him before taking a moment to look at the larger scene in front of me. We had come in from behind them and had a fairly good view of the back of the barricade. There were five men in sight, all of whom were watching the other direction.

We waited, lying on the cool leaves, and I did my best not to wonder what else might be crawling through the leaves, looking for a new home on the inside of my clothes. Ticks I knew about, and immediately began having creepy crawly feelings all over my body. It was all I could do not to flick my arm when I saw the slug slowly inching its way up my sleeve toward my face. I tried to brush it off quietly, but my finger made a soft *swish!* on my jacket. The leader shook his head at me.

I went back to watching my target, and happily didn't have long to wait. A couple of minutes later, I could see the group come to attention.

"Someone's coming," one of them said, the breeze bringing his words to our ears.

"Who is it?" the M2 gunner asked.

"Looks like one of the recon groups," the first to speak replied.

I couldn't see the group, but expected it was our people. The group at the barricade relaxed slightly, but then one of them pointed and yelled, "That's not them!" and everyone jumped into motion. I flipped off the safety as the lead hunter yelled, "Fire!" and looked through the sights at the M2 gunner. He was just leveling the enormous weapon when the first of my bullets hit him in the back. A second and a third followed as quickly as I could get the rifle in line again, and he slumped, never having fired a shot.

A second person jumped up to the gun, and I fired again, hitting an arm. The person—a woman I could see as she turned—looked to see who'd shot her, and I hit her again in the chest. She fell backward onto the bed of the truck, then slid off the opposite side. It seemed like everyone around me was firing, and I could hear the other group firing as well, but I couldn't see any more targets.

"Cease fire!" I yelled. I yelled it again as I stood. I wanted to go check out the enemy, but I didn't want to run in front of the idiots who seemed to be shooting just to shoot. I finally got their attention, and I moved forward at a jog, not wanting to get shot by the other group that was approaching, either.

Amateurs, I thought with a shrug, but when I tried to think about me professionally doing something like this, nothing would come. I was really growing to hate the random thoughts that would spring unbidden into my memory. *Why could I remember bits and pieces, but not everything else?*

I walked around the truck, checking the enemy forces. All were dead, some gruesomely so, so I jumped up onto the flatbed, ready for the next phase of the night's activities. It didn't take long before we were loaded and moving. Although it was unlikely that anyone had heard the firing—it was seven miles away and almost 2:00AM, there was no sense giving them time to prepare.

Several buses followed us as the truck turned around and headed toward Maplesville, and I joined the rest of the group—I couldn't call the motley crew an "assault force"—in tying a strip of red cloth to my upper left arm to identify me as one of the "good guys."

The people onboard the flatbed with me were an interesting study of the human condition, from one end of the spectrum to the other. There were several who were either crying or misty-eyed— men as well as women—all the way to people who were excited about having just participated in an assault that led to the killing of another group of people, and who were actively looking forward to doing it again.

While I realized we needed people toward that end of the spectrum—people who were able and willing to kill—in this new world, that was probably how we had come to the state we were in. The world had gone to war and torn itself apart because there had been too many people who were willing to kill—or to have others do it for them, anyway—as well as people who were willing to carry out orders to do so. Look what it had gotten us.

I shook my head. What the hell did I know? I was one of those people who had allowed myself to be used by those types of people.

Happily, the drive wasn't that long, and I wasn't forced to dwell on either the world or my place in it for very long. We rolled into Maplesville and the truck stopped at a major intersection along its version of Main Street, where we had good fields of fire in all directions. One of the buses stopped short of our intersection and another went a block further. Without a word, everyone but me jumped off the flatbed or unloaded from the buses and went about their grim work.

I manned the M2 on the back of the flatbed, content to let them do the house-to-house searches this time. It was their fight, not mine, and my body was already complaining about my overutilization of it. I was content to scan the roads leading into Maplesville for people without the red identifier and listen to the random shots being fired as the houses were cleared. The town could have been anywhere in the American countryside before the war, with little shops on both sides of the street.

It was almost peaceful, aside from the periodic bouts of gunfire, and I have to admit to zoning out. I don't think I fell asleep—quite—but then a burst of gunfire rang out close by and someone yelled, "Look out!"

I snapped fully awake, but it took me a couple of seconds for my brain to catch up with what my eyes were seeing. It took even longer to process it.

The thing—it had to be the Geno Freak that Jacobs mentioned—had emerged from whatever hole it lived in, and I watched as it tore apart a four-man patrol group. The Freak was larger than a normal human—at least seven feet tall—and faster than anything that big had a right to be. The monster was dark-skinned and shiny across the length of its body—it wasn't wearing any clothes—and it blended into the night, making it hard to see.

It was facing away from me, and I watched as it took a swipe at one of the men. It had to have a blade of some sort in its hand, as the man's throat exploded in a spray of red visible in the light provided by the town's small street lamps. The man was thrown to the side, but the monster was already in motion. Before the body hit, he had already torn the arm off a second person with a twist and a yank, and punched a third man so hard in the chest that he went flying backward—airborne—at least eight feet through the air. The fourth person in the group was a woman, and she screamed.

It was cutoff as the Freak latched his jaws—not a full crocodile mouth, but jaws that extended at least eight inches from his face— around her throat and pulled back, ripping it out in another spray of blood. As the woman's body fell, the creature looked around, licking its lips with a tongue long enough to do so.

At least three of the people were dead, and I wasn't worried about the fourth as I cut loose with the M2. The Freak saw me as I did so, though, and it leaped to the side, faster than I could train the gun on it. It jumped a fence and blurred as it ran behind a church, moving so fast I could barely see it, much less hit it with the .50 caliber rounds. I took a good chunk out of the church before I could stop myself, but I figured God would understand; *that thing needed to die!*

Having made it behind the church, I lost sight of it. If there was one thing I knew, though, it was that I was *not* chasing it around in the dark; I would stay right in the middle of the intersection, with as much light as possible to see it. I scanned back and forth between the sides of the church, not knowing which side it would appear from, but then saw it had a third option—it had run halfway down the block, and sprinted across the street before I could get the barrel of the M2 around to it.

People began running toward the flatbed, yelling and asking questions, but I didn't have time for them. My concentration was locked in on the abomination that was now stalking me. I tried to keep watch on both sides of the line of buildings that ran toward me, but it again did something unexpected—it didn't come from either side; instead, it leaped off the roof of the library and sprinted toward me.

It only stopped once, to grab a woman along the way and toss her at me. I would have fired at it, anyway, in spite of the woman, but I was too busy ducking the flesh missile to operate the weapon. I straightened, only to have it leap onto the flatbed and hit me. I didn't even see it, but it catapulted me backward off the flatbed.

My body is a lot denser than most people's, and I didn't fly as far as he expected. He looked down at me and—although the crocodile mouth didn't move—his eyes indicated his puzzlement. Now in the light, I could see that his dark, shiny color came from the scales that covered his body and that he was—rampantly—a human male, which was a lot more than I'd wanted to know.

It shrugged and walked over to the M2, and tore the weapon from its mountings with its two huge, webbed claws. The Freak hefted the gun once, then threw it at a man who was on the street gawking up at him. The barrel impaled the man, and threw him backward five feet on impact.

Although there were now a number of people nearby—all of them standing around gawking, too amazed to do anything—it turned to look back at me, and jumped off the flatbed in my direction as I stood. I drew my pistol from its holster, and the creature blurred. Before I could pull the trigger, it slapped the pistol from my hand, leaving bleeding furrows marking me from my wrist down. It tilted its head back and made a loud noise, but it took me a second to realize what it was—it was laughing at me.

I took a couple of steps back, looking from side to side for a weapon I could use. I knew I couldn't outrun it on my best day, and today was far from it. After a couple of seconds, the creature stopped laughing and paced toward me. I could see my death approaching...stalking me; the Freak was far stronger and faster than I, and we both knew it. I needed to be faster—much faster.

As I had that thought, I could feel my adrenal glands kick into overdrive, and my body surged with energy unlike anything I had ever felt before. I covered the two steps between us faster than I'd ever moved, pulling my knife as I advanced. I don't know if I was as fast as the Freak, but I was faster than he expected. He didn't get his hands up to block, and barely turned aside in time.

He *did* manage to twist though, and instead of my knife driving through his heart, it only scored a line across his right shoulder as he turned and moved to his left. His right hand snapped back as he moved, and I ducked a blow that would surely have broken my neck. The Geno Freak took two steps away from me and roared a challenge, then dropped into a ready position as if to grapple with me.

There was no way I was going to wrestle the Freak; there was no way that could end well. I stepped back, looking for another option, all the nerves in my body aflame with the desire to move, to strike, to kill the beast. Before I could come up with a plan though, it charged me with its arms open wide.

I feinted left, then down to the right, under his arms, diving at his legs. He leaned forward but missed me, and my shoulder hit him in the knees. The force of the impact cracked my collarbone and stopped me in my tracks, but I was enough of a roadblock to make the Geno Freak cartwheel over me.

He hit the pavement like a ton of bricks, flat on his back, and I heard the air *whoosh!* out of him. I spun, my shoulder on fire, and raced over to him as he struggled to sit up. I grabbed him from behind and tried to run my knife across his throat, but the scales were too thick and turned my blade. He reached behind with his left arm and grabbed mine, and I nearly blacked out as he wrenched my arm so hard I could feel the broken collarbone separate.

I held on with my right arm around his throat as he tried to drag me around from behind. Like the kid with the tiger by the tail, I was unable to do anything to him but hold on—to let go meant certain death. He got my arm far enough around where he could grab it with both of his webbed claws, and he adjusted his grip in preparation for throwing me. Or snapping my arm off; I wasn't sure which, but I knew I only had a moment left before I was going to be in a world of pain.

Unable to do anything else, I jabbed the knife up into the underside of his mouth, and I found the skin and scales much softer and more giving there; *the knife penetrated!*

With a strength born of desperation, I pulled it out and jabbed it as hard as I could, sinking the blade all the way to the hilt. The Geno Freak froze, then seized as all his muscles contracted at once, and I lost my grip on the knife as I was bucked over his head onto the pavement in front of him.

I maintained a tenuous grip on consciousness as I hit—hard—and was able to push the stars back from my vision as I rolled onto my side, then onto my stomach, holding my left arm as close to my chest as I could to prevent any further damage. The gravel on the road bit into my arm, but I ignored it as I struggled to my feet to find the Geno Freak twitching about spastically, while a circle of about ten people stood around it watching.

All of them were armed, and I walked over and took a pistol from the closest woman, without asking, and emptied the entire magazine into the creature's head from underneath its chin. One of the men on the other side of it was coated in gore when he didn't move fast enough to get out of the way; I didn't care, nor would I have minded if he'd been hit. All I knew was that I was going to put the Freak down for good.

When the pistol ceased firing, I walked back to the woman I'd taken it from, handed it back to her, and said, "You've got the rest of them."

Then everything went as black as the asphalt I collapsed onto.

Sometimes you reach your limits in this Fallen World.

* * * * *

Chapter Thirty-Seven

"I thought I told you I couldn't be using up all of our supplies on one person," Doctor Briggs said as I woke up. I recognized the room. If it wasn't St. Vincent's again, it was a very close facsimile.

"Not...my...fault," I said.

"Oh?" she asked, surprised. "Do tell me why that is."

"You told me not to stand in the way of any more bullets or knives," I said, my voice growing stronger. "You didn't mention anything about wrestling giant half-crocodile/half-man crossbreeds."

The doctor chuckled. It was the first time I'd seen her look amused. "Honestly, I'm sure it never would have dawned on me to do so." The smile left her face. "I guess I should thank you. Had you not killed that...that thing...I'm told that eventually its minions would have used us all as livestock."

"Happy—" I coughed and got a little twinge of pain from my shoulder. Not anywhere near as much as I would have expected. I mentally sighed—I'd probably been out again for a while this time, too. "Happy to help," I finally finished. "Did you see it?"

The doctor shuddered. "Yes," she said, her voice much softer than it had been before. "It was awful. There were also some...other things it had sired. They were all...awful." She shuddered again.

"But they're all dead now, thanks to you," Jacobs said.

I rolled a little and found him sitting in a corner behind me. I nodded once to him.

"Once you killed the leader, it took the heart out of the rest of them, and the last few gave up. It didn't make it any easier at the end, but it's over now, and we were able to make contact with some other survivors down toward Selma that we may be able to trade with. It's a long way with gas being scarce and all, but we're going to put together a wagon train and see what we can do."

I nodded at him again when he stopped and looked at me funny. "What?" I asked as he kept looking at me.

"Is it too early to ask if you'd be interested in a job as a caravan guard?" he asked. "I came up as you fought that Geno Freak. I've never seen anyone move as fast as you did."

"Not fast enough," I said, holding up my hand, which was so heavily bandaged it looked like a club. "That thing was a lot faster."

"Well, you moved faster than anyone I've ever seen. You also absorbed that blow when he punched you off the flatbed. He punched one of my other men like that, and it killed him—crushed his entire rib cage through his organs. I saw my man afterward—it looked like he'd been run over by a semi, and you got up as if nothing had happened."

He stopped and looked at me, and I shrugged.

"There's a lot more to you than meets the eye," he continued. "You also weigh a lot more than someone your size should. They told me you were heavy the last time we brought you here. I didn't think anything about it then, but I helped lift you this time, and they weren't kidding; you are *a lot* heavier than what you look."

I shrugged again. "I don't know what you want me to say," I finally replied. "I've already told you everything I know about me. I'm not one of those Geno Freaks, if that's what you're trying to get at.

Not that I know, anyway." I looked at Doctor Briggs for confirmation.

"No, you're not a Geno Freak," the doctor replied. She appeared to want to say more, but then shut her mouth.

"But what?" I asked.

"I didn't want to say anything else in front of him," she said, nodding to Jacobs. "Doctor-patient confidentiality."

"That's fine," I replied. "I'm not hiding anything...that I know of, anyway."

She nodded. "To be totally honest, I'm not sure what you are," she said. She held up her hand to silence me when I opened my mouth. "Let me finish please." I nodded. "Okay, what I wanted to say first is that you are *not* a Geno Freak, so you don't have to worry about that."

"So I'm just normal flesh and blood?"

"Well, no," she replied. "Actually, you're neither normal flesh, nor blood." She shrugged. "I don't know what—or how—it was done to you, but you have been made into something...I don't know how to describe it. You are a human...only more. Your muscles and bones have been enhanced and are higher in density than a normal person."

"I knew I was a little stronger than most people..." I said.

"You're a *lot* stronger than most people, and you're a lot better at absorbing punishment than the average person," Briggs said.

"I'd vouch for that," Jacobs added. "Based on what I've seen, anyway."

"Your nerves have also been tweaked—I think to make you faster—and your blood is able to carry a lot more oxygen than a normal person, increasing your athletic performance. Your lungs have also been tweaked, and I wouldn't be surprised if you were able to breathe oxygenated water." She shook her head. "I don't know how all this was done, but you have been developed—or modified—to be more than a normal person."

She looked at me expectantly, and I looked over to Jacobs. He was giving me the same look, as if both of them expected me to have a breakthrough with all of this information and tell them something.

"Sorry," I said, "I don't know anything about it." Which was true—to a point. Although I expected those changes must have had something to do with being an Agent, I still didn't know that for certain, nor did I know how those changes had been made. I could definitely see the advantages that an Agent would have, though, with all those modifications.

Ultimately, I shrugged and smiled at Jacobs. "It must not be too bad, if you still want to hire me on as a guard."

It was Jacobs turn to shrug. "I don't know anything about all that stuff," he said, "but you've never been anything but honest with me. You've done what you said you would—and more—and have helped out this city more than the next five people. Whatever—and whoever—you are, I don't think you're a criminal or someone who's evil. If you were, we'd all be in a lot of trouble. You could have turned on us at any point, but didn't. Hell, you even fought the Geno Freak for us…and he would probably have eaten most of us alive. Literally.

"The bottom line is that—whatever you are—I trust you, and trust isn't something you find much anymore in this world. If you want to stay, I've got a place for you."

"Thanks," I replied. "Maybe I'll be back, someday. This seems like a nice enough place, and it's encouraging to find a place where the rule of law still holds."

"I figured you'd say that," Jacobs said. He pointed out the window toward the parking lot. "We brought your car here, and the town has paid your hospital bills and stocked the car. You're free to go, whenever you feel up to it."

"Thanks, Jacobs, I really appreciate it."

He nodded once and started for the door, but turned and looked at me again. "You take care of yourself, okay? And, once you find what you're looking for, y'all come back and see us now, you hear?"

I nodded once, and he left.

If you look, compassion can still be found in this Fallen World.

* * * * *

Chapter Thirty-Eight

I rested for two more days and drove off after a quick goodbye with Doctor Briggs. I thought she might actually have had a tear in her eye, but whether that was because of the dusty nature of the hospital, or because she was losing her favorite experiment, I didn't know. She muttered something about how there'd now be a lot more medical supplies for everyone else, and then I was on the road.

The car was pretty much as I had abandoned it, with the exception of a .50 caliber hole in the door. As it turned out, there were two layers of kevlar in the door paneling, and the second had stopped the round. That was good to know, although I doubted the window could have done the same.

Jacobs had done a great job provisioning the car, and I think I actually drove off with more ammo and supplies than I had arrived with. As I almost got killed twice in order to get it, including nearly getting eaten alive by a giant Geno Freak, I'm not sure how great a deal it was, but I ended up alive, re-provisioned, and on my way, so I was as happy as a man who didn't know who he was could be.

The journey north started out better than most of my other recent excursions, and I was all the way to the outskirts of Birmingham in less than an hour, having only had to run two roadblocks where the defenders made—at best—a half-hearted attempt at stopping me. It wasn't even worth giving them the finger for trying. Don't get

me wrong—I totally *did* give them the finger—but their efforts barely justified it.

The Geiger counter started going crazy as I approached Birmingham—it had obviously taken a hit or two—so I took the bypass
around the city, running another two roadblocks along the way. Perhaps the folks in northern Alabama didn't have as much ammo as
their cousins in the south? Perhaps they hadn't been fed as well?
Ignorance and apathy—I didn't know and didn't care—I was just
happy to blow on by the barricades without being in a whole lot of
danger. And, thanks to their involvement in my life, I was able to
improve my skills in driving on grass to the point where I rarely lost
control anymore.

My car acquired a few more bullet holes in the outer sheet metal,
but in general, I was rather pleased with my progress.

After a couple of hours on I-59 and a crossover onto I-24, I was
rapidly approaching Chattanooga when things returned to normal,
which is to say, "shitty." I had just gotten my first sight of the Ten-
nessee River when I came to the bridge that wasn't. Where the
bridge used to cross Lookout Creek, there was now nothing except
the river, flowing quickly under the 80-foot-wide gap. Worse, as I got
out of the car to look at it, the Geiger counter began climbing. It was
too early to know for sure if Chattanooga had been wasted, but that
was looking like the way to bet. Still, I hadn't seen Boudreaux yet, or
any indications of his passage, so I went back to the last big intersection and cut over to Highway 41, which roughly paralleled I-24 into
the city.

I made it a little further past Lookout Creek on the other road,
but then the Geiger counter went crazy. I was within a couple of
miles of my destination, but unless I wanted to glow at night—which

I really didn't—I was going to have to try something else. Boudreaux had an army of helpers—I knew he wouldn't have risked going any further either, so I had to have missed him somewhere along the way. Either he went down a different road...or he got wiped out, which I felt was less likely. If I'd made it this far on my own, he probably had, too.

With that in mind, I turned back south, climbing up Lookout Mountain. Maybe a view from above would help me figure out what to do. Unfortunately, the mountain was heavily wooded, and there wasn't any way to look back into the city. On the good side though, the radiation levels fell quickly as I headed south, so at least I had that going for me.

I drove along, continuing south along the spine of the small ridge, not really sure what I wanted to do. I needed to stop and think, but the area was well-populated, and I didn't want to give anyone a shot at me in the open. I would need gas soon, as it was reaching a critical level, but I'd seen plenty of people since I reached the outskirts of Chattanooga and didn't really want to stop. Although none of them appeared ready or willing to accost me, I wasn't really in a trusting mood. There were a number who held out hands to me as I breezed through some of the intersections, but I avoided them and kept going.

I made it about two miles farther, then ran into a roadblock at the entrance to Covenant College. Although the three men at the barricade were all armed with rifles, they were slung and none of them seemed to be in a hurry to shoot me, so I allowed one of them to approach the car without trying to back up and make a getaway.

He made a motion for me to roll down my window.

"Can't!" I yelled through it as best I could. The armored window blocked sound almost as well as bullets. "It's broken!"

The man scanned the inside of my car. Happily, I'd put all of the extra stores in the trunk, out of sight. All he could see was that I had a rifle and pistol. I could see a calculating look in his eyes—while the weapons might have been enough for him to try to take them, if he did so, he had to know I might be able to use them, and he ran the risk of becoming dead, rather than better armed. Common sense won out over avarice in the end.

"You need to turn back," the man said, finally. "There's a war zone up ahead."

"A war zone?" I asked.

"Yeah. Some folks from Florida thought they could come through and take what they wanted from us, but we called up the militia. We got 'em trapped up at the college." Something must have crossed my eyes, because the man stepped back away from the car and moved to the front of the car. "Where you from, anyway?" he asked.

"Clanton, Alabama," I replied. I'd removed the tags from the car on the thought that no one really needed to know where I was from or how far from home I was.

"And whatcha doing up here?" he asked. "That seems a long way from home, with gas so scarce."

"I hadn't heard from my grandma, and my mom asked if I could go take a look. She lived in Chattanooga."

"Well, if she was downtown, she's dead," the man replied. "Chattanooga took one right on top of the City Diner. You won't be getting any more cake from there...not for a long while."

"Well, shit," I said, trying to look distraught. "Mom's going to be sad."

I could tell by the look on the man's face he wasn't buying it. His rifle slid off his shoulder and down into his hands. That was my cue I'd overstayed my welcome. "Okay, well, I have to get back to my mom," I said. I put the car into reverse and started backing away.

"Stop!" the sentry ordered. Avarice and distrust had won out in the end, apparently.

I spun the car around, and he fired, putting a chip in the center of my back window. The other two fired as well, and I could hear impacts on the car as I gunned the motor, although none appeared to penetrate or hit anything vital. They hit the car another couple of times before I made it to the next corner and out of sight. I checked the gauges and everything appeared fine, but the handling was off slightly. The little yellow tire light illuminated right at the same time I figured out what had happened—they'd hit at least one of my tires.

That put me into a quandary—did I get as far as I could before trying to change the tire? The men at the barricade probably knew they'd hit my tire and might come looking to catch me when I stopped. Or, since it seemed like there was a decent chance I'd just found Boudreaux's group, did I stop and try to link up with him? I shook my head as I contemplated. There really wasn't anywhere good to stop along the way to fix the tire, and I'd come all this way to meet Boudreaux...

I made a decision and pulled off down Frontier Bluff Road, a side street which ran off to the left, further into the forest and slightly down the backside of the hill. There were a few houses buried deep in the woods that it serviced. I passed them slowly and coasted to a stop a little further up the road and got out of the car. I had to know if it was Boudreaux, and I had to know now, even if the guys at the barricade sent someone out looking for me.

Sometimes you just have to do what feels right in this Fallen World.

* * * * *

Chapter Thirty-Nine

Once I got out of my car, I could hear gunfire, and I knew I was close. It sounded like it was coming from just over the hilltop, but in the thick trees, I couldn't tell for sure. I grabbed my pack and threw it over my shoulders, as well as all the ammo I could carry. With my pistol in its holster and my rifle in my hands, I set off toward the sporadic gunfire. As I listened, it seemed more like nuisance fire—just meant to keep people's heads down and irritate them.

I doubted it was Boudreaux's men; as Agents, they would be better disciplined. They wouldn't waste rounds just to be irritating, especially if they were holed up somewhere; they would be conserving their ammo.

The random fire, though, let me figure out where they were, and I crept through the woods doing my best not to think about what I was doing. As I reached the edge of the woods, I could see a road and a number of large buildings that sat on the crest of the hill. There were a couple of small buildings on my side of the street a little way off to the right, but there didn't seem to be anyone there.

It didn't take long to figure out where Boudreaux's men—if they were really his—were located. It was the enormous building on the left at the top of the hill. At least five stories high, the building would have made a great castle, were it not for the windows, many of which had either been shot out or broken out to allow the defenders to fire through. The structure even had what looked like a bell tower on one end of it, and I could see motion in it—it made for a perfect sniper's nest, and I stepped back into the forest—if I could see them, they could see me, and I didn't want them to kill me after getting this close. If I was Boudreaux, I would have a sniper-trained Agent sitting up there picking off the opposition as they showed themselves.

A couple of smaller buildings were next to the fortress-like building, and off to the right as well. There may have been buildings on the other side of the fortress, but I couldn't see them from my vantage point.

I could, however, see people in a number of places around the building, keeping it under observation. Most weren't firing, and might have been trying to get a shot at the people inside the building, but not much was currently happening. It looked like a stalemate, where the people on the outside were hoping to starve out the folks on the inside. Neither side looked particularly like they wanted to change the status quo.

As I watched the situation for a few minutes, I realized one thing—it was going to be really hard to get to the building without being shot. By my "friends" even more so than my enemies.

* * *

I watched the siege for a couple of hours, staying inside the tree line and, I hoped, out of sight of the sniper in the tower. All I could hope was that he'd see me sneaking around and figure out that I wasn't with the people who had them holed up in the building.

What I didn't understand was why they were there in the first place. If Boudreaux had an army of supermen, how had he allowed himself to be trapped like that? Alternately, why didn't he stage a breakout? If I knew either of those answers, I was pretty sure I could help them…but I didn't, and I couldn't figure out a way to communicate with the people inside the building without getting shot.

I was going to have to get closer, which meant going into one of the buildings that were next to the main building and trying to signal from there. Dangerous—as it would mean putting myself into contact with the enemy—but not as foolhardy as standing in the open where both sides could shoot at me.

I waited until dark to move, staying in the cover of the trees as much as possible. The buildings were at the top of a hill, which meant a sprint uphill across the overgrown lawn, with at least a little of it under the watchful eye of the shooter in the tower. I got as close as I could before making the final sprint to the smaller building.

There was a building a little further down that had seemed to be their headquarters, with more people coming and going throughout the day, but there had been plenty from this one, too. As I approached it, I decided it was a maintenance building for the college, where the engineers and their minions had worked to keep it running.

I ran up to the back of the building and took a minute to catch my breath before sneaking a peek into one of the windows. There was only one doorway in, and on the other side there appeared to be a lounge area. Several people were sitting around and shooting the breeze by candlelight while having a drink. There was no way I was going to sneak past them, nor did I think I could bluff my way past.

Not seeing any other way to do it, I drew my pistol and burst into the room. The three may have thought themselves tough warriors—they were big and burly, with bushy beards—but caught unaware, they all went down in my initial barrage.

I raced across the room to check them, but heard a door open across from me. I spun, but the man was already running back out the way he'd come. I fired into the door a couple of times, but didn't hit him. "It's one of them!" he yelled as he ran. "There's one in here!"

I loaded a new magazine, grabbed a candle, and went to follow him, but he was gone when I opened the door. I knew I would need to go up two stories, so I looked for the stairs. I found them at the end of the hall by two non-functional elevators. As I opened the door into the stairwell, I could hear the man. Judging by the sounds, he'd gone up the stairs as well.

I quickly went up one flight, and could hear several voices from the floor above me. Deciding discretion was the better part of valor, I set the candle down, and slipped out the stairwell door. As I suspected, there was a hallway that ran the length of the building, which I could just barely see in the moonlight coming through the windows.

I went as quickly as I could to the other end and found another stairwell that I used to go up. As quietly as I could, I eased open the door and looked down the passageway to see a group of people huddled at the other end. Apparently, no one had thought about the second set of stairs, and they were all arrayed at the stairwell—one person held the door open while the other three pointed pistols into the yawning abyss.

I crept as silently as I could toward them, and had made it to within 20 feet when one of them sensed my presence somehow. As he started to turn, I shot him, the flash of my pistol strobing in the dark hallway and messing with my vision. I had them all pegged though, and I fired a couple of rounds into each of the ambushers with guns. Only one got off a shot, and it buried itself in the wall between the guy holding the door open and myself. I shot him an extra time for scaring me.

That left the guy who had been holding the door, which he'd let go in all the gunplay. The man was young—probably a college student who'd never seen gunplay like that before. "Don't kill me," he whined.

"I don't want to," I said, "and if you just tell me what's going on here, perhaps I won't have to."

"O—okay," he stuttered. "You—you're not one of them?"

"No, I'm not. I was just passing through looking for someone, and your guys attacked me. So, who are those people in the next building, and what's going on here?"

"From what I heard," the young man said, "some out-of-towners came and holed up in the building next to us. Some of the locals took exception to it and told them to leave. There was a gunfight, and a lot of the locals were killed. That made everyone else mad, so they put together a big group to trap them in that building. I got recruited to help with that. The leaders thought we'd starve them out, but then realized there was a cafeteria in the building, and there's probably still some food that hadn't gone bad…which is making this take longer than everyone thought."

"I see." I thought for a moment. "How long is it going to be before someone comes to find out what's going on here?"

"I don't know…"

"Think harder," I said, pushing the barrel of my pistol into his stomach.

"Uh…well, the shift changes in about an hour. Someone would come then, if they don't come to find out what the shots were all about."

"Okay, here's what's going to happen, then. If you help me out for a few minutes, I will let you go."

"Really?"

"Really." I smiled. "I don't want to kill you, kid. Didn't want to kill them either, if I'd had the choice." I shrugged.

"So what do you need me to do?" he asked.

"I need a light source. The candle is fine, but I need a match or something to light it." I indicated the men. "Search them and see if you can find some matches."

"I have matches," he said. "I'm in charge of candles."

"Awesome," I said. Finally, something that went my way. I motioned him toward one of the doors that lined the hallway. "Now we go in there and signal the men in the building next to us."

"We'll get shot if we do that!"

"I hope not," I replied. "I have a plan."

"Do you know them?"

"I don't know. I think I may know who they are. If so, I think I can end this whole confrontation."

"Really?"

I chuckled. "Yeah, really."

"That'd be great," he said as he went in. "A lot of people have died here." I surveyed the room in the moonlight. "So," he asked, "what do you want me to do?"

"Well, come away from the window, for the first thing," I said. "You're no good to me if you get yourself shot."

He jumped like someone had hit him with an electric prod.

"Now, give me your T-shirt."

"My T-shirt?"

"Yeah," I replied, "I want to make a white flag. You know, like, 'Hey, don't shoot us?'"

The shirt came off like he saw a co-ed waiting for him in bed, and he handed it over to me.

"One last thing," I said. "Bring that easel over here and see if you can find a black marker."

He brought both of those to me, and I wrote on the paper.

"Okay," I said. "I'll take care of this. You just stand out of the way of any of the windows and light that candle."

"Now?"

"No, why don't we wait until the sun comes up and light the candle then?"

"But why—"

"Yes, light the candle now!" I exclaimed. Kids these days.

He pulled out his matches and lit the candle. It wasn't bright, but I figured it would have gotten the attention of everyone in the building alongside us. I picked up his T-shirt and waved it in front of the window without putting more than my hand in front of it.

Hopefully, they got the message.

I risked a peek out the window, but couldn't see anyone across the intervening 50 feet. I pushed the easel out in front of the window, with the single word, "Boudreaux?" on it, then leaned forward and looked out the window again.

Across the small courtyard, a light snapped on, and a man's face was briefly illuminated. He nodded twice, then the light went off. A gun fired outside, and the window the man had been behind shattered. I doubted he'd want to highlight himself like that again, and hoped he didn't think I was trying to draw him out to be killed.

I quickly wrote, 'I'm coming over,' on the easel.

"So, what do we do now?" the kid asked.

"Now we put the candle out, so we don't highlight ourselves anymore," I replied.

He blew out the candle, and I opened the window. The ground rose on this side of the building, so it was only about a six foot drop to the ground, very manageable.

"Here's where I leave," I said, scooping up his T-shirt. "Tell your friends to be on the lookout for a white flag tomorrow."

"You—you're taking my shirt?" he asked.

"Better than taking your life," I said. He nodded vigorously. "I'll bring it back tomorrow."

I turned and slid out the window, then looked at the 50 feet of open space between the buildings. It seemed like forever. Summoning my nerve, I burst forth from the cover of the building and ran toward the door on the other side of the courtyard as fast as I could. Of course, someone shot at the movement, and I heard the *crack!* as the bullet went past, but then I was across, and I lowered my shoulder to ram through the door.

Someone opened it as I was about to crash into it and I dove forward, sprawling across the entryway floor. The door slammed shut behind me, and I rolled over to find the dim outlines of four men with rifles pointed at me.

Very slowly, I raised my hands. "Hi guys," I said. "I'm looking for Mr. Boudreaux."

"And you are?"

"I don't know," I replied. "I'm one of you, I think, but the war killed my imprinter and left me with nothing. I'm also a good friend of Mr. Boudreaux's nephew."

"You believe him?" one of the other men asked.

"Perfect alibi," a third said. "There's no way to prove the story, right or wrong."

"Well, how many people even know about Agents?" I asked.

"If you were an Agent," the first man said, "and you got left with nothing from the imprinter, then how do you know about imprinters and Agents in the first place?"

"I didn't, for the longest time," I replied, "and I wandered around for a long time trying to figure out who I was, but then I met up with Mr. Boudreaux and helped get him to Pensacola. While I was there, I talked to a few of your Agents and figured out what must have happened."

"And just where was this imprinter," a new voice asked.

"Boss, should you be up?" the first man asked.

"I'll lie down again in a minute," the new man said, "but first, I want to see who this is." He walked up to me and stared at me in the dim light. "Where are you from?"

"I woke up in New Orleans," I said. "I have no idea if I'm really from there, though."

"You're not."

"What? How do you know?"

The man snapped on a flashlight and held it under his chin. "I'm Luc Boudreaux," he said. "I'm the head of the Agent program, and I know everyone that I accepted into it."

My jaw dropped. After all I'd been through to find the man, here he was, finally in front of me. I was at a loss for words, and my jaw just hung open as I stared at him.

He chuckled and turned out the light. "So, if the imprinter failed, you don't know anything about yourself."

"No," I said, shaking my head. "I don't know anything. I appear to have some skills in my muscle memory that would tend to make me believe I'm an Agent, but I don't know what kind or who I am in real life."

Boudreaux coughed and slumped a little, and two of the Agents grabbed him and supported him. "Let's get you back to bed," the first man said.

"Okay," Boudreaux replied. They turned to leave.

"You guys mind if I get up?" I asked the other two men who were still pointing their guns at me. They withdrew their rifles, and I stood and joined the procession to Boudreaux's bed. I had to smile.

Sometimes lost things *can* be found in this Fallen World.

* * * * *

Chapter Forty

I followed Boudreaux up to the second floor, where they laid him on a bed in one of the dorm rooms, then we all went into the passageway where the first man who'd spoken started giving out assignments. When all the others had left, I said, "Let me guess; you're Williams, right?"

"Yeah. How'd you know?"

"I met your counterpart in Pensacola."

The man nodded. "Makes sense."

"So what's going on here?"

"We were returning to Pensacola when Mr. Boudreaux took a bullet. We decided to hole up here until he was well enough to travel. Unfortunately, the locals took exception to us using this building. There was some nastiness, in which the locals got the worst of it even though we lost a couple of Agents, and then they went and got a bunch more people and blocked us in." He shrugged. "When Mr. Boudreaux is ready to travel, we'll break out of here. They think they're holding us here; we just haven't chosen to go anywhere else."

"When will he be ready to travel?"

"We don't know."

"You do too know," Boudreaux's voice came weakly from the room. "I'm dying, but I'm not dead quite yet."

Williams shrugged. "Without medical attention, he may not make it."

"So what are you doing about that?"

Williams snorted. "Medical attention? Around here? It doesn't exist."

"I happen to know where it does," I replied. "It's only a few hours south of here in Clanton, Alabama. They put me together a couple of times."

"You're an Agent, though," Williams said with a shrug. "You're hearty. You'll heal from most things if just left alone."

"No, they have a hospital, with medical supplies, a doctor, and everything. And they like me; I helped them out. If we could get him there, they would take care of him."

"Well, that's all good and everything, but there are about 100 people around us right now who'll try to kill us if we leave. My job is to keep Mr. Boudreaux safe; I can't get him to a car with all of those people outside who want to kill us."

"Maybe I can talk with them," I said. "You guys killed a bunch of them, which may have closed down the lines of communication. I'm new; maybe I can work something out with them."

"You kill any of them?" Williams asked.

I looked at the floor. "Well, yeah, but no more than six or so. They may not hate me *too* much."

"As inbred as this area is," Williams said, "every one of those guys had a brother or a father or a son who now wants your blood."

"Isn't it worth at least trying?"

"Of course it is," Boudreaux called. He started coughing again and then added in a softer voice, "Come here."

Williams and I walked into his room and approached his bed.

"Let him talk to the locals," Boudreaux said. "He may not know it, but he has negotiations skills as part of his imprint."

"But he didn't get the imprint," Williams replied.

"That's true, but he's been imprinted a number of times. Sometimes, after enough imprints, you pick up the muscle memory of different skills. It's also possible that he may remember some of the softer skills, too. One thing's for certain, Williams; you're not the person to negotiate anything."

"No sir, I'm not. I just kill people."

"And you're damn good at it," Boudreaux said with a sad smile. "Let's hope Collins here can remember what *he* was good at."

"Collins?" I asked.

"Yeah, you're Joshua Collins. That's your real name. Your Agent name is Stephen Spade, Hostage Rescue Team Leader."

My jaw dropped. It all made sense. The things I'd done. The things I couldn't allow—like people being taken hostage—it all made sense. I could do a room entry, because I would need that. Sniper? Yeah, me, too. I closed my mouth and nodded. I knew who I was, and everything was right. Now, I just needed an imprinter, so I could get "me" back. I'm not sure which me I wanted—not yet—but the first thing we needed was to get out of here and back to Clanton so Boudreaux could get fixed up. We needed to have a chat, but not yet. He wasn't up to it, and I needed time to process. But chat we would.

Some things take time in this Fallen World.

* * * * *

Chapter Forty-One

I waited for the sun to come up before signaling the people surrounding our building, figuring that whoever was in charge out there was probably sleeping and would be in more of a mood to negotiate if he weren't dragged from his bed at two in the morning. It also took me a little time to get used to the idea that I would be doing hostage negotiation from the side of the hostages. It just seemed...weird, somehow, and it took me some time to adjust.

After the sun rose though, there I was again, waving the kid's T-shirt first in the window, and then reaching outside to wave it so that everyone outside could—hopefully—see it.

"In the building!" a voice yelled. "We see the white flag. What is it you want?"

"I'd like to talk with whoever is in charge out there. See if we can't work out a solution so we can all go home."

"How do you intend to have this talk?"

"I'm coming out."

"Come on out."

"Promise not to shoot me?"

There was a pause that was a lot longer than I would have liked, but the voice finally said, "Yeah, come on out. We won't shoot you."

"Don't worry," Williams said, clapping me on the back, "I've got my best sniper on the roof. If they shoot you, he has orders to kill them in return."

"And that's supposed to help me, how?"

Williams shrugged. "Won't help you much at all. But it *will* be one fewer asshole we have to get past."

I frowned at him and headed toward the door, but stopped on the way to point out the building that held their headquarters. "Come get me if I don't come back, okay?"

Williams shrugged again. "If that's what the boss says to do."

That also wasn't very helpful, but I opened the door and walked out into the main campus area for the college. Someone waved me over to another one of the buildings, and I jogged over, feeling pretty naked in the killing zone between the two forces. I wasn't scared, I just didn't want to be standing in the open if someone decided they didn't feel like honoring the truce.

The man led me into the building and relieved me of my pistol, then led me down a corridor and into an office space where three men were waiting for me at a conference table. One man sat at the end of the large wooden table while the other two men stood behind him, one on each side, with rifles at port arms like he was some sort of third world dictator.

"I understand you want to talk," the man said with no preamble. "What is it you want to talk about?"

"Hi," I said. "I'm Joshua Collins. Who do I have the pleasure of talking to?"

"The person that holds your life in his hands. What do you want?"

"We'd like to leave, with no further injuries to either side."

"Sure," the man said. "Give us the guy in the orange shirt and the guy that joined you last night, and the rest of you can all leave."

As Luc Boudreaux was the only person I'd seen in an orange shirt, I knew that wasn't going to happen—nor did I particularly feel like turning myself in to him. "Sorry," I said, "but I can't give you those people. What I can do is tell you that so far, the men in that building have been holding back. If they really wanted, they could have killed all of you, whenever they pleased."

"They ain't so tough," the man to the right of the leader said. "I killed one of them on the way in."

"Then you're a very lucky man," I replied. "Those men are—" I didn't think they'd know what Agents were, so I fed them something I figured they would, "—special forces troopers, and they could come assault you guys whenever they wanted."

"I doubt they could," the leader said, "or they already would have done it." He shrugged. "That's my bottom line. The guy in the orange shirt and the guy who arrived last night. Give me them, and the rest can leave."

"Can't do it," I said, "but I can trade you weapons, ammo, and food for our freedom."

"Got plenty of all those. The two men, or nothing."

"I can't give you them."

"Then we have nothing left to talk about," the leader said. "Get him out of here."

The toughs led me back through the outer office, where several people were now standing around talking. One turned around, and it was the kid from the night before.

"That's him!" he yelled pointing at me. "That's the guy that killed Kenny!"

"I—" That was all I managed to say.

Something hit me in the back of the head, and the lights went out across this Fallen World.

* * * * *

Chapter Forty-Two

I woke up gagging from the bucket of water thrown into my face. I couldn't wipe it off, as my hands were chained to the frame of the bed I was laying on. I tried to move my feet and found they were similarly shackled.

The leader was there, along with several other men and one woman.

"You're making a big mistake," I said. "They will come get me, and when they do, they will kill all of you."

"Thanks for the warning," the man said, "but we've doubled our guards. They won't get out of the building alive. And as for you, before too long, there won't be much to save."

He punched me in the face, and my head rocked to the side. The man had a nice halo of stars as I looked back over to him.

"They told me you were heavy," he said as he rubbed his fist. "What are you made of, rock?"

"Iron," I said, smiling. "I eat my carrots."

"Oh, a funny guy, eh? We'll see how funny you are when we cut off your genitals and shove them into your mouth."

I tried, but couldn't come up with anything funny to say to that.

"Nothing to say, huh?" the leader asked. "Well, then. Let's get started."

He hit me again, and the beating commenced in earnest, punctuated periodically by slaps from the woman, who apparently was the mother of one of the people I killed. She didn't appear to care that they'd been trying to kill me, and all I had done was defend myself.

I passed out a few times—from the pain and the abuse—but was always woken up again by a bucket of water to the face. They went until they got tired, then switched in new people. What they lacked in technique, they made up for with sheer enthusiasm. I was aware of several broken bones and some major internal damage by the time I finally passed out for good.

* * *

Gunshots woke me up, eventually, overly loud in the tiny room I was being held in. I didn't feel any additional pain, but I was admittedly in so much pain at the time I'm not sure I would have noticed bullets hitting me.

"Damn, you look like shit," a voice said. It may have been Williams, but my eyes had swollen shut some time earlier, and I think at least one of my ear drums may have ruptured. "So much for being a negotiator."

I tried to remind him I hadn't actually been imprinted for it, but think I only said, "Mugh…" before passing out again.

* * *

When I woke up again, I instantly recognized my surroundings. I should; I'd spent enough time in my room at St. Vincent's.

"Ugh," I said.

"You truly are the bad penny that keeps turning up," Dr. Briggs said. I didn't have to look; I knew her voice and level of sarcasm as intimately as I knew the hospital room.

"Mah," I mumbled.

"I see you make friends everywhere you go, Ishmael," a male voice said. It sounded like Jacobs.

"Not Ishmael," I said, struggling to speak correctly through a couple of missing and cracked teeth. "I'm Collins, Joshua Collins."

"Well, at least I now have a name to put your files under," Dr. Briggs said, "although I thought I was done having to waste our precious resources on you."

"Sorry," I muttered. I was able to get one eye half-open, but everything was blurry.

"Don't thank me," Dr. Briggs said. "You can thank your buddies who brought you in. They were very insistent about me taking care of you."

"Sorry," I muttered again.

I saw a white blur, and then her voice whispered in my ear. "I would have done it for you anyway." Something brushed my cheek, and I swear I saw an eye, which would have meant... *it was her lips on my cheek?!*

Before I could ask, though, I passed out again. I'm not sure whether it was from the damage I'd taken or the shock of her kissing me.

Strange things happen in this Fallen World.

* * * * *

Chapter Forty-Three

"**B**oy, you must have been a mess if I healed up faster than you did," Luc Boudreaux said as he came into my room.

I was almost functional again. I could open my eyes and see pretty well out of one of them. Most of the worst trauma marks were fading into the background patchwork of previous scars, and they told me I'd be able to walk the next day, 'If I was a good boy.'

For once, there was no driving force—I didn't have anywhere I needed to go or anything I needed to do, so I actually intended to be good. For once.

"Hi, Mr. Boudreaux," I replied. "Yeah, I was pretty messed up when I got here."

"They told me," he said with a nod. "Sorry. I hoped you'd be able to do a better job negotiating."

I shrugged. "Well, I didn't have the imprint, and it probably wouldn't have mattered much anyway. I killed their leader's kid on the way in the night I met you; he was bound and determined I was going to pay for it. I was just bound."

Boudreaux chuckled. "Like I said, sorry about that. When I heard they hadn't let you go, I authorized Williams to get you back and get us all out of there." He sighed. "I hadn't wanted to kill them all…"

"That's what had to be done, though," I said. "They knew you were the leader and wanted to kill you, too."

"Well, then, I don't feel so badly." He pointed to the chair. "Mind if I sit?"

"Not at all," I replied. "We need to talk. I have some questions I need answered."

"Figured as much," he said, dropping heavily into the chair. "There's no one so confused as someone who hasn't been imprinted yet."

"Tell me about me. Did you know me…before?"

"Yes, I did. We actually were friends growing up. We went our own ways for a time—you into the service and me into management. I was at the funeral for your wife and son. They were killed in a hostage situation that went bad, and you said you wished there was something you could have done to help them, to ensure what happened to them never happened to anyone else.

"We had just started the Agent program, and were looking to diversify it a little. We knew we needed more skill sets than we had. Ninjas and assassins, we had in plenty, but we needed people who could act within the law, but who were able to take down bad guys when needed. It just kind of clicked that a hostage rescue team was what we needed, and you were the perfect person to lead it."

"Who was Spade?"

"He was a Delta Force team leader, one of the last we had. You talk about elite…he had been everywhere and done everything. We were lucky to get him. We paid him millions to get his imprint, and it was worth every penny. We filled out your team with other elite operators—a couple more Delta guys and some DEVGRU folks from the U.S. Navy's SEAL Team Six. You successfully completed every mission we sent you on. You were one of my best…and when you weren't that, you were one of my best friends, although it was too dangerous to spend any time together."

"I want to get me back," I said, looking him in the eye.

"I'm sure you do. Which 'me' are you talking about?"

"I don't know. It seems to me that Spade is needed a lot more than Collins in this new world."

"That is certainly true. While Collins has some skills due to his time in the service, Spade takes those skills to a whole new level and adds in some other ones as well."

I nodded. "I've seen some of that. Even though I don't remember the skills, I have the muscle memory for some of them, and if I just let them happen—without thinking about them—I can do a lot of things."

"Yep, a fully loaded Spade would be pretty handy these days."

"So how do I get him back?"

"With some difficulty, I believe."

"Well, you can't just taunt me with him, and then refuse to tell me how to bring him back."

"Oh, I'll tell you, but it isn't going to be easy." He sighed. "I take it something went wrong in New Orleans. That was where you were going right before the bombs started falling. There was a situation, and we sent you there to get imprinted, even though you had just finished a mission and were taking some vacation as Collins. Unfortunately, the situation degenerated quickly, and the bombs and missiles started."

"I was in the imprinter when that happened," I said. "I guess I'd been prepped and had Collins removed and stored, but hadn't gotten the load for Spade yet."

"Any chance we can go back and finish it up there? In New Orleans?"

I shook my head. "Unfortunately, I burned down the building before I knew who I was or what I was doing."

"Damn it!"

Although I'd thought the same thing, many times, since I'd come to realize who and what I was, even I hadn't said it with quite that much vehemence. "What?" I asked. "Surely, there are other copies of the Spade and Collins imprints."

"There were only three copies of the Spade imprint—we didn't want the competitors to get hold of them and find out what we were doing. They were at the Corporate HQ in Charlotte, in Philadelphia, and at a secret facility in New Orleans, in case you were a long distance from the other two places and we needed you up to speed quickly."

"Okay, so I go to Charlotte. It's not that far."

"Perhaps you didn't hear me say that it was at Corporate HQ. What do you think was the first target they hit in the corporate war?"

I sighed and looked at the floor. I didn't even have to say it; it was apparent that one was gone, too. "And Philly? They got nuked too?"

"No." Boudreaux shook his head. "I almost wish they would have, though." He shook his head again. "When you found us, we were coming back from Philly. Although our original destination was Chattanooga, when we found out it was nuked, we tried to get to Corporate HQ. When we found out that was gone, too, we went to Philly. That place was...awful. I lost several Agents there. The depths of depravity people will sink to...and how quickly..." His eyes took on a haunted look as he remembered.

"But you found the imprinter?" I asked when he didn't continue after a few moments.

"I never saw the imprinter, but I saw its handiwork," Boudreaux said. "Clowns. They made dozens...maybe hundreds of clowns."

"I take it they're the scary kind, not the funny ones."

"Yes, 'The Clown' was an assassin imprint we had. We only used it once, and I told the people to destroy it. Not only was the clown an outstanding assassin, he was also totally psychopathic, something we didn't realize until we'd turned him lose on a mission. It cost us five Agents to take him down when he refused to come back in after the mission. Some of the things he did…horrible. I knew that imprint had to be destroyed, and I ordered it to be done away with."

"But it wasn't," I said. It wasn't a guess.

"No, apparently, it wasn't destroyed," Boudreaux replied. "Someone found it and had made some, and when we approached the building where they were, hundreds of clowns came out to meet us. I don't know how many people they actually imprinted or how many people were just dressed up as clowns and didn't have the actual load, but we didn't stick around to try and fight through them. If even half those people had been imprinted…we would have all been killed."

"So you just left them?"

Boudreaux shrugged. "There was nothing we could do without a huge loss of life, so we left. As psychopathic as the clown is, they'll eventually turn on each other and do us all a favor. Until that time, though, I intend to avoid Philly at all costs. We were headed back to Pensacola when you found us."

That filled in the discrepancy for where Boudreaux had been all that time; he'd gone to Philly and back. It didn't help me, though.

"So, how are we going to get me a Spade or Collins imprint?"

"There's no way we can," Boudreaux replied. "Nothing is worth taking on the clowns. Nothing. And even for a friend, I will not send my people into that circus and get them killed. There aren't enough good people remaining on this planet; I won't needlessly kill off the remaining ones I have. You're welcome to go there, but you're going to need friends. Probably thousands of them, if you want to take on the circus."

"But it can be done?"

"Of course. Anything can be done; it's just a matter of how many casualties you're willing to take in order to accomplish your mission.

I wasn't prepared to take the number of casualties it would have cost."

Not having me—at least one of my personalities—wasn't acceptable. I wanted Spade, but failing that, I would take Collins. Maybe I could find a nice country doctor in small-town Alabama to get married to and live out my life in peace. But I needed, "me." I couldn't—no I wouldn't—continue in this weird nothingness where I wasn't anyone. I would find friends, then take on the clowns, and I would get back my life. At least one of them, anyway.

It's important to know who you are in this Fallen World.

# # # # #

ABOUT THE AUTHOR

A bestselling Science Fiction/Fantasy author, speaker, and publisher, Chris Kennedy is a former naval aviator and elementary school principal. Chris' stories include the "Theogony" and "Codex Regius" science fiction trilogies and stories in the "Four Horsemen" military scifi series. Get his free book, "Shattered Crucible," at his website, https://chriskennedypublishing.com.

Chris is the author of the award-winning #1 bestseller, "Self-Publishing for Profit: How to Get Your Book Out of Your Head and Into the Stores." Called "fantastic" and "a great speaker," he has coached hundreds of beginning authors and budding novelists on how to self-publish their stories at a variety of conferences, conventions, and writing guild presentations, and he is publishing fifteen authors under five imprints of his Chris Kennedy Publishing small press.

Chris lives in Virginia Beach, Virginia, and is the holder of a doctorate in educational leadership and master's degrees in both business and public administration.

Titles by Chris Kennedy

"Red Tide"

"Janissaries"

"The Search for Gram"

"The Mutineer's Daughter"

"Asbaran Solutions"

"The Golden Horde"

"Alpha Contracts"

"A Fistful of Credits"

"A Fiery Sunset"

"Dark Moon Arisen"

"The Replicant War"

* * * * *

Connect with Chris Kennedy Online:

Facebook: https://www.facebook.com/chriskennedypublishing.biz

Website: https://chriskennedypublishing.com/

Patreon: https://www.patreon.com/ChrisKennedy110

* * * * *

Like this book? Please write a review.

* * * * *

The following is an

Excerpt from Book One of The Devil's Gunman:

The Devil's Gunman

Philip Bolger

Available Now from Blood Moon Press

eBook and Paperback

Excerpt from "The Devil's Gunman:"

I eased the door open and braced for gunfire or a fireball.

I got neither. I swept the entryway with my rifle's sights. Nothing more offensive than some high school photos glared back at me, and I didn't hear anything running down the hallway or readying a weapon. There were no shouts from police or federal agents, either.

What I did hear, from the living room, was incessant chatter underscored by the occasional interjection of a laugh track. The chatter was accompanied by the soft peripheral glow of my television. Whoever had broken into my house was watching a sitcom.

"I'm unarmed," a man's voice rang out. "So put down the rifle, and let's have a talk."

"The fuck we will," I shouted back. "You broke into my home!"

I moved down the hallway, keeping my rifle on the opening to the living room.

"That's part of what we have to talk about," the voice said. I peered around the corner and saw a young Caucasian man. His pale features and dyed blue hair did little to mask the malicious smirk on his face. He was dressed in an oxford shirt and slacks with a skinny tie, as though he couldn't figure out if he wanted to look like he'd just joined a band or an investment firm. He wore a silver tie clip with a red blood drop on it.

I stood there with my rifle sights on his head.

"I'm here as a messenger," he said and flashed his teeth. I saw pointed incisors. That was enough for me. "This is peaceful, Nicholas. No need to be violent."

I lowered the rifle. I didn't like the prick's condescending tone; he sounded like he enjoyed the sound of his own voice. Those types were always eager to give up information.

"Okay, let's talk. Who's the message from?" I asked.

"I hold the honored post of Emissary of the Lyndale Coven," he said politely, examining his nails. "We've taken a professional interest in you, and Coven leadership sent me."

"Oh yeah?" I asked. "What for?"

"To dictate the terms of your surrender," he said, locking eyes with me. His hands twitched, then curled slightly. I imagined him leaping off the couch and knocking me down. I fought the urge to bring the rifle to bear, keeping it at the low ready.

"Thought your kind needed an invite," I said.

The man snarled.

"We both know who built this house. I have a standing invite. The coven master says that the Duke no longer wants you, so you're fair game. Our agreement, which I have right here, has the details."

He pulled a no-shit scroll out of his suit jacket and put it down on my coffee table. I glanced at it. The Lyndale Coven seemed to be under the impression that I belonged to them. I read the word "slave" once, and that was enough for me to decide I wasn't interested.

"No dice," I said.

"These terms are much more charitable than those the Coven Master wanted," he said, warning in his voice. "Oath breakers aren't normally given this kind of clemency."

I didn't have much idea what he meant about oath breakers, but I wasn't going to play ball with this pompous fuck.

"Not charitable enough," I said. "Why do you guys want me? Running out of blood from young clubgoers and runaways?"

The young vampire smiled again, flashing his teeth with what I'm sure he thought was menace.

"It'll certainly improve our coven's standings with the Duke if we prove we can clean up his loose ends. I'm sure you'll make an excellent blood thrall. We'll be taking a pint of blood every month, as—"

I raised the rifle and sighted in on his head. He sighed, and rolled his eyes.

"Look, you primitive ape, guns won't—"

I fired three times, the rounds earth-shatteringly loud in such a tight place. He screamed in pain and terror as the holy rifle's bullets tore through him, the wounds leaving bright blue caverns of light.

His screaming echoed in my head, so I kept shooting. I fired the rest of the magazine until there was nothing left but a corpse, riddled with holes and glowing softly, and me, standing there in my gunpowder-fueled catharsis.

I dropped the mag and slapped in a fresh one, savoring the sound of the bolt sliding forward and knowing that if the emissary had any friends, they too, would be introduced to the kinetic light of St. Joseph.

"Anyone else here? I got more."

* * * * *

Get "The Devil's Gunman" now at:
https://www.amazon.com/dp/B07N1QF4MD.

Find out more about Philip S. Bolger and "The Devil's Gunman" at:
https://chriskennedypublishing.com/philip-s-bolger/.

* * * * *

The following is an
Excerpt from Book One of The Shadow Lands:

Shadow Lands

Lloyd Behm, II

Available Now from Blood Moon Press

eBook and Paperback

Excerpt from "Shadow Lands:"

The combatants, for lack of a better term, were both resting at the edges of the dance floor. To the left was a very butch-looking blonde in what looked to be purple leather, along with her entourage, while to the right, a petite, dark-skinned Hispanic in a princess outfit stood, surrounded by meat popsicles wrapped in leather. Vampire fashions make no damn sense to me, for what it's worth. There were a few 'normals' huddled against the far wall, which showed signs of someone's face being run along it, repeatedly. Sure enough, the London 'Special' was in the DJ booth. He killed the sound as soon as he realized we were standing there.

"Ladies and gentlemen, may I introduce the final players in our little drama, the Reinhumation Specialists of the Quinton Morris Group!" the Special said into the mike.

"Fuck me running," I said.

"With a rusty chainsaw," Jed finished.

The two groups of vampires turned to face us.

"Remind me to kick Michael in his balls when we get back to the office," I said.

"You're going to have to get in line behind me to do it," Jed replied.

"You can leave now, mortals," the blonde said with a slight German accent. She had occult patterns tattooed around her eyes, which had to be a bitch, because she would have had to have them redone every six months or so. Vampires heal.

"Like, fershure, this totally doesn't involve you," the Hispanic said, her accent pure San Fernando Valley.

"Jed, did I ever tell you how I feel about Valley Girls?" I asked, raising my voice.

"No…"

"Can't live with 'em, can't kill 'em," I replied, swinging my UMP up and cratering the Valley vampire's chest with three rounds into the fragile set of blood vessels above the heart. Sure, the pump still works, but there's nothing connected to it for what passes as blood in a vampire to spread. On top of that, company-issue bullets are frangible silver, to which vampires have an adverse reaction.

With that, the dance was on. The damn Special in the DJ booth at least had the good sense to put on Rammstein. *Mien Teil* came thundering out of the speakers as we started killing vampires. Gunny ran his M1897 Trench Gun dry in five shots, dropped it to hang by a patrol sling, and switched to his ancient, family 1911. I ran my UMP dry on Valley Vamp's minions, then dropped the magazine and reloaded in time to dump the second full magazine into the Butch Vampire as she leaped toward the ceiling to clear the tables between us and the dance floor. As soon as Butch Vamp went down, the remaining vampires froze.

"Glamour," the Special called, stepping out of the booth. "I can control a lot of lesser vampires, but not until you got those two randy cunts thinking about how much they hurt."

"You. Fucking. Asshole," I panted.

Combat is cardio, I don't care what anyone else says.

"Yes?" he replied.

I looked him over. He was wearing a red zoot suit—red-pegged trousers and a long red jacket with wide shoulders over the ubiquitous white peasant shirt, topped with a red, wide-brimmed hat. He even had on red-tinted glacier glasses.

I felt his mind try to probe mine, then beamed as he bounced off.

"My that hurt," he replied.

"You know, we don't work with Michelangelo for nothing," Jed replied. Apparently the mind probe had been general, not specific.

I went through the messy side of the business—staking and beheading—assisted by Capdepon. Crash helped Jed sort out the normal survivors, followed by prepping the live lesser vampires for transport. The Special leaned against a wall, maintaining control of the lesser vampires until we could move them out. Once all the work was done so the cleaners could move in, and the lesser vampires were moved out of Eyelash, I stepped wearily to the Special.

"What's your name?" I asked.

"You can call me," he paused dramatically, "Tim."

I kicked him in the nuts with a steel-toed boot. Even in the undead, it's a sensitive spot.

* * * * *

Get "Shadow Lands" now at:
https://www.amazon.com/dp/B07KX8GHYX/.

Find out more about Lloyd Behm, II and "Shadow Lands" at:
https://chriskennedypublishing.com/imprints-authors/lloyd-behm-ii/.

* * * *

Made in the
USA
Middletown, DE